# WILD JUSTICE

*A Peach and Blake Mystery*

When Tamsin Hayes decides to kill her husband, she sets in train a series of events she could never have predicted; for there is a seedy side to Tim Hayes, which the police are already investigating when he is violently murdered. Was he dispatched by his wife? Or by one of the other suspects who emerge once DCI 'Percy' Peach and DS Lucy Blake begin their investigation?

# WILD JUSTICE

J.M. Gregson

**Severn House Large Print**
London & New York

This first large print edition published 2010
in Great Britain and the USA by
SEVERN HOUSE PUBLISHERS LTD of
9-15 High Street, Sutton, Surrey, SM1 1DF.
First world regular print edition published 2009 by
Severn House Publishers Ltd., London and New York.

British Library Cataloguing in Publication Data

Gregson, J. M.
  Wild justice.
  1. Peach, Percy (Fictitious character)--Fiction. 2. Blake,
  Lucy (Fictitious character)--Fiction. 3. Police--
  England--Lancashire--Fiction. 4. Detective and mystery
  stories. 5. Large type books.
  I. Title
  823.9'14-dc22

  ISBN-13: 978-0-7278-7893-9

Severn House Publishers support The Forest Stewardship Council
[FSC], the leading international forest certification organisation. All
our titles that are printed on Greenpeace-approved FSC-certified paper
carry the FSC logo.

Printed and bound in Great Britain by the
MPG Books Group, Bodmin, Cornwall.

'Revenge is a kind of wild justice, which the more man's nature runs to, the more ought law to weed it out.'

Francis Bacon

*To the librarians of New Zealand, sturdy and consistent evangelists for literature.*

# One

It was in the first week of January that Tamsin Hayes decided to kill her husband.

It was a wholly rational decision. She was quite sure of that. Mrs Hayes was quite good at making decisions. She did not like people who shilly-shallied, who talked on and on about the issues involved, as a way of avoiding a verdict. When the solution to a problem was startling or unpleasant, when the only solution was a radical one, such people did not want to confront it. Tamsin had no such problem: it was obvious to her that in this case there was now only one way to proceed. The man had to go.

Decision-making was one of the things which had divided her from Tim in the first place: she saw that quite clearly now, with the benefit of hindsight. Even when they had been newly-marrieds and quite fond of each other, a quarter of a century and more ago, he had been unable to follow a train of thought to its proper and inevitable conclusion. They had made decisions about furniture for their new house which had seemed to her simple enough, only for her to find her new husband changing them without any consultation.

Tim Hayes must be a good decision-maker when he was at work, or he wouldn't have been so successful; that was the argument which people always put to her when she complained about his treatment of her. Maybe that was so; he had certainly driven the business on from small beginnings to something which was now quite grand. But he had always excluded her from discussions about the business. By now, it was far too late for her to take an interest in his work, even if he had been willing to allow her.

It was strange how clear these things could be at four o'clock in the morning. She had been awake for at least two hours now and what she must do had become ever clearer to her.

She slipped from between the silk sheets – Tamsin Hayes had never taken to duvets – and moved silently to the window, sliding the heavy curtains a foot apart to look at the night sky. A clear, cold winter night, with a thousand stars visible in even the small section of the firmament she could see. The face of the man in the moon was clearly visible in the navy sky; if he was conscious of what she had just decided to do, he was quite impassive about it. Naturally so; in the face of the cosmos and what she was looking at now, the concerns of one woman in North Lancashire were surely puny and irrelevant. The vastness of the universe made the removal of one small, irritating man a trivial irrelevance.

Tamsin shifted her gaze a few degrees and looked at the sky above the great black mound of Pendle Hill. The fell seemed larger and more dominating by night, when the long, very black outline and the abrupt descent to the fertile valley beneath it were all that you could see against the sky. No city of any size between here and Scotland; she remembered her dead father telling her that when she was a wide-eyed and impressionable little girl. She liked that thought, liked the idea of a rural landscape stretching away from North Lancashire through the Yorkshire Pennines and up to the higher hills of the north.

It gave her a feeling of privacy, a certainty that what she was planning would remain her secret and hers alone. She was quite calm, but she shivered a little on that thought. That was no doubt because the night was cold. There was a frost out there; she fancied she could see the whiteness on the lawn as it sloped away towards the invisible gates, even now. She stole softly back to the big bed and slid her whole body, including her head, beneath the sheets for a few moments, shutting in her warmth, isolating herself with her own body heat and the delicious notion she had developed through the night.

The man she was going to kill had chosen to sleep with her tonight, instead of going to his own room in the big, echoing house. He lay on the other side of the queen-sized bed, but Tamsin had no intention of snuggling closer to him to steal a little of his body-warmth, as a normal woman would have done. She found to her surprise that she enjoyed thinking of herself as abnormal. She had never really done that before. It was the decision to remove this unsatisfactory man from her world which had empowered her and made her unique. This difference from the rest of her sex was pleasing, even exciting.

Tim Hayes was snoring. He lay on his back with his mouth slightly open and the long snorts coming irregularly. He moved one arm up beneath his head, breathed more quietly for a few seconds, then snatched in breath abruptly and resumed his noise more erratically, in the pattern which would normally drive a wakeful companion to anger and retaliation.

Yet on the other side of the bed, Tamsin Hayes listened to the cacophony and stared at the invisible ceiling with a contented smile upon her lips. Snore away, unconscious, faithless husband. You do not know it, but you do not have many snoring nights left.

# Two

Tim Hayes had no idea that his days were limited. He enjoyed his normal breakfast of cereal and toast and showed not the least sign of nervousness.

As his wife watched him, she felt empowered. The fact that Tim did not know he was to be killed gave her a feeling of control over him and her own destiny which she had not possessed in years. She offered to get Tim his toast, to fetch the marmalade from the larder for him, and was gratified when he looked at her curiously. He could not make out the reason for this unexpected benevolence; he had no idea what was to happen to him.

Tamsin looked at him dispassionately, for the first time in months. He was a good-looking man for his age. She affirmed that with a little frisson of surprise; her hatred for him had become so intense that it was a long time since she had even considered such things. He was now forty-eight; his plentiful dark hair was greying a little at the temples, but becomingly so: it gave him that touch of gravitas which he no doubt thought was appropriate to the successful businessman. His large grey eyes were wide and clear as he looked at her curiously and then went back to his paper. He was running just a little to fat, but his expensive suits disguised that. He put away the glasses he now used for reading as he finished his mug of tea.

Tamsin Hayes savoured the feeling that she knew something which Tim did not. She rather than he was directing their lives now. However badly he might treat her in the days to come, whatever contempt he showed in his conversation, whatever women he chose to consort with at her expense, she would know that his days were limited. She, and not he, would decide how long he could continue these insults to her. He had lost his power to hurt her.

It was that thought which made her decide that there should be no hurry over this. She had to get it right, if it was to give her real satisfaction. She felt nothing but contempt for those silly women who picked up a knife and killed a husband in a red mist of fury and were promptly arrested. Blind passion, which penalized the killer as much as the victim. There was nothing clever about getting yourself locked away in a high-security prison for years. The smart thing was to leave people wondering who could have done this awful thing, to be the wide-eyed, horror-stricken wife in the aftermath of it. The canny thing, in fact. In her youth, she had always been delighted when her father had called her a 'canny lass'.

This would need careful planning. There was no hurry: she could put up with anything Tim threw at her, now that she knew it was only a matter of time. She was going to enjoy considering the various methods by which the man was going to meet his end, just as she would enjoy the eventual selection of the one which was most effective. Revenge is a dish that tastes better cold, the proverb said. For all that Timothy Hayes had done to her over the last twenty years, this would be revenge indeed.

He left as usual with scarcely a word to her and without telling her which of his enterprises he proposed to visit. She could not remember when he had last kissed her, any more than she could pinpoint the time when she had last wanted him to kiss her. She stood at the front door and watched him reverse the big blue BMW out of the garage and then glide almost noiselessly away from the high country house. The winter sun was gilding the flanks of Pendle. The hill looked much less sombre in the bright morning light than when she had looked out on it during the night in the exultation of her decision.

She stood for a moment, relishing the sharpness and clarity of the January air, before she went back into the house.

An hour later, her intended victim had no thought of his wife. The electronics firm which had been the start of his success was still profitable, though he used it now partly as an innocent front for his other enterprises. He dictated a few routine letters, sent a memorandum to his sales director to say he had promised delivery within three days, and collected the information which had come in during the last two days when he had not been here.

Clare Thompson, his personal assistant, handled the routine stuff very competently when he was not around. Though she was golden-haired and blue-eyed, she was much less vacuous than the conventional and now very old-fashioned stereotype of the dumb blonde. At thirty-eight, she was carefully but expertly made up and her fair skin carried the becoming light tan which was rare in Brunton at this time of year.

When you were the mistress of a boss who had so many opportunities, you had to give careful attention to such things.

She reminded the man she always took care to call Mr Hayes in the office that he had two meetings with important clients later in the week. He nodded, itemized the documents he would need for each encounter and gave her instructions that he should not be disturbed in the hour before these visits, so that he could prepare himself thoroughly for them.

Clare Thompson made a note on her pad of these directions, though she had known that they would come. Tim Hayes might be excitingly unpredictable as a lover, but he was both consistent and thorough in his working practices. She had decided a long time ago that she liked that in him. She could not have respected a boss who did not plan efficiently, whatever the attractions of power as an aphrodisiac. A certain danger in private conduct was acceptable, even desirable, but diligence and common sense were necessary to keep the professional ship upon an even keel.

Tim Hayes watched her out of the corner of his eye as he gave his instructions. He felt the little frisson of sexual excitement he had known so often before at the spectacle of a woman soberly dressed in a grey skirt and long-sleeved white blouse, with every hair on her expensively coiffured head impeccably in place. She worked hard at her role of personal assistant and was highly efficient in it. That was what made her wildness in the bedroom even more attractive to him.

The head of Hayes Electronics walked over to straighten the Renoir print on the wall which he fancied was marginally askew. On his way back to his desk, he paused behind the chair in which his personal assistant sat so demurely. He ran the back of his index finger gently down her spine, felt the tingle of desire which the contact brought to both of them.

'Thursday night as usual?' he said softly.

At ten o'clock, Tamsin Hayes was still not dressed. She was shocked to realize that she must have spent a full hour staring out unseeingly at the winter garden and relishing the new circumstances of her life. Well, that didn't matter, she decided. You needed time to accustom yourself to the idea of being a killer. Or rather, of being the instrument of justice: that was a higher mission altogether.

This hour of contemplation had been an indulgence, but a necessary one. But now she must get back to normal: it was essential that the daily, mundane routine of life should be preserved, if she was to carry this off successfully. She stretched herself deliciously, took a last look at the frost-bound vista outside, and then went upstairs and showered. She did not know yet how she would spend her day, but she rifled through her wardrobe and selected the expensive trousers she had bought last month, then slid her only mohair sweater luxuriously over her shoulders. It was an important day, the first day of the new life she had awarded herself: it was important to dress properly for it.

Tamsin looked across from her wardrobe to Tim's, as if she might project a little of her hatred of the man by glaring at his possessions. Seeking to relieve a little of the tension which had fallen upon her suddenly when she was dressed, she went across and opened the door which concealed his clothes, as she had not done for years. She did not at first see what she sought, but when she felt inside the jacket of a dark blue suit, she found it.

The pistol was in its small black holster, the

one made to fit under the armpit of a jacket. She reached in gingerly, forced herself to take out the weapon and examine it. It felt unexpectedly cold and heavy in her small hand. It was a Smith and Wesson. She had never known the name before and it meant little to her. Yet the knowledge felt like one more step in her empowerment. She found that she had a smile on her face as she went back down the stairs.

She made herself a cup of coffee, a little stronger than usual, and went into the room she had furnished as her study. She selected herself a book from the bookcase her husband had never used and sat down in the single armchair. It was an afterthought which made her go back for the dictionary of quotations she had not consulted in years.

She hadn't been quite certain who had said it when she recalled the phrase, but there it was in black and white for her. It was old Francis Bacon, that dusty arbiter of Tudor ethics, who had first pronounced the words. Tamsin liked the fact that the thought was four hundred years old; the centuries seemed to give added weight to the pronouncement: 'Revenge is a kind of wild justice'.

Tamsin Hayes settled down with her coffee to begin the delicious task of planning her justice.

Tim Hayes had left his plush office at Hayes Electronics for an altogether more seedy room at the Brunton Casino.

This was a glamorous name for a gambling club in the grimy old cotton town. It was a lucrative but not at all glamorous enterprise for the man who owned it. There was no well-groomed personal assistant here, no polished desk and well-organized files. Most of the business done here was not recorded. Hayes sat behind a table with telephones and made the calls himself.

Not only the environment but the persona of the man who controlled it was changed here. Hayes was not the urbane man who operated at Hayes Electronics, with a polite word for most and the occasional tender one for his personal assistant. Female croupiers operated during the evenings at the gaming tables in the long, low-ceilinged room where the business of the place was conducted, but this was otherwise largely a male world.

And the miscellany of males who passed through it reflected the dubious nature of the activities which were conducted from this base. Some of them wore expensive coats and drove expensive cars. Others had more basic transport and adopted a humbler dress; jeans of various quality and states of repair were common, perhaps because of the anonymity afforded to the wearers by this universal form of cover. Whatever their status and degree of opulence, most people who came and went here had acquired the habit of keeping a wary eye on what was happening around and particularly behind them.

The man who came to see Hayes this morning behaved like that. He parked his shabby Ford Focus carefully a hundred yards away from the casino and checked all movements in the street around him before he entered. He looked watchfully around the floor of the big room, deserted at this hour, ignored the cleaners, nodded automatically at the one face he knew, that of a man in shirt sleeves who was reading a tabloid newspaper behind the bar.

Leroy Moore was of Jamaican parentage, but he had never seen that remarkable island. He had never known his father and he was not sure how genuine his first name was. Though he had long ago accepted it, he had a vague memory that his mother had conferred it upon him in place of something more mundane when he began his patchy school experience at five.

Moore had spent the first twenty of his twenty-four years in the Moss Side area of Manchester. As a consequence, he was not just streetwise but slum-wise, even sewer-wise. He had a mass of black, frizzy hair. He was black, squat and almost perpetually smiling. The smile was the impression you carried away from a first meeting with the man; it was accentuated by his large and perfectly white teeth, so that it seemed to linger for a moment when he departed, like that of a sinister Cheshire cat.

Leroy never went anywhere without the knife he regarded as one of the tools of his trade. He felt its comforting presence in the pocket of his leather jacket as he went in to see his employer.

'You're late, Moore. Do you think that time doesn't matter?' asked an unsmiling Hayes.

Leroy hastily removed his habitual smile. 'Sorry, boss. It took me time to park.'

They both knew it was a token excuse. But Hayes had made his point. 'I've work for you to do.'

'Name it, boss.' Moore looked at the single chair on his side of the table but the man in the suit did not ask him to sit down.

'Simpson. He's behind with his rent. Again.'

'He paid last time, Mr Hayes.'

'Yes. After a warning. This time he's had his warning and hasn't responded. He needs a sharper reminder.'

Leroy let his smile steal back in the face of this humour. It didn't do to miss a boss's joke. 'I'll see to it.'

'You will, yes. It's what you're paid for. It's what you do.'

'It's what I do well, boss. You won't have cause to complain.'

'Discreetly, mind. I don't want the fuzz making any connection with me. Which means I don't want them making any connection with you. Understood?'

'Understood perfectly, boss!' Leroy thought of flicking a quick salute at him, then decided against it. His smile broadened as he said slyly, 'What degree of reminder would you like,

Mr Hayes?'

Tim allowed himself a small, grim smile, recognizing the attempt at subtlety from an unusual source. 'No deaths. Not even broken bones, unless it's a jaw or a rib. A severe roughing up, I'd say. A sharp reminder, as I said.'

'When?'

'Weekend, I should think. Away from work, so that any connection won't be clear. Don't take any risks – there's no immediate hurry.' Hayes smiled the smile of a man in control who appreciated his power. 'In the unlikely event of him paying up in time to save himself, I'll let you know.'

Moore nodded three times emphatically, as if registering some complex thought instead of a simple instruction. 'I'll see to it, Mr Hayes. Do I let you know when it's done?'

'No. I'll hear about it, soon enough. And if you need help, choose carefully. I don't want gorillas who don't know when to stop. And I don't want thickos who sound off to their mates about what they've done or can't keep their mouths shut if they're questioned.'

'OK, boss. You can rely on me.'

'I hope so, for your sake.'

It was a dismissal. Moore, who had looked so carefully to right and left as he came through the almost deserted casino, looked straight ahead and this time ignored the curious gaze of the man behind the bar. He slipped out quickly, as if he hoped that a swift exit would not be noticed.

# Three

Detective Chief Inspector Denis Charles Scott Peach, universally known to his CID colleagues in Brunton nick as 'Percy', was having a difficult Wednesday.

After a morning in court with a bench of magistrates he found particularly uninformed and unworldly, he had seen three young bully-boys get away with suspended sentences or community service for crimes of violence. They had departed after thumbing their noses, literally as well as metaphorically, at him and at DC Brendan Murphy, who had arrested them at the cost of facial injuries and bodily bruising. The world, in Percy Peach's considered and informed opinion, had gone mad.

He had passed on that view to his chief when summoned to his penthouse office on the top storey of the massive new police station. This structure was itself an acknowledgement of the fact that crime was a growth industry in the twenty-first century. And Thomas Bulstrode Tucker, Chief Superintendent in charge of the CID section at Brunton, was in Percy's view an arsehole. This is a technical police term for a senior officer of bungling incompetence with self-interest as his only guiding principle.

The man Peach had long ago rechristened as Tommy Bloody Tucker had been absent for the first two days of the working week and was now demanding that his DCI bring him 'up to speed' on everything important that had happened since his last appearance at the station on the previous Friday. Tucker had not caught up with modern technology and saw no reason to do so, with his retirement only two or three years away, so that emails and the like remained things of mystery to him. This at least allowed Peach to be selective in what he chose to highlight; he was now seeking furiously for items which might bring him a little light relief.

'We had a preacher in the station on Sunday night, sir,' he said mysteriously.

'A preacher?' Tucker spoke with the wonderment which might have greeted the mention of an animal previously thought extinct.

'Yes, sir. A man who delivers sermons and gives moral or religious advice. Sometimes formally from a raised enclosed platform known as a pulpit, but also often from—'

'Yes, yes, I know what a preacher is, you idiot! What – what denomination was he, this preacher?'

'Methodist, sir.'

'Not very important nowadays, the Methodists.'

Peach toyed for a moment with a delicious

23

vision of John and Charles Wesley rising from their graves as militant evangelists to strike down this pillar of ignorance with the weighty Methodist hymn book. He contented himself with a modest, 'They have a proud history in Brunton, the Methodists.'

'Fuck history, Peach.'

He's like Henry Ford, but without the scholarship and intellectual distinction, thought Percy. 'Yes, sir. Is that the latest official police policy towards our national inheritance?'

'Don't be impertinent, Peach. I was merely recognizing a fact of life. Merely reminding you that the Methodists are not as important on our patch as they were fifty years ago.'

'I follow you, sir. You were taking account of history, as you might say, sir.' Peach nodded twice and donned the expression of innocent puzzlement he reserved specially for his chief.

'Take it from me, Peach, no Methodist carries any real clout nowadays.'

'Five and a half thousand hymns he wrote, Charles Wesley.' Percy stared dreamily at the wall behind Tucker and shook his head in admiration.

'Not a Methodist yourself, are you?' Tucker stared at him as if accusing him of some unspeakable sexual perversion.

Peach came delightedly back to the real world and gave his chief his most impish smile. Beneath his shining bald head and jet-black moustache, this was a chilling phenomenon. 'I'm not sure you're allowed to ask me that, these days, sir. But as we're such good chums, I don't mind telling you that I have no connections with Methodism. I'm more of a lapsed Papist myself, sir. Altar boys and celibacy and incense and A-level guilt, in my day, sir. I understand that some or all of these have now been abandoned.'

'Your religion is of no interest to me, Peach,' said Tucker loftily, effortlessly ignoring the fact that he had just enquired about it.

'Yes, sir. Most C. of E. people say that.' Peach enjoyed the odd gnomic pronouncement. He stared at a point two feet above Tucker's head with an inscrutability which would have been the envy of a poker player.

'Don't distract me, Peach! You're diverting me from the facts. Why was this Methodist preacher in our station?'

'He was involved in a punch-up, sir.'

'I see.' Tucker steepled his hands and pressed the tips of his fingers together in the gesture he had lately adopted to indicate that he was coming to a balanced decision. After several seconds he said abruptly, 'I think we should throw the book at the bugger!'

Peach was amazed once again by Tommy Bloody Tucker's ability to leap to the wrong decision without any attempt to assemble the facts. He contented himself with a dry, 'Admirably decisive, sir.'

Something in his junior's manner alerted

Tucker. With an unusual burst of perception, he said, 'You've let the sod go, haven't you?'

'He was only in the station for two hours, sir. In my opinion, he should never have been here.'

Tucker smote his empty desk theatrically. 'We need a crackdown on violence, Peach. The public is calling for it.'

'Yes, sir. In that case it might be a good thing that the assailants of this elderly man are still in custody.'

'Assailants?'

'Yes, sir.' Peach decided that it was high time that his chief superintendent learned at least some of the facts of the matter. 'The Methodist lay preacher was a man named Thomas Douthwaite, sir. A man of seventy-two years who attempted to protect a young lady who was being threatened with sexual assault by the two young men we still have in custody. Mr Douthwaite, who is of impeccable reputation and previous conduct, sustained a cut over his left eye and some bruising to the chest. He should in my opinion have been taken to A. and E. at the hospital, but the young uniformed officers brought him here. Apparently he was anxious to make a statement denouncing his attackers.'

Tucker frowned hard at the backs of his hands. 'These young thugs mustn't be allowed to get away with this, Peach. You're much too soft on incidents like this, in my opinion.'

The notion of Peach being soft on anyone,

least of all young thugs, would have caused widespread astonishment among Brunton's criminal fraternity as well as its police service. 'I'm sure we can prepare a case which even the Crown Prosecution Service will be prepared to take on, sir.'

'They'll have me to take on if they don't, Peach.' Tucker jutted his chin aggressively, and for a few seconds the two men were united in the police contempt for the pusillanimous lawyers who would take on only cast-iron prosecutions.

'These hoodlums are awaiting a final interview, sir. Would you like to do that yourself, and show them the full force of Brunton CID in action?'

'No!' Tucker as usual shied away with horror from any direct contact with the crime face. 'You know I make it a policy never to interfere with my staff in the day-to-day business of the CID section.'

'I do indeed, sir. In that case, I may see them myself.'

'That seems a very good idea, Peach. And you have my permission not to pull any punches in the interview. My orders, if you wish to phrase it that way.'

'Oh yes, sir, I think I might. Show the less experienced lads and lasses downstairs that there is a firm and fearless hand at the top.'

'Fearless?' Tommy Bloody Tucker did not like that word.

'I'll certainly let Messrs Iqbal and Hussain know that there is to be no quarter given and that these tactics come directly from the top. I might well—'

'Those are Asian names, Peach.'

'Yes, sir. Thuggery knows not the boundaries of race and religion in the twenty-first century.' Peach was rather proud of that; his fiancée's injunction to order the *Guardian* was paying off already.

'This puts rather a different complexion on things, you know.'

'I agree, sir. It gives us the chance to show that race and creed don't matter when it comes to policing crime. That whatever the colour of your skin and whatever the religion you purport to follow, there is no escape from the long arm of the law in Brunton.'

'Perhaps we should consider whether there might be mitigating circumstances in this particular—'

'None whatsoever, sir. I've made sure Mr Douthwaite's injuries were fully photographed. There is quite an appealing range of colours apparent in the chest bruising. I'll make sure the press officer knows that you were the driving force behind the prosecution when he briefs the local hacks. It might even make the nationals, if we stress the hard-line policy. You might even consider one of your famed media briefings to explain yourself fully. "The copper who has no time for political correctness and racial soft soap," I expect they'll call you. Something along those lines, anyway.'

'Peach, you'd better put the full details of this in writing and bring it to me for an executive decision. In the present sensitive climate of opinion, I might well need to review the—'

'Too late for that, I'm afraid, sir. The young villains have been charged with common assault. Come before the magistrates tomorrow morning. The young lady's agreed to give evidence against them. Open-and-shut case, I'd say.'

Tucker smiled wanly and made a final attempt at rebuke. 'I can only hope the magistrate will be more aware of the delicate state of race relations in this town than my detective chief inspector appears to be.'

'I think we can rely on satisfyingly severe sentences, sir. Custodial, if these thugs have previous histories of violence.'

'Thugs? You really should moderate—'

'Your word, sir, if I remember right.' As I invariably do, in your case, you old fraud, thought Percy with bitter satisfaction.

'Who – who is Chairman of the Bench tomorrow?'

'Councillor Abbas, sir. Believes in making an example of people who share his Pakistani origins and his Muslim faith. I think we can be confident that justice will be done tomorrow morning. Good afternoon, sir.'

Percy paused by the window as he went back

29

down the stairs to savour the clear and brilliant red of the January sunset. Not such a bad day, after all.

Matthew Ballack had known Tim Hayes for more than twenty years. Each of them knew more about the other than any other person on earth.

They had started Hayes Electronics together over a quarter of a century ago, making computer parts in premises which had once been a grocer's shop but which had failed with the relentless advance of the supermarkets. They had recognized the importance of the microchip which was to drive forward the domination of the personal computer, and obtained early concessions and supplies. They had prospered until the nineties, when the British silicon valley had spread out along the M4 in Berkshire and Wiltshire.

They had used the early profits from Hayes Electronics to fund other and more dubious enterprises, so that the slowing of their PC profits did not damage them. Even the collapse of the dot.com boom in the early years of the new century did not greatly affect them, since by that time they were reaping rich returns from gaming and betting shops. The risks here were high but the profits for the successful were even higher, whilst the possibilities of money-laundering for returns from fraud and the sex industry were almost infinite. Neither of the men admitted their involvement in such things, even to their intimates. And both of them had realized early in their careers that they should have very few intimates.

Hayes was careful as well as intelligent, but Ballack had an Achilles heel. He was a gambler himself. He brought to the partnership an unrivalled knowledge of the betting industry and its possibilities. When a Labour government anxious to replace the tax on smokers had first relaxed the laws on gambling and then positively encouraged it, Hayes and Ballack had been in a position to use their profits from electronics in this new, squalid, but highly profitable expansion.

Unfortunately for him, Matthew Ballack had not been able to kick his gambling addiction.

He had made a grandiose announcement of his rejection of his habits, pointing out ponderously the truism that business and pleasure did not mix, that a man could no more be a gambler and run betting shops than he could be a publican and a drinker. Tim Hayes listened, and doubted, and studied carefully what happened next.

Matthew Ballack did not defraud his partner. He never attempted to fiddle the books of their shops or to take what was not his from them. But he dissipated the handsome profits he was making from businesses new and old by betting huge sums with the big chains like Ladbrokes and William Hill. And like all addicts, he believed the great coup, the huge betting success which would wipe out all his previous losses, was just around the corner. He staked ever larger and rasher sums and lost most of his considerable fortune.

And all the while, his partner watched and waited. The partnership had begun with only the minimum of written agreements, so that when Tim Hayes judged that the right moment had come and Matthew Ballack was at his lowest, he had divested himself of its trappings and taken control of the business himself. That moment had been five years ago.

'I've been a fool!' Matthew Ballack had declared vigorously but conventionally. Like most addicts, he thought he had been pursuing his vice in secret, when those close to him knew that something was wrong and Tim Hayes had been following his every move for months.

'A fool indeed,' nodded Tim calmly. 'I warned you off betting many years ago, Matt, but you ignored my advice.'

It was the nearest he would come to an apology for what he was about to do. He did not cut Ballack off completely: somewhere, a written agreement of partnership still existed. Rather than try to destroy that, he simply ignored it. The man knew too much about the more dubious side of their moneymaking for him to fling him out completely. Besides, if anything went wrong in the future, if questions were asked about drug-dealing or prostitution, it might be useful to have a convenient scapegoat to hand.

But Ballack was now to act not as a partner but as an employee. He was allowed to retain a minor role in charge of the now very small research and development department at Hayes Electronics and the token managership of one small backstreet betting shop, on condition that he joined Gamblers Anonymous and gave evidence of complete reform.

Matthew made his token, hopeless protests against his humiliation. 'We came up together. We've been through so much. You owe me more than this,' he protested pathetically.

'I owe you nothing,' said Hayes viciously.

'You can't do it. We have agreements.'

'I can and I will. We've never bothered much with written agreements. You're lucky I didn't let you go the whole hog and put yourself on the streets.'

'Ros left me last year and took the kids.'

'Wise woman. She should have gone earlier.'

'She took the house and I have to pay maintenance. The business is all I have left.'

Tim saw that the man was near to tears and exulted; the sight moved him not to sympathy but to domination. 'Correction. Had left. You're lucky to retain what I'm offering. Take it or leave it.'

Matthew Ballack had taken it, of course. He'd had no option. In the shock and the humiliation of his distress and his addiction, he had been unfit to make a fresh start anywhere else. He had thought that he might be a junior partner, with status maintained despite the drop in his income, but, as the months stretched into years, Hayes made sure that he was more and more marginalized. Other men, hard men whom Matthew did not know, were brought in to occupy the posts and to do the things he had once done.

Today, although Matthew Ballack did not as yet know it, was to mark one more stage in his degradation.

He knew he should suspect something when Hayes arranged to meet him at home instead of in the casino where he was still officially based. Ballack lived in a small flat near the centre of the town, in an area which a century ago had been the most expensive part of the prosperous cotton town, with high Victorian houses and spacious gardens filled with geraniums and lobelia and snapdragons.

Those days were long gone. The gardens were now concreted over to accommodate cars in various stages of roadworthiness, whilst the once-proud houses were rabbit warrens of flats and bedsits, housing a floating population. Few people stayed for long. Those who could afford it moved out to something better, those who failed ended in squats, or in the prisons which were the inevitable destination for an ever-increasing minority of them.

Matthew Ballack had one of the better residences in this down-at-heel area, a large bedsit on the ground floor of what had once been an elegant Edwardian semi-detached. He was the longest resident, and he paid his modest rent on time, so he was the landlady's favourite tenant. If she wondered privately why he did not move on, she had far more sense than to ask. In fact, once Ballack had paid the maintenance to his wife and children, which had been computed on his income in palmier times, this was all he could afford.

Tim Hayes had been here only once before; he decided that it must have been at least three years previously. He looked up at the high, smutty ceiling, with its marks of damp in the corner of the outside wall, then at the faded wallpaper, with its strips torn away by the children of some previous tenant. The light was on because of the early dusk, but the single bulb had no shade.

Hayes turned his attention to the occupant. Ballack was almost the same age as him, but Tim thought he looked at least ten years older than his forty-nine years. Most of the hair on his large head had gone; the fringe and the thin covering he combed over the top of his skull looked lank and greasy. He had not bothered to make himself tidy for this meeting: Tim wondered whether that was deliberate, whether he was offering the only pathetic defiance left to him. One of the buttons on the stomach of his shirt was undone, which accentuated the pot belly which bulged over the belt of his trousers.

His broad nose had grown more bulbous in his decline, and the once sharp brown eyes on each side of it were watery and slightly bloodshot.

Hayes deliberately ignored his former partner's appearance. Instead, he glanced again at the walls and the ceiling, at the shabby kitchen area at one end of the big room, and said, 'I'm surprised you stay here, Matt.'

'I don't have much choice. What did you want to see me about? Why the mystery?'

'No mystery, Matt. I just thought it better to do this in private.' He sat down in a threadbare armchair, stretched his legs unhurriedly, stared with approval at the shine on his expensive leather shoes for a moment, as if it was necessary for him to assure himself of his own quality in this place where squalor prevailed. 'No business remains successful by standing still, Matt.'

'I don't need the clichés. I understand business as well as you do, Tim.'

Hayes looked again at the peeling wallpaper, the shabby suite, the scratched table and the outdated kitchen area. His smile was more infuriating to his host than any frown could ever have been. 'If you say so, Matt. The point is that decisions have to be made. I need to take account of what is expanding and what is declining in my empire.'

'It would have been "*we* need to take account" and "*our* empire" at one time.' Matthew Ballack had no idea why he made this hopeless protest. Perhaps it was because he wished to delay the unwelcome news he sensed was coming.

'Those days have gone, Matt. That was your fault, not mine.' For a couple of seconds, Tim sounded genuinely sorry about that. Then he addressed himself to turning the knife in the wound. 'I need a younger man to take charge of the betting shop. The government is freeing things up. With a bit of luck, we'll be able to turn ourselves into a proper, Continental-style casino in the next year or two. I need someone with his finger on the pulse.'

'You mean you're kicking me out.' Ballack spoke with dull resignation; everything about this clandestine meeting made sense now.

Tim Hayes smiled, deliberately unhurried, deliberately relaxed. 'I'm moving you sideways, Matt. Into a growth area. You could look upon it as a promotion.' The irony in his smile said that it was certainly not that.

'What is it you want me to do now?'

'A job that's right up your street, Matt. Management of an area in which your personal experience will be invaluable.' He paused to savour that phrase, watching the heavy features of the man in the other armchair as recognition of its implications dawned on him. Then he nodded and smiled. 'I want you to take responsibility for the welfare of the most attractive of our female employees.'

There was a pause of several seconds before

Ballack said dully, 'You're putting me in charge of the brothels.'

'Come now, Matt! You know that's a term we never use. That would be acknowledging that such places exist! You know that Hayes Electronics needs to be morally beyond reproach.'

'You want me to make sure the tarts give us their forty per cent. That they pay up for their protection and look cheerful.'

'Not cheerful. Beautiful, Matt. Comely, even. Cheerful isn't enough for people in their trade. Not for the best ones, anyway. And we only want the best ladies working for us, don't we, Matt?'

'You want to put me in charge of a business which officially doesn't exist. To kick out ageing toms when they reach their sell-by dates.'

'That's the idea, Matt. I knew you'd appreciate what was involved, or I wouldn't have chosen you. Of course, there'll be more positive things, too. You'll have to recruit new, young, attractive staff and install them in our properties – I expect you'll enjoy the auditions. And all the time you'll need to pretend that this aspect of our business doesn't exist. Discretion is the watchword, as always. But I know that I can rely absolutely upon your discretion, Matt.'

'You mean you know things which will ensure that I keep my mouth shut if the fuzz come sniffing around.'

'You see things very negatively these days, Matt. But of course I bear such things in mind.

One considers everything, when making the appointments in different sections of the empire.'

'Do I have a choice?' The question which invited further humiliation was out before Matthew Ballack could prevent it.

Hayes leaned a little further back in his chair, raised his eyes to the damaged ceiling, let them travel unhurriedly again around the walls of this dingy room. 'You could always look for something elsewhere, I suppose.' He brought his gaze back sharply to the face of his erstwhile partner. 'But I have to tell you frankly that I'd be disappointed if you did that, Matt. I'd like to keep you with Hayes Electronics, if at all possible.'

Moments later, Tim Hayes stood for a moment beside the big BMW in the shadow of the high building. He looked up and down the shabby street, relishing in that moment not only how far he had come but how far Matthew Ballack had fallen. Then some belated qualm of conscience overtook him. He looked towards the orange light behind the curtains which did not meet in that high, depressing front room and was sorry for the man who had to live there.

The feeling did not persist. As he turned up the heating and eased the big limousine away from the place, his mind turned swiftly to his next concern.

# Four

Darren Simpson was fond of his children. Nevertheless, both they and he were secretly relieved when Sunday was over and it was time for them to go back to their mother. It wasn't easy to fill the day in January. Boys of four and six were quickly bored when they were away from home and their familiar toys.

He saw his wife and the new man through the uncurtained window as he drove up to the house. It was almost as if they wanted him to see them, he thought sourly. He didn't want to speak to Hetty, but he had to ring the bell and see the small boys safely into the house. They ran straight in when the door opened, without a backward glance at him. He heard them shouting a greeting to the man who now shared his former wife's bed. Hetty said as if she did not much care, 'They been all right for you, have they?'

'Yes. They had a bit of a bust-up with each other this afternoon, but it was soon over. They're good kids, really.'

'You're behind with the maintenance again.'

'I know. The lads aren't going short though,

are they?' He glanced at the Jaguar in the drive.

'We've had this argument before. That's got nothing to do with it.'

'No. Well, things are tight for me. January's always a slack month in betting shops, after people have spent up at Christmas. And several days of racing have been abandoned because of frost.'

'Not my problem, I'm afraid.' She thrust her head forward in that aggressive, bird-like gesture he had thought beguiling when they were eighteen.

'The Focus needs new tyres. And the shop isn't in the best part of town, as you know. I'm finding it difficult to raise the rent, let alone to—'

'Not my problem, as I said. I don't want to take you to court, Darren.'

She shut the door before he could make any rejoinder. That was just as well, because he couldn't imagine what he might have said.

He felt very depressed as he drove back into the town. It was just as well the flat over the betting shop came cheap, or he wouldn't have survived this long. He couldn't think of anything he could do to increase turnover. Advertising was useless; everyone knew that betting was an industry in which you were notoriously at the mercy of outside influences. Apart from the vagaries of the weather which sometimes meant there was little sport left to bet on, far too many favourites had won in the last few weeks.

Sometimes he thought he'd just get out and start anew somewhere else, somewhere a long way away. But if you left debts behind you, they had a habit of seeking you out.

It was probably because of his increasing despondency that Darren Simpson did not notice the headlights of the vehicle which remained a steady hundred yards behind him.

The shop and the flat above it were in complete darkness, looking anything but welcoming. He felt very weary as he pulled into the small walled parking area behind it: the boys were good lads really, but a day with them in his cramped accommodation and in the corporation park was pretty wearing. He turned off the engine and sat still in the darkness for a moment or two.

The street was deserted as he rounded the corner. He had his key out and had almost reached his shop when he saw the two figures in the doorway. They wore anoraks with the hoods up. He couldn't see their faces in the gloom. It wasn't until he was very close to them that he realized that both of them were black.

He turned, tried to run, but found an arm round his neck. The coarse material filled his mouth, smelling of petrol and tasting foul. 'I've no money on me,' he rasped desperately. The voice sounding in his ears was that of some other frightened creature, not his own. 'Not more than a couple of quid at most. You're welcome to it, but it's all I've got. Honest it is!'

Their silence made him go on talking, even shouting, as if his ceasing to speak would be the signal for something damaging.

Leroy Moore said, 'Shut up, Simpson. This isn't a mugging.'

They knew his name. This wasn't random, then: he had been targeted. He still could not see faces, but the light from the distant street lamp flashed intermittently on the whites of eyes. 'Who are you? What do you want?'

'Your rent for this place. Here and now.'

'I haven't got it. I'll pay this week. Somehow I'll pay this week.'

It was the other man, the man who hadn't spoken, who hit him first. A blow to the cheek, breaking the flesh, doing heaven knew what to the bones beneath it. A knuckleduster: Darren felt the metal in the wound even as he gasped. Then a blow came from the other side, hard into his ribs, doubling him up fiercely, so that the blow to his chin was redoubled in force, buffeting his head back on his neck as if it had been that of a doll. He felt the top of his head hit the handle of the door as he went down, felt his ear tear against the edge of the step beneath the door.

He screwed himself into a feral hunch as the kicking began. He did not shout for them to stop. It took him a moment to realize that the gasps of pain were coming from him. They kicked him systematically, with the one who had spoken delivering blows at his stomach and

43

his vitals, the other man alternating with a boot-ing of his back and his thighs and his buttocks. He wondered how long it would go on, how soon he would pass into unconsciousness.

But Leroy Moore was a professional, if there could be such a thing in this barbarous trade. Hayes paid him, and Hayes had told him he didn't want serious, life-threatening injuries. Moore flung a fist against the chest of his brutal assistant and said abruptly, 'That's enough!' The man aimed a final boot at the small of the back of his prone victim, like a child brought in from play who gives a last, valedictory kick at a football.

Leroy looked down at their victim, checked that he was breathing, listened for the groan which might mean that Simpson was still con-scious. He looked up and down the street, which remained deserted. It was quieter and less dangerous here than Moss Side, where he had learned his vicious skills. He spoke the words which had become almost a formula to him: 'It's a warning, Simpson. Pay up and pay up on time. Otherwise next time you may not get the chance!'

There was a short, mirthless, scarcely human laugh from his companion at this. It was the first sound the man had uttered throughout their business.

Ten miles away from the shop doorway where the injured Darren Simpson lay, a very different scene was being enacted by a very different trio.

DCI Percy Peach was at the home of the woman who was scheduled in a few months to become his mother-in-law. That conventional target of politically incorrect comedians was in fact one of Peach's favourite people. His fiancée, Detective Sergeant Lucy Blake, who was normally both intelligent and resourceful, found the combination of the two far more than she could cope with.

Percy's picture was on the mantelpiece beside that of her dead father. Both photographs showed men in cricket whites, and the pictures stood like icons upon this cottage altar. Her father's picture was in black and white, showing a shy man, weary but happy, ascending the pavilion steps at Blackpool after taking six wickets in the Northern League. Percy Peach's picture was in colour: it had been taken only three years previously. A cap worn at a jaunty angle covered his bald head, making him look much younger. The words written beneath in Agnes Blake's neat, careful hand told the reader that this was 'D.C.S. Peach leaving the field after another unbeaten Lancashire League half-century for East Lancs'.

Agnes Blake had been a cricket fanatic for sixty years. Percy's three initials had forged an immediate link with her. Agnes was one of the few people who now recognized them as those of Denis Charles Scott Compton, the dashing cavalier of English cricket in the ten years after the Second World War, and in Agnes Blake's formidable opinion the most attractive and gracious of all English cricketers. Compton had been a hero of Percy's long-departed father, who had determined on these Christian names for him. An unromantic police service, with no respect for sporting tradition and a penchant for alliteration, had long since determined that the man should be simply Percy Peach.

The three had enjoyed one of Agnes's special high teas. Roast-ham salad had been followed by her delicious baking, which her daughter tried to resist and Percy made hay with. Scones had been followed by flapjacks and Agnes was now preparing with some ceremony to cut into the fruit cake she had prepared specially for the occasion. 'This is Simnel cake,' she announced portentously. 'We should really have it on mid-Lent Sunday, but as this is the nearest you busy young people are going to get, I've got it out today.'

'It looks most impressive, Mrs B,' said Percy reverently. He struck a note of humility Lucy never heard from him save in her mother's cottage. She shot her man a molten glance, which he ignored with practised aplomb.

Agnes smiled at him as fondly as if he was the son she had never had. 'It has a layer of marzipan in its centre, as well as on top,' she explained proudly. 'Let's hope it tastes as good as it looks.'

It did, and Percy Peach told her that it did, and Agnes Blake was absurdly pleased. Lucy agreed that the cake she remembered from her childhood was as good as ever and went to replenish the teapot. She heard the hum of animated conversation between the two soul mates she had left behind and immediately regretted her absence. Percy's impish sense of fun was not to be trusted at the best of times; when he got together with her mother there was no knowing what would happen. Except that whatever it was, her interests would probably suffer. She waited impatiently for the kettle to boil.

Agnes Blake looked very pleased with herself when her daughter came back into the living room, whilst Percy Peach bathed her in the blandest and most contented of his vast range of smiles. An ominous silence prevailed as Lucy replenished their teacups. With the meal completed apart from this final drink, hostess and visitor had moved from table to armchairs. Percy now stretched his short legs as far as they would go in front of him and lay back like a cat contemplating a post-prandial nap.

Agnes Blake said happily, 'We've been discussing the timetable for the wedding whilst you were out, love.'

Lucy knew she should never have left them alone. She said determinedly. 'Autumn, we agreed. Some time in October, perhaps.'

'Spring,' said her mother decisively. She

almost winked at the recumbent Peach, then thought better of it; daughters insisted upon maternal decorum, even when it was least appropriate.

From the depths of his armchair, Percy said sleepily but insidiously, 'I don't think we ever agreed on autumn, love.'

'That's right, our Lucy, we didn't!' Agnes Blake was in like a flash: you had to admire such reactions in a seventy-year-old, thought Percy. 'Spring's the time for weddings – it's traditional.'

'Traditional,' echoed Percy dreamily.

'It's the beginning of February now,' said Lucy firmly. 'Far too late for us to make the arrangements for a spring wedding.'

'I'll do all that for you,' said her mother firmly.

'And I'll help, Mrs B. It's high time she made an honest man of me.' Percy gave the delighted lady the smile of a man anxious to help.

'*I* can't be ready for then,' said Lucy Blake massively.

'Nonsense! You're almost ready now. I should think you've completed your trousseau. I saw you in Lingerie Lucille last week. Aaaa-aaraaagh!' In deference to the age and dignity of his hostess, this was not the long, low-pitched growl of sexual desire which Percy was prone to when he cornered Lucy in private in her underwear. He produced instead a much more refined and high-pitched wail, which was presumably meant to encompass aesthetic as well as more basic gratification. Lucy found it a chilling sound.

'There you are, then!' said Mrs Blake emphatically. It was not clear whether she referred to Percy's ululation or his earlier statement of the bride's readiness. 'We need to fix a date.'

'October,' said Lucy firmly.

'April,' said her mother.

'How about early May?' said Percy, his round face a picture of innocent enquiry and willingness to help.

Agnes Blake nodded. 'All right. I'm willing to compromise if you are, our Lucy.'

Lucy shook her head gravely and played her trump card. 'We won't be able to book anywhere for the reception. May is far too early: everything suitable will be gone.'

From some mysterious recess of her armchair, Agnes Blake produced a small leather-bound diary, like a magician triumphantly concluding a successful trick. 'It's a good thing I made a couple of provisional reservations for the beginning of May, then, isn't it, love?'

'You two have planned all this!' Lucy looked accusingly at her fiancé. He shook his head sadly at such cynicism and sighed theatrically.

'I'd say you should be grateful for the foresight of your loving mother, my dear. Without her, it seems the dates you now seem determined to have might have been impossible.' Percy gave her the beam he reserved for his

49

most outrageous assertions.

Lucy Blake had the now familiar sense of being outflanked by these unlikely allies. 'We haven't even finalized the guest list.'

Her mother held aloft the diary triumphantly. 'It's all in here, love. All ready to go. We agreed it on Boxing Day, if you remember – you took several hours over it.'

'You wore me down, you mean! And you made sure I was pissed at the time!'

*Language*, our Lucy! I shall have to watch you at this wedding. I don't want you getting tipsy and upsetting the guests.'

'I'll keep my eye on her, Mrs B,' said Percy solicitously. 'I quite agree, we can't have her losing control and showing her bloomers to all and sundry!'

Agnes Blake apparently found this a most amusing image, when her daughter had hoped that she would be outraged. 'It's this man here you'll have to watch!' Lucy said desperately.

'Why would that be?' said Percy, looked very hurt. 'I'm sure that on the day I shall control myself perfectly, with the prospect of a honeymoon with my beloved as the prize.' Lucy had never seen anyone nod unctuously, but Peach now achieved it effortlessly.

'Saturday the third looks like a good day.' Agnes's attention was all upon her diary and not her daughter. 'As it happens, I have an option on Marton Towers for that date.'

'You've planned this, haven't you? The pair

of you have ganged up on me. As per bloody usual.' Lucy glared from parent to fiancé and back again. Percy managed to look as if his tender soul was very hurt by the accusation, but her mother did not trouble to conceal her triumph.

'Language, our Lucy,' said Percy primly. 'Well, it looks as if I shall have to accede to your request for a spring wedding. It will be tight, but if that is what you want, your mother and I will do everything we can to help you.'

'It's a pincer movement.'

'I don't think you should talk about our love life in front of your mother. It's not seemly.'

'I shan't give up my career,' said Lucy despairingly. She looked at her mother with a sudden, disturbing shaft of love. 'I know you want grandchildren, Mum, but there's no immediate hurry, is there?'

'There is when you're seventy and counting, our Lucy.' Agnes had had her only child at forty-one. She was determined to see the next generation whilst she still had the energy to enjoy it.

'The law is very accommodating to working mothers nowadays,' said Percy loftily. 'I believe there is even paternity leave available.' He pronounced the phrase carefully, as if naming some mysterious religious practice. 'And don't forget I'm ten years older than you. I know that life seems to stretch eternally for thoughtless girls like you in the blaze of youth, but your mother and I are conscious of time's winged chariot at our heels.' He shook his head and smiled sadly, a reaction often induced by his poetic strain.

'I'm twenty-nine!' snapped Lucy.

'All the more reason to get on with married life and produce your children, then,' said her mother triumphantly.

In the car on the way back to Brunton, Lucy Blake reiterated what she felt she had always known. 'You're a bastard, Percy Peach.' But it was said with no great bitterness, almost with a note of admiration.

'I do my best,' said Percy complacently.

'There'll be a lot to arrange.'

'I suppose so. We'll have to hope the criminal fraternity of Brunton give us an easy ride for a month or two.'

But the events of the next few weeks would show that not even Percy Peach could control everything.

# Five

Tim Hayes was getting tired of Clare Thompson. Mistresses had a limited shelf life, in his cynical view, and this one had almost run its course.

The sex was good: better than good. He had no complaints about that. But Clare was getting clingy – with his experience, he knew the signs. She was talking as if they had a long-term future. Before he knew it, she'd be sounding him out about divorce. Sometimes he thought that wouldn't be a bad thing; Tamsin was a cold fish nowadays. But she was going to come into a lot of money when her parents died, and they were in their eighties.

He certainly wouldn't move out of one marriage and into another. The sex wouldn't be as exciting, for a start. The fact that it was all a dangerous secret was one of the things which drove things on for Clare Thompson, whether she realized that or not. The breathless evenings stolen away from her jealous husband were exciting to her, as they would never have been if the affair had been open. She enjoyed the contrast between her everyday efficiency and reliability as his personal assistant in the office and her physical abandon between the sheets. She was the librarian who took off her glasses and shook down her hair and became an entirely different creature, a force of nature exulting in her own desires.

Their working relationship was another complication, of course. She was the most efficient secretary he had ever had – he still thought of her as that, though the role nowadays extended much further. She knew how he operated, she knew the world of Hayes Electronics, and she didn't ask awkward questions about his other and more dubious enterprises. The electronics company was the respectable face of his business empire, and Clare Thompson was eminently the respectable face of Hayes Electronics. She was patently honest herself, and if people tried to poke their noses into other and more suspect aspects of his prosperity, she would be entirely convincing because she knew nothing.

He didn't want to lose her as his PA. But if he said she wasn't to come to his flat in the town any more, would they be able to go on working together? She might leave, of course, might feel unable to work for a man who had cast her aside. If she didn't, he wouldn't want to sack her: he certainly couldn't prove that her work was unsatisfactory and he wouldn't want to try.

As if to emphasize that, Clare Thompson came into his office now with letters for him to sign. She had drafted three of the routine ones herself and he could not fault them. He told her so and she gave him the small, constricted, working-hours smile with which she always greeted professional compliments.

She lingered a little longer than usual by his desk, then stopped as she reached the door, looking down at the documents in her hand and not at him. 'Tomorrow night as usual?' she asked.

'I can't make it this week. I have an important meeting with a new investor tomorrow night, I'm afraid.'

'OK. Next week, then. Unless we can arrange something before—'

'Next Thursday night as usual. I'll look forward to it!'

He knew her well enough to realize how much it had cost her to ask the question. She was a proud woman, who had never made the first move before. It was flattering to have her so keen, but he was too long in the tooth to let that sway his judgement. The writing was on the wall: she was getting much too involved. In a little while, she would become cloying.

As a lover, it was time to be rid of Mrs Clare Thompson.


'I want to order a book.' Tamsin Hayes felt she looked very conspicuous, when that was the last thing she wished to do.

She wanted to duck out and order something banal and boring like a cookery book. The story she had thought up didn't seem even faintly convincing now. She said in as neutral a tone as she could manage, 'I'm writing a book, you see. I'm having a go at a crime novel. It's about someone who did a poisoning in the 1960's, but wasn't found out at the time. I know that very few novels get published and it's probably hopeless...' She tailed away, aware that she was talking too much, perhaps drawing attention to herself when she least wished to do so.

'You fill in one of these forms. There's a charge of eighty-five pence.' The girl scarcely looked up from the list she was compiling.

Her boredom was a splendid sight for Tamsin. She'd thought of doing this on the Internet, but some compulsion against sending anything out in writing to the world at large had held her back. Then she had set out to place an order for the book at the bookshop in the High Street, but had decided that it would draw more attention to her than a borrowing from the library. It wasn't a big, impersonal Waterstone's, but a quiet little shop run by an enthusiast who would remember things.

Tamsin filled in the author, Gustav Schenk, and the title, *The Book of Poisons*. It looked very damning as she looked down at it: she'd have liked something less specific, but presumably a specialist book on poisons had to be clearly titled.

She took a deep breath, waited for two people taking books out to have them stamped and clear the area, and then went back to the desk with the completed card. 'This book was published in 1989,' she said. 'It may well be out of print now. Perhaps I should—'

The girl glanced down at the card, showing her first real interest in this nervous client. 'Specialist non-fiction books tend to stay around for longer. I'm pretty confident we'll turn up a copy for you somewhere within the library service. It may take a little time. We'll let you know when it comes in.'

'It's just for a little research. In connection with this book I'm planning to write.' Tamsin felt a compulsion to repeat herself, in case the young woman had not been paying attention to her explanation the first time.

'You said that, yes. I'm sure we'll get it for you. It may take a week or ten days.'

Tamsin thanked her and left as swiftly as she could. She might never even use whatever information the book could give her. It would be just another string to her bow, another possibility for the dismissal of this husband she had now determined was to go. There were several other possibilities; when she had the full picture, she would make her decision.

Before she went back to the big, empty house, she took a walk by the winter Ribble. The river was flowing dark and silent, looking almost as if it shared her secret. She pictured the library girl looking thoughtfully at the title she had ordered after she had gone, and wondering what unspeakable crime this middle-aged woman was planning. Even though people tended to stretch it out much later, you were middle-aged at forty-six; there was no doubt about that.

But what did that matter, when you were soon to begin a new and much more exciting life? When Tamsin Hayes arrived home, a strange, private smile was lighting up her face.

Clare Thompson felt very guilty about her husband. He had done nothing to deserve what she was doing to him. Rather the reverse, in fact: he deserved a wife who was loving and faithful. Clare told herself that she still loved him, whatever that elusive word meant. Fidelity had gone some time ago.

Jason Thompson was a year older than his wife, though she thought that he now looked considerably older than her. He was a schoolteacher and looked like one, she thought, although she was aware that teachers had as wide a range of physical types as any other profession. Jason was bespectacled; his myopia gave him a perpetually slightly bewildered air. He was of average height, but his extreme slimness made him look taller. He had carroty, unruly hair, which was fading a little but hardly improving with age. He wore the sports jacket and tie which in more conformist times had been the standard pedagogical dress: Clare had always been thankful that he had at least eschewed leather elbow patches. He knew a lot about geography, but he looked nerdish, even geekish. That didn't prevent Clare from being very fond of him, even now, when her passion for Tim Hayes made her wonder if she had ever really been in love with her husband.

Jason, on the other hand, had never had any doubt that he loved Clare. He was highly sexed and easily jealous. It was not a good combination in a husband who was being betrayed.

He had brought home a takeaway Chinese meal, as he usually did on a Thursday. He noted that his wife was eating more than her usual share and taking her time over it. 'Aren't you going to badminton tonight?' he asked casually. 'You'll be late unless you get your skates on.'

'I'm not going tonight.'

'Why's that?'

'The women I usually play with aren't going to be there. It's someone's fortieth birthday party and they're all going to it.' It had seemed a convincing enough story when she had thought it up. Now it sounded decidedly thin. She wondered how good a liar she was: she had never needed to lie before her affair with Tim.

'Didn't they invite you?'

'I don't know them all that well. I only see them at badminton. I think they've known each other for years.'

'Poor Clare!' He stroked her hair, let his fingers linger on her neck, ran them down her spine. 'We'll have to make sure you have a good night in, won't we? Make sure you don't miss your exercise.'

She thought of Tim Hayes's fingers on her spine, of the little tingle that brought to her, of how she had been looking forward to spending this night with him. She said hastily, 'If you go and sit in the lounge, Jason, I'll bring our coffee through in a few minutes.'

He sipped his coffee and studied her intently as she sat opposite him on the other side of the fireplace. She turned the pages of the paper restlessly, trying not to be aware of his scrutiny. He said, 'I expect you're missing your badminton. Missing the exercise and the company.'

He put a strange emphasis which she found quite disturbing on the last phrase. Clare said, 'I wasn't even thinking about it. It's good to have a night at home, actually. I had a hectic day at the office.'

Jason went on as if he had not heard her. 'It must be very dull for you, stuck at home with an old fuddy-duddy like me.'

'It isn't and you're not.' He was still looking at her in that intent way. She did not dare to look up and meet his eyes. She found that she had turned to the sports pages she never read. Some football manager she hadn't heard of had been sacked. She stood up and was surprised how tense she was, what a release she felt in simple physical movement. She walked across and switched on the television, then resumed her seat with a sigh and affected interest in the police drama she never watched. But he was still watching her and she found she couldn't sit still. She gathered up the cafetière and the coffee cups and took them into the kitchen. It was an immense relief to be away from that observant presence.

Jason was behaving oddly. But he couldn't know anything, surely? She had been very careful and discreet, knowing how violently he would react to even a suspicion of adultery. That's what he called it when he spoke of these things: others used terms like 'playing away', but Jason preferred the old-fashioned term, with its suggestions of religious and legal significance. She washed up noisily, though he had told her that he would do it. She stayed as long as she could in the kitchen, refusing to think about the things she might at this minute have been doing with Tim, trying to concentrate on what she might do to please the man she had left looking at the television.

He was immediately alert when she went back to him. 'You've been a long time.'

'I tidied up a little. Listened to a couple of phone messages. Set the table for the morning.'

'There weren't any messages when I came home from school.' He said it quietly, reflectively, as if he did not wish to make it a challenge.

She said, 'What's on the box tonight? I'm not usually here on Thursdays.'

'No. You have more exciting things to do. Well, it's not usually a good night for telly. In fact, there's nothing worth watching at all.' He looked at her challengingly. 'We could have an early night. Make our own amusement. Like we used to do in the old days.' There was a touch of strain in what should have been a smile of friendly, intimate lechery.

She had known that this was coming, she told herself. His outlet for tension of any kind was always sex. And why not? He was good at it, and it was good for him; he was usually much more relaxed after it. And he was a good lover: she still felt very tender towards him, whatever she did with Tim. That was something set apart, a compartment quite outside her life here.

Clare stood up and walked across to him, smiling down into his face as he looked at her expectantly. 'There's life in the old dog yet.' She ran her fingers through his unruly hair, then down his arm until she grasped his hand.

'I'm thirty-nine, not sixty. And you're thirty-eight. In your sexual prime, I believe.' He led her unhurriedly up the stairs.

She would enjoy this, she told herself determinedly. She would shut out those images of that other and more spacious room, of that other man who had so much power and wealth and knew so much more about life than Jason. She went into the en-suite bathroom to compose herself and to get into the right frame of mind; she wasn't finding that easy, with her husband's eyes so unswervingly upon her.

He was in bed when she got back into the

room. She was glad that there was to be no complicated foreplay, no preliminaries which would require an elaborate response from her. She slipped out of her underwear and slid between the sheets beside him, shivering a little at the cold, hoping that he would think that it was the chill which provoked her nervous giggle.

He held her tight against him for a moment, burying his head between her breasts. She was glad to be free of those relentless brown eyes. He stroked her back, running his right hand down to the curve of her bottom and then allowing it to investigate the warm, damp recesses within. She reached her hands around his slim back, felt the big muscles tensing there, felt with relief the stirring of her own response.

Jason kissed her hard, his tongue active and exploring. Then he thrust her legs apart and entered urgently, gasping with the pleasure, pumping as if she would be snatched away from him if he took too long over this. It was rough, but lovingly rough. He shouted his love as he came; held her at his climax for a long, exultant moment as she worked against him and moaned her own moment of ecstasy; remained hard within her long after she would have thought it possible.

She lost all sense of time as they subsided and lay quiet in the big bed. She thought he might have sunk into a post-coital doze, but presently Jason stirred, stroked the back of her neck gently, and whispered, 'Much better than the telly.'

'Mmmm.'

'Was it all right for you?'

'You know it was.'

'You were quieter than usual.'

'You have enough energy for the two of us, when the urge is upon you.' She felt him reach for her hand and wrap his fingers in hers.

He sat up and looked down at her affectionately. 'Do you want a cup of tea?'

On a sudden impulse, she slid her feet to the carpet. 'I can do better than that. I'm going to get us a different kind of drink.'

She slipped on her dressing gown and went swiftly down the stairs. She found that it was a relief to be on her own for a couple of minutes, but she did not feel the disquiet she had felt earlier when he had fixed her for so long with that intense look. It had been as if he was examining her for something. But that look had gone with the sex, as she had known it would. Whatever it was that had disturbed him, he was relaxed now.

She allowed herself a large glass of white wine and poured a generous measure of the malt whisky he loved, then set the glasses carefully upon the small silver tray and carried them carefully up the stairs. Jason was lying on his back, with his arms behind his head and his ruffled red hair against the headboard. She was beset by a sudden, unexpected tenderness as she stood by the bed: her husband's thin arms and torso looked very vulnerable as he lay below her.

He turned the whisky tumbler thoughtfully in his hand. 'Cut glass.' He took a sip, ran it round his mouth appreciatively. 'And single malt. This must be a special occasion which has escaped me.'

'No special occasion – we don't need one. Unless it is to celebrate your continuing and undiminished virility.' She slipped back beside him, felt the comfortable warmth of his body against hers, enjoyed the familiar marital intimacy which comes with the years, the closeness which makes no demands that you should conceal your wrinkles and always look your best.

He slipped his arm beneath her head and they lay and looked at the ceiling. There was a faint and intermittent hum of traffic from the road outside, reminding them that the world went on out there, accentuating rather than diminishing their feeling of comfortable isolation. It was then that Jason said very casually, 'Your badminton kit doesn't get dirty.'

She wondered if he felt her body stiffen against his. He must surely have done so. 'No?'

'I took it out to wash it before you came home today. It was completely clean.'

'Yes.'

'You must have worn it to badminton for the last eight weeks, by my reckoning.'

In her panic, she had not known what to say, but his words came to her like a prompt to a failing actress. 'Not eight weeks, Jason. You must think I'm a real slut! I wash it every two or three weeks. I did it on Saturday, whilst you were out at the football.'

'It looked brand new. Almost as if it hadn't been worn.'

'It is quite new, you know. I replaced my gear for the new season, when I got my bonus from work. And the new washing machine you got is much kinder to fabrics than the old one.'

'I see.' He seemed to relax very gradually beside her, as if he had weighed her words and decided to accept them.

Something told her she must consolidate this. She turned towards him, put her arms round his neck, kissed him lightly on the forehead. 'You're a funny old thing. Fancy thinking me such a slut. Anyway, at least if I'm a slut, I'm your slut!' She kissed him on the lips, more passionately this time, and felt desire stirring anew within his slim, sinewy frame.

She rolled on top of him and he made love to her again, more slowly this time, with more consideration for her pleasure and less for his own fierce drive. She muttered words of love into his ear, then the more urgent, basic four-letter words he loved when he was excited, as she rode him expertly to his climax. He hissed urgently into her ear. '*My* slut! My beautiful, beautiful, beautiful slut!'

Jason Thompson slept the sound sleep of happy exhaustion through the night. His wife's rest was more disturbed. At three in the morning, her head ached and her dry eyes stared sightlessly into the darkness.

There was no getting away from it. She really was a slut. And Jason's discovery of her unworn badminton clothes had nearly exposed her. She would need to be even more careful in future.

# Six

Matthew Ballack had been wondering for a few days what he was going to do. His first reaction had been that he couldn't take this latest humiliation from Tim Hayes. Being left in charge of the man's developing income from brothels was surely the last straw. You took the risks of breaking the law without the lucrative returns that might accrue. He would be paid a pittance for his unofficial management of the prostitutes, whilst the profits went to Hayes. The man had gone too far this time: Matthew had taken quite enough lying down. He'd get himself another job and make a completely fresh start.

And then reality took over. A man of forty-nine without much in the way of formal qualifications and no real skills to market wasn't going to find it easy to find new work. The downward spiral of his career from part-owner of a prosperous firm to general lower-executive dogsbody would be obvious to any prospective employer, however imaginatively he compiled his application letter. Moreover, any worthwhile concern was sure to contact his present employer, and he could rely upon Timothy

Hayes to scupper any application he might make.

Matthew decided that he would bide his time and keep his eyes and ears open. He knew a lot of people around the town and even further afield. Someone in Lancashire, someone who needed experience and reliability, was sure to want an able man like him. When that time came, he would delight in telling Tim Hayes exactly what he could do with his stinking job.

Like many men of his age who come upon hard times, Matthew Ballack did not choose to confront the harsh realities of his situation.

He did realize, however, that for the moment he would have to do the job, stinking or not. If he neglected it, Tim Hayes would be only too ready to note his shortcomings and diminish him still further; he had no doubt of that. Matthew decided that he would get to know some of the workers he had never seen before. Every manual of management dictated that you should have a detailed knowledge of your workforce, that you should be fully aware of the strengths and weaknesses of the people responsible to you. Only that way could you plan efficiently and set yourself real and attainable goals: some of the old clichés which he thought he had forgotten came sourly back to Matthew from a distant and more optimistic past.

He got the names of the girls who worked the streets under their protection and picked out three names at random. Different ages and different areas were the only distinctions he made. Show them that someone in control of their destinies cared; raise morale a little even in this dubious and dangerous industry. The fact that someone in charge was keeping checks and had their interests at heart would pass round on whatever grapevine operated in brothels. Thursday morning would be a good time to call, Matthew decided: in this trade, they surely wouldn't be as busy midweek as at the weekends.

He didn't know quite where he expected people like this to live, but he was surprised by the first house he visited. It was semi-detached, built in the 1960's in a dull but highly respectable road. Most of the residences here had recently fitted double glazing and neatly kept front gardens. Matthew checked the number and the name of the road again carefully before going up the path and ringing the bell by the front door.

The man who answered the door was stocky and heavy, with a paunch far too big for a relatively young man – Ballack took him to be no more than forty. He had inappropriately round and cherubic features, as if some sculptor had left off after half-forming a face. The incongruity was emphasized by the fact that he had not shaved for at least three days. He opened the door no more than eight inches and said suspiciously, 'Whaddyerwant?'

Matthew felt he should be brandishing some

kind of document to vindicate his authority, like a policeman's warrant card or a meter-reader's proof of authenticity. Titles such as 'Brothel Controller' or 'Whoremaster' flashed across his racing mind. He said, 'Is Sandra Rhodes here?'

'Who wants her?'

'My name is Ballack.' He took a deep breath, trying to make the next phrase impressive. 'I'm her employer. It's in connection with the cleaning-service rotas.' That was the code they used. You needed something uncomplicated, with such a variety of backgrounds, not all of them English, so the girls who sold their bodies were all officially self-employed part-time cleaners.

The man opened the door a little wider, peered at him for a moment, and then said with a sudden and surprising switch towards deference, 'You'd better come in, Mr Ballack.' He led him down a surprisingly spruce and well-carpeted hall and called upstairs, 'Sandra! Visitor for you. It's important.'

The room where he left Ballack had probably originally been a separate breakfast room with a kitchen beyond it, Matthew decided. The two were now one, and had been fitted with an extensive range of units and kitchen appliances. Washing machine and washing-up machine were neatly dovetailed into the line, adjacent to the new sink. The fridge-freezer doors matched those of the surrounding cupboards. He had time to observe these details at leisure, for it was a full three minutes before the woman he sought came into the room.

He thought when he saw her that she had used the delay well. She wore a dark blue dress with an interesting but by no means daring neckline and court shoes which emphasized the excellence of her legs. The single ornamental slide in her blonde hair matched the gold bangle at her wrist. Her face was carefully and expertly made up. She could hardly have presented a greater contrast with the male figure upon whom she now carefully shut the door.

'Matthew Ballack.' He smiled and held out his hand.

She hesitated for a moment before she took it. 'Sandra Rhodes. I don't operate here. If you want to—'

'I'm not here as a client!' he said hastily. 'I'm your employer. The man who makes sure of your safety and provides you with a place to work.'

'Who takes forty per cent of everything I make.'

'It doesn't come to me personally. I work for the people who take the profits, like you.'

'Big consolation to me, that is.' She walked across to the radio and switched it on.

To his surprise, the announcer told him it was Classic FM and a Strauss waltz filled the room with its incongruent lilt. 'Nice music,' he said lamely.

'You mean toms shouldn't like classical? It should be all Radio One and soft-porn TV for

72

the likes of us, should it?'

'Not at all. But do we have to have it on just now? It doesn't make it easy to talk.'

She gestured towards the door and said in a low voice, 'It's so Big Ears out there can't hear, see? What he doesn't know won't hurt him.'

'I'm sorry. Perhaps I shouldn't have come here. If you think it's going to—'

She smiled at him for the first time. 'He knows all about what I do, the idle bastard. It's paid for all this and more.' Her gesture took in the new kitchen and the house beyond it. 'So long as he gets his beer and his fags, he doesn't really give a bugger. But I like him to know as little of my business as possible.'

Ballack got the picture. Drawing unemployment benefit, living off his woman, flashing his money and boasting to his pals whilst he lost his money in the betting shops: Matthew knew the type and the temptations only too well. Not for the first time, he was amazed by what women put up with. What on earth could this cultivated creature see in that bundle of dependency out there?

He had never expected to be using the word cultivated when he set out to visit his chosen sample of his new working staff. He said, 'I can't change the forty per cent. I don't fix it and it's not in my power to change it. You get somewhere safe to work and protection from pimps who'd like to muscle in. You could have worse arrangements.'

She shrugged. 'I suppose you're right. Anyway, I don't have a choice, do I? If I tried to work my patch on my own, I'd soon have a face I couldn't work with, wouldn't I?'

He wanted to deny it, but he knew she was right. 'We wouldn't want to lose you. You know the score. You're an attractive woman who knows how to draw the punters and how to keep her mouth shut. It's a combination we like to encourage.' He knew very little about her, but he was sure that this much at least would be true.

'And a combination which will be chucked on the scrap heap, as soon as it gets a few wrinkles. I know the score.' She looked him sharply in the face for the first time. 'You haven't come here to tell me I'm finished, have you?'

'Not at all!' Matthew said hastily. 'I just like to get to know my workforce and let them get to know me. So that we're not just names to each other, you see. And of course, if there's anything you're concerned about, I'd like to know about it. There are limits to what I can do, but I'll certainly listen to you and do whatever I can.'

She looked at him for what seemed a long time before she spoke again. 'You haven't been involved in this game before, have you?'

'Not directly, no. The managing director thought that someone more senior should take control of this side of our activities.' Matthew brought out the sentence he had planned in the car; it had sounded more impressive and convincing there than it did here.

'The more anonymous we are the better, in this game. So long as the punters pay up and I don't get cut or beaten, you won't get complaints from me. Except about the forty per cent, which you've already said you're not going to change.'

The uncomfortable knowledge that she and not he was controlling this interview came upon him. She offered him coffee but he refused, anxious only to get out of this strange place before he lost all face. This woman he had unconsciously expected to be ignorant and fawning, to be grateful for this small attention volunteered to her by the man in control of her destiny, was dictating things. She seemed not only to know much more than him but to be both resilient and realistic. He stood up and smiled down at her as brightly as he could. 'Well, it's been good to get to know you a little. You'll be a face to me now, you see, instead of just a name.'

'It's not my face the customers are interested in, after the first few minutes.' She smiled wryly and without self-pity at the facts of her life. He was almost at the door when she put her hand on his arm and said abruptly, 'How much longer have I got?'

She was thirty-five, and he knew in that moment of sudden fear why she had groomed herself so carefully before she came down to meet him. There was nothing so pathetic and so dispensable as an ageing tom, nothing so desperate as a woman who felt the doors of this lucrative but dangerous trade closing against her. He wanted to reassure her, but he knew that he had no power to do so. Perhaps, indeed, there was no power on earth which could do so.

But if he kept this new role, it would fall to him in due course to tell her that she was finished. He said with false heartiness, like a man offering reassurance to an ageing relative in hospital, 'You're all right for a good few years yet, I'm sure, Sandra!' He clasped her hand briefly for a moment before she opened the door and allowed him to flee.

He wondered as he drove away how he would be able to make dismissals like that. He had thought of himself as hard and efficient, but he couldn't do this new job, if indeed it was a job. His hatred of Tim Hayes throbbed in his temples as if it had a pulse of its own.

The girl had wide brown eyes, a spontaneous, infectious smile, a figure which curved with the supple, unthinking grace of a nineteen-year-old, skin the colour of milky coffee.

Tim Hayes watched her through the one-way glass of the window of his office and congratulated himself on his decision to come to the casino tonight. This was definitely a better way to spend his Thursday evening. The wisdom of his decision to ditch Clare Thompson was confirmed for him by this vision of youth. As her employer, he must surely be an attractive proposition.

There was no hurry. The casino staff hadn't seen him for months, because of his regular assignations with Clare. He had caught them on the hop, five minutes late opening and with two of the tables not fully ready for business. There was no real damage to trade: the first hour was always very quiet. But he had shown his people that they could not relax, that the boss was likely to drop into the place at the most unexpected times.

This one-way window in his office was similarly an excellent addition. The staff and the punters couldn't see him, but he could see them at any moment he chose. He glanced out only occasionally, and usually not for long, but his workers knew that they might be under observation at any time during their evening. It was a cheap but highly effective spur towards efficiency.

He watched the floor filling up for a while, then opened the top drawer of the filing cabinet. The girl's name was Jane Martin; he checked her name, age, address and background. Quite a clutch of GCSEs and A levels, with good grades. She was no fool, but he would have expected that. There was a lot of competition for croupier posts; for some reason it was seen as a glamorous job. Perhaps it was the British obsession with money. You handled plenty of that, as the punters bought their chips and embarked on their hopeless quests.

He watched Jane Martin intermittently as the evening wore on. She was not only attractive but efficient. A pretty, cheerful girl always drew out the money more easily than the most polite and efficient of men. The clients tended to hesitate and then decide on another fifty or a hundred pounds beyond the limit they had set themselves when a girl like this one smiled at them. Men were perpetually stupid, but that was the basis of his business: the overwhelming majority of punters here were men, though they were increasingly often accompanied by women. That was something he encouraged. All men liked to be seen as big spenders, when they had a woman at their elbow to impress.

Tim Hayes waited until the girl went for her break at half past ten. He gave her a couple of minutes in the small staff room at the back of the building before he emerged from his office. He moved among the tables, nodding to clients he recognized, checking quietly that all was in order with members of his staff; there was no need to make his intentions too obvious.

She had coffee and a biscuit in front of her when he went into the rest room. There was only one other person there, a burly doorman who was relaxing for twenty minutes before his busiest hour of the night, which was always after the pubs shut. Hayes caught his eye and flicked a glance towards the door. The man left with the briefest of words to the girl at the table; when your employer made his intentions clear, you didn't hang about.

Jane Martin looked at him curiously as he sat down opposite her. 'You're new here, aren't you?' she said.

Tim liked that. It helped when girls made a gaffe like that. It got them off on the wrong foot, made them more anxious to please, more malleable. 'Not entirely new, no. I'm your boss, actually.'

She was as embarrassed as he'd hoped. 'I'm sorry, sir! I never realized. It was Mr Ballack and another gentleman who appointed me. They said I'd see you eventually, but I wasn't quite prepared to meet you like this.' She spoke well, but with a marked Lancashire accent, which seemed to him an intriguing contrast with her exotic hue and figure.

'You blush as becomingly as you do everything else, Jane Martin. I've been watching you during the evening, you see, and I've been pleased with what I've seen. But I didn't think anyone with that gorgeous colouring could do a good blush! We learn new things all the time, don't we? I'm Tim Hayes.'

He thrust out his hand, took her smaller one in his, shook it heartily, held it for just a little too long as she said, 'Jane Martin. Pleased to meet you, sir.' She slid her fingers from beneath his as soon as she could and glanced at the small gold watch on her wrist. 'I suppose I'd better be getting back to work, hadn't I? Don't want to break the rules the first time I see the boss!'

Her nervous giggle was music in his ears. He let it flicker away into the corners of the small room. 'There's no hurry. You're entitled to your full rest allocation. You've only been in here for ten minutes: I can't be seen to be exploiting my staff, can I?'

He must have watched her come in here. Jane found that a little disturbing. She wondered just how much he had been watching her during the evening. She went hastily back in her mind over her actions during the last few hours; had she done everything a croupier should? Still, he seemed to like her, which had to be a good thing. And he was a good-looking man, the boss, for an oldie. She'd tell her boyfriend that, in due course: it didn't do any harm to keep your man on his toes, the magazines said.

Hayes gave her his most winning smile, the one which said he was powerful but human. 'Do you like it here, Jane?' He lent forward, fixing those limpid brown eyes with his own keen grey ones, stealing his hand on to the top of hers. 'Please be absolutely honest, now.'

His touch didn't frighten her; she was quite flattered by it. She didn't feel at all threatened; a pretty girl like her didn't reach the age of nineteen – nearly twenty, as she told anyone who asked – without learning to handle male attention. It was rather nice to have this attractive, powerful man treating her as a human being, not just an employee.

Jane Martin had not had an easy life, but she had retained a surprising degree of naivety.

Now she couldn't think what to say. She didn't want to let anyone down when she was talking to the boss. She felt stupid as she said feebly, 'I like it here. People have been very kind to me.'

'I'm sure they have. It must be very easy to be kind to you, Jane. Even I feel like being kind to you.' He pressed her hand to emphasize the words.

'I suppose it really is time I was back at work now.' She slid her hand from beneath his, smiled apologetically, began to get to her feet.

'There's really no need. No one will come in here looking for you.'

For the first time, she felt real apprehension. 'Nevertheless, I feel I should get back, Mr Hayes. It must be getting busy out there.'

'Nonsense. If you're with me, no one's going to watch the time. And if I can't enjoy a private chat with a pretty girl like you, what's the point of owning the place?' He gave her his open, winning smile. 'And thanks to me, your coffee's gone cold. Let me get you another.' He leapt up and went over to the machine on the far wall of the room.

He slid his coin into the slot, hummed a little tune whilst he filled the beaker, kept his body between himself and Jane Martin as he slipped the tablet of Rohypnol into the beaker. 'There you are, dear. I'm only too glad to see you drinking coffee and not alcohol.'

'It's forbidden at work.' The words came quickly. And meaninglessly: he made the rules, so he must surely know that. She added clumsily, 'I don't drink much, actually, even in my leisure time.'

'And probably don't smoke either. A sensible girl, if I'm any judge, as well as a pretty one!' He laughed heartily; she saw that he had perfect, expensive teeth and a couple of fillings.

'You're right. I tried it at school and after I left – I think everyone does that. But I never got beyond five a day and I never really inhaled.' She laughed more naturally this time. It was a relief not to have to pretend you were sophisticated with this man who seemed to understand you.

'Don't go away. I'll be back in a minute.' He went out quickly and shut the door behind him. He said to the man who patrolled the floor and controlled the staff, 'Arrange cover for Miss Martin, will you? The lady won't be completing her shift tonight.'

'Will do, sir. It's not particularly busy.' The man had more sense than to make difficulties or ask for explanations.

When he went back into the rest room, he and the new girl conducted a conversation which became gradually easier as the drug took effect. He watched her drink the coffee, knew that it was only a matter of time now. He asked her about her home life and she was flattered that he should be interested in it. He leant forward and said earnestly, 'You should have gone to university, with your qualifications. Why didn't you?'

'Circumstances. My mum hasn't got a man. I felt I should help out with the money at home.' She didn't usually volunteer this to strangers, but this man was hardly a stranger now, was he? She confessed shyly that she played the violin at home, admitted that she liked classical music, as if confessing to some sort of youthful perversion.

Tim professed himself delighted with these revelations, explained that he would be back in a moment, then left her again. Alone in his office, he looked at her application form again and made a swift phone call. 'Mrs Martin? It's Brunton Casino here. Just to let you know that your daughter is working a late shift tonight. She said you're not to worry when she doesn't come home. Apparently she's made arrangements to stay with a friend.'

The sleepy voice said all right, told him she'd got her own place now and then thanked him as an afterthought for making the call. He hadn't even been asked for his name.

He went back to the rest room, asked her about her violin playing, scratched his memory and told her that the Beethoven violin concerto was one of his favourite pieces of music. This time when he took her hand in his, she made no attempt to withdraw it. The date-rape drug was obviously everything people claimed. Not that he needed it, of course. But when you were a busy man, it helped to hurry things along a little. When he moved his chair beside her and slid his arm around her waist, she made no objection.

It was time to go.

Jane felt a little unsteady when she walked, slid her arm through his as she got to the door. He grinned at her, then detached himself. 'Better if we go through the main room without touching each other, I think.'

She looked at him uncomprehendingly for a moment: her mind didn't seem to be working as quickly as usual. Then she gave a conspiratorial chuckle. 'That would be much better, wouldn't it?'

He nodded at the man he had spoken to twenty minutes earlier as they crossed the floor between the gaming tables. The worker knew what was going on all right, but he'd have more sense than to talk about it. And he didn't know and would never know about the Rohypnol.

Outside, the girl, relieved that she had made it across the floor without stumbling, fell against him in her relief. 'I feel quite woozy. Almost as if I was a little pissed!' She giggled at the impropriety of the word, then clasped his waist as they made their way to the big car with his arm round her.

He stowed Jane Martin in the front passenger

seat, looking appreciatively at her carelessly exposed thigh, feeling the lust rise within him as he set off towards the flat.

Thursday night had improved no end.

# Seven

The houses here had been built in terraces, cramped and close. The streets were also narrow. The nineteenth-century landlords had wanted as many houses as possible to the acre, as near as possible to the mills where the occupants were to work, and they had not been hampered by the building regulations which were introduced during the next hundred years.

These were not the worst houses built in that era: they had not had to share the rudimentary services and sanitation provided. Each of these dwellings had been given a single cold tap within the house and a privy at the end of a narrow flagged yard at the rear, which the night-soil men of the time emptied once a week. Brunton had never suffered from the cholera epidemics which had decimated the great cities of the empire on which the sun never set.

The terraces which survived slum clearance had been much improved by their occupants in the years after the Second World War. It was King Cotton's grip on the area which had been the raison d'être of the town. Ironically, it was as his control declined that the people who had once rented these houses prospered. They now had the money first to buy them and then to improve them. The proud new owners had introduced indoor sanitation and hot water to the grimy brick dwellings, had converted them into what the most popular phrase of the time proudly termed 'little palaces'.

It was quiet here at eleven o'clock on a Friday morning. On a dull, mild February day, the light in the narrow street seemed even dimmer than that in the centre of the town. A thin tabby cat hurried along thirty yards away, but there was not a single human presence in the street. That was the way DCI Percy Peach wanted it. When you were visiting a snout, you had to be very careful to do so in secret.

He parked beside the Pakistani corner shop a hundred and fifty yards away. He covered the ground to the house quickly, a squat, quick-striding figure, wearing a grey suit which was a little too stylish for the area. The door opened straight onto the street. It slid wide at his first knock. The sinewy hand motioned him into the house; the thin, crafty face looked quickly to right and left before the door was firmly shut upon the world outside.

'Kitchen, Enid,' the man said firmly as he followed Peach into the room. The thin, grey-haired woman in the pinafore allowed herself a single curious look at the visitor before she disappeared.

The television glared at them from the darkest

corner of what had once been the front parlour of this two-up and two-down house, its morning programme crazily optimistic about the spring fashions, which were being given free publicity by the determinedly bright presenters. The man who sat down at the table with his smartly dressed visitor had twisted teeth and stale rather than stinking breath; Peach, who was used to pressurizing people in confined spaces, had smelt much worse. The eyes above those teeth darted restlessly about, as if even in his own home the man feared there might be hidden traps. When you were a police informer, you could not be too careful.

'You said you had information, Ron.'

The head nodded repeatedly on the neck which seemed too thin for it, like that of a toy doll in the back of a car. 'Good stuff, Mr Peach. You can rely on Ron Peggs.' He nodded slyly and looked at Peach's jacket, wondering which of the pockets might contain the fee he was hoping to negotiate.

Peach produced a wallet from his inside pocket. He watched Peggs's face as he peeled two twenty-pound notes and a ten and spread them on the table with elaborate slowness beneath the man's widening eyes. The thin hand stretched longingly towards the notes, but Peach clamped his own broader palm firmly upon them. 'Facts first. Then we trade, Ron. And I control the terms.'

The thin, greedy face nodded eagerly. 'It's

good stuff, this, Mr Peach. Worth more than that.' But his eyes said that he would take the fifty willingly.

'I'll be the judge of that, Ron.'

The man looked automatically at the blaring television and then at the door through which his wife had disappeared, though it was apparent that no one could hear them. 'Hayes Electronics.'

'A name, Ron. No more than a name.'

'A front, Mr Peach.'

'You think we don't know that?' Peach's poker face told the man opposite him not an iota.

'Tim Hayes is up to things, Mr Peach.'

'And you think we weren't aware of that? I'm disappointed in you, Ron.' The black eyebrows lifted fractionally in surprise, the corners of the chief-inspectorial mouth dropped fractionally, expressing his regret that the man should waste his time with such generalities. He leaned so close to Peggs that he could see the grime on the scalp beneath the thinning hair. 'I hope you're not wasting my time, Ron. I'm a busy man.' His hand drew the notes back a little towards him on the table.

The gesture brought Peggs near to panic. 'It's good, this, Mr Peach! I've got real information for you. I didn't know how much you already knew, did I?' His voice rose in the old lag's familiar whine of protest.

Peach gave a theatrical sigh. 'Let's have it

then, Ron. Stop trying to make it more than it is. I'll decide what it's worth when I hear it. So spit it out!'

Ron Peggs poured his knowledge out, gave everything he knew all at once, when he had planned to release it in crafty gobbets and maximize its price.

Peach's face was a mask of concentration now: this was the real business of his visit, and it was information CID had not had previously. He rapped out the occasional terse question, but otherwise listened intently for three, perhaps four, minutes. At the end of this time, he lifted his hand from the notes and slid them across the table to his informant.

Ron Peggs pocketed his fee eagerly, glancing automatically towards the closed door and the invisible female presence beyond it. His voice rasped with a chesty excitement as he said, 'There's more to come, Mr Peach. I'll get you more.'

'But carefully, Ron.'

'Don't worry about me, Mr Peach! I can look after myself.' A small, absurd pride crept for a moment into the battered face.

'I'm not worried about your miserable skin, Peggs. I'm worried about these people realizing that we're on to them. If that happens, you'll be dead meat and they'll cover their tracks.' He might be exaggerating the threat, but there was no harm in that, with men like this.

The narrow, volatile eyes glinted as they

recognized a rare opportunity. 'It's dangerous, like you say, Mr Peach. Because of the risks, this stuff's got to be worth plenty.'

Peach nodded. He'd used the stick quite enough. Best to depart with a juicy carrot left dangling. He leaned forward, ignoring the breath which had grown more noxious with the man's excitement. 'It could be worth as much as a monkey, this, Ron, if you come up with everything you're promising.'

'I'll deliver, Mr Peach. You can rely on me.' The man's eagerness was almost touching. This was far more money than he had dared to hope for.

'We're going to need a lot of detail for a monkey.'

'I can get detail.'

'It will be the usual terms, mind. Half when we have enough to bring charges. Half when we have a successful prosecution and men go down.'

'I can get it, Mr Peach. Ron Peggs won't let you down!' He was pathetically anxious to convince. Five hundred pounds was more than he had ever seen in cash.

'Discreetly, mind. We don't want him to know that we're on to him or the evidence will disappear. And you don't want him to know you're feeding us or you'll disappear.'

'I know that, Mr Peach. I'll be discreet.' He pronounced this strange word he had never used before carefully, as though handling a strange new concept, then tapped the side of his twisted nose three times. 'Let me show you out the back way. More discreet, like.'

Peach went down stone steps from the back door, down a sloping flagged yard, through a wooden door which Peggs struggled to unbar, and out onto a cobbled back entry which ran between the rear elevations of two terrace rows. He was back at his car and starting the engine within one minute.

As Peach drove thoughtfully back into Brunton, Jane Martin was ringing her boyfriend. 'You're probably busy, but I have to speak to you. I'm sorry.'

Leroy Moore knew immediately that something was wrong. Jane wasn't a girl who made a fuss over small things: that had been one of the things which had attracted him to her. 'What is it, Jane?'

'It's something that happened last night. I don't want to speak about it on the phone. I'm sorry.' She couldn't stop apologizing, couldn't cast off this blanket of guilt.

'Last night? Did one of the punters at the casino turn nasty?'

'No. Nothing like that. I told you, I don't want to talk about it on the phone.' She choked back a sob.

'I'll come round.'

'It's my day off. There's no need to hurry. Just come when you can.' This time she could not control herself: she burst suddenly and violently into tears, surprising herself as much as her listener.

'I'll be round as soon as I can, but that might not be until late this afternoon. Don't let anyone else in.'

Leroy Moore put down the phone and stared at it wonderingly for a moment before he moved. If anyone had hurt his Jane, they'd have him to answer to.

Friday afternoon would be the best time, Tim Hayes decided. Get it over with quickly, give her the weekend to come to terms with it. With any luck, he and Clare Thompson would be able to resume a normal professional relationship as boss and personal assistant when the new working week came round.

By three o'clock the day's business was done. He pictured the girls in the small factory behind the offices watching the clock and waiting impatiently for their weekend to begin. POETS day, they'd called it when he started work in there with just two other people, and they probably still did: 'Piss off early, tomorrow's Saturday'. They'd been happy days, in many ways, with the business building rapidly and the sky the limit. Happier than now, he sometimes thought, when business here was slack and Hayes Electronics operated merely as a respectable front for more dubious and infinitely more profitable enterprises.

Had he really been happier when there had been all kinds of restraints upon him, rules defining what he could and could not do? Had he needed the disciplines of the law and the normal practices of industry to give him the satisfaction in his success which he nowadays he found so elusive? That was surely a ridiculous notion, wasn't it? He'd built up a big and varied company; he had everything he wanted, nowadays. He could behave exactly as he wished without having to answer to anyone. If he seemed to be perpetually running after something just out of reach, to find happiness always transitory, to see real content perpetually just round the corner, that was surely just some personal flaw which he could remedy with a minor adjustment.

It was time to set aside reflection, melancholy or otherwise, and move into action. Action would dissipate gloom. He buzzed the intercom and asked Clare Thompson to come into his room.

Clare had taken considerable pains to look her best today. They hadn't seen each other on Thursday night, so she wanted to make him as regretful as she was about the omission. She wore a neat grey skirt which was absolutely conventional office wear; it was provocative only in that it was just a little too tight for her, accentuating the neat, rather abrupt curve of what Tim called her derrière, when he was in the right mood. A good bra was always a sound investment; raising and rounding her small breasts beneath the cream of her simple linen blouse, it gave her confidence.

Clare Thompson brought her shorthand notepad and her ball-pen with her: she was as conscious as her employer was that it was the contrast between her neat business appearance and her abandoned private behaviour which contributed to the excitement she aroused in him. She was proud of her shorthand; fewer and fewer secretarial staff were proficient in it nowadays.

'Sit down, Clare.' He waved expansively at the armchairs, waited until she was seated with her pad at the ready, and then came round the big desk and sat down opposite her. 'It's been a quiet week for business.'

'Yes. We seem to have been quiet for months now. Is everything going all right?'

'Well enough, well enough. There's a lot of competition, nowadays, but we'll survive.'

'I do hope so. Some of the girls are feeling a little anxious, I think. Frankly, there isn't enough work to go round, sometimes. I hope we aren't going to have to face redundancies.'

'I shouldn't think so.' Tim made a vague, impatient gesture of dismissal with his right hand. She tried not to think of the passion that right hand could arouse when it caressed her; they were much closer today than they usually allowed themselves to be at work. 'This isn't about business, Clare. Except that I hope what

I'm going to say won't affect our working relationship.'

It came like an attack on the very core of her being. Those dull, formal, conventional phrases hit her like blows to the solar plexus. She could not breathe, could not respond with words of her own. And her brain was affected too; it would not work properly to form any sentences of her own which would fend off this assault, would stop him from going any further with this.

He wasn't even looking at her – not seeing her, anyway, however accurately his eyes were trained upon her. He went on calmly, 'I've decided it's time to end our affair, Clare. It's run its course, I think. In my experience, a quick break is much the best, in the long run. We'll both have our regrets, of course we will, but believe me, you can't let these things die a lingering death. We've had our fun. Let's remember the good times!'

'Fun!' The word came from deep within her, in a voice she had never heard before. It was the cry of a wild animal in the most vicious of traps. 'I was never in this for fun! I was in it for the long term. You said you were too, when I tried to fend you off in the early days.'

'I don't do long term, Clare. You must have deceived yourself.'

He was perfectly calm. Worse than that, he was cold as ice. She wanted to fling herself upon him, to wrap herself around him in passion, to remind him of what they were like together, what they could still be like. She wanted to hold him, to transfer some of her own desperate need through the physical contact, in some childish miracle of transferred feeling. Instead, she said sullenly, 'I gave myself to you as I've never given myself to anyone. Does that mean nothing?'

He noted exultantly that she was already speaking in the past tense. The break-up was always embarrassing, but it would be over soon now. 'I'm sorry you feel like this, Clare. It was good, but it was never for ever. I thought you understood that as clearly as I did. I want to remember it as being good. You will always be a little special for me.'

She knew as clearly as if she had names before her that he had used that last sentence to other women. That is what it was, in the other sense of the word: a sentence. 'You'll be saying next that you want us to remain friends. That you'd like to feel we could console each other when times are bad.'

He hadn't been going to go as far as that. He had no intention of remaining close to her, and he certainly didn't want her bringing her troubles to him. But he gave her an urbane smile and said, 'Is friendship such a bad thing? Isn't it the civilized way to conduct one's life?'

Clare knew again in that moment that this was a conversation he had conducted before. 'Civilized?' All her outrage came out as she shouted the word across the six feet which separated them. 'You weren't so damned civilized when we were in bed together, were you? You weren't talking about short-term attraction and remaining friends then, were you? Since when did we decide to be civilized?' She mouthed each syllable of the repeated word individually, hissing out her contempt for him and all he now stood for.

Tim Hayes stood up. 'I'm sorry you feel like this, Clare. I'm sure that when you've had a little time to think about it, you'll agree that my way is best. As I said at the outset, I hope that we can go on working together. There is in my opinion no reason why we should not do that. I hope to see you in the office on Monday. If you find it impossible to work here in the future, I shall of course give you every assistance I can in finding a suitable post elsewhere.'

She said nothing. He had prepared all this before she set foot in the room. He was no doubt ready to move on now to someone else. Someone younger and prettier and even more naive than she had been, no doubt. She would not look at him as he stood above her, would not give him the satisfaction of seeing the agony in her face. Instead, she stared downwards, noting how the grey skirt which was a little too tight had ridden up, exposing the thigh she no longer wanted him to see.

Tim Hayes stood motionless above her, seeing the turmoil in her but not wanting to acknowledge it. He had given her the signal to go and to end this when he stood, but she had not heeded it. After a moment, he said quietly, 'I'm going to leave you now, Clare. Take as long as you need to compose yourself and then take what's left of the day off. There is no more business today.'

Clare Thompson sat for a long time in the chair when he had gone. She listened to the factory closing down around her, to the laughing, happy voices of the women workers, first in the cloakrooms, and then in the car park beyond the unlit windows of the boss's office.

It was quite dark when she slipped out of the room, through her own deserted office, and out to her car.

# Eight

At the very moment when Tim Hayes was terminating his affair with Clare Thompson, Chief Superintendent Thomas Bulstrode Tucker was contemplating an early departure to the bosom of his family. That anodyne phrase masked a harsher reality, as clichés often do.

Tucker had no children: the bosom in this case was the formidable one of the wife whom Percy Peach always thought of as Brünnhilde Barbara. Mrs Tucker was a woman of Wagnerian physique and temperament. The lady detested Peach as fiercely as her husband did, though for different reasons. Never having applied her formidable will and energies to police work, Barbara Tucker did not have Peach's comprehensive knowledge of T. B. Tucker's disabilities.

Mrs Tucker thought that her husband allowed his DCI to take far too many liberties, that Tucker as head of Brunton CID should put Peach firmly and permanently 'in his place'. Tucker, though he dared not confess such things to Barbara, knew exactly why he could not take such bold action. Peach brought him results: the results which drove the complex machine of police reputations and promotions. Without Peach, he would never have become a chief superintendent. He had had to accept Peach's promotion to detective chief inspector at the same time, but that had been a small price to pay for the boost to his prestige and forthcoming pension, both of which were steady beacons in Tucker's murky world.

Now, just as Tucker was taking a last look at the view over the town from his penthouse office and sidling towards an early weekend departure, Peach arrived to frustrate his plan and complicate his world. And as usual, Percy divined from Tommy Bloody Tucker's guilty demeanour exactly what his chief had been contemplating.

'On your way out, were you, sir?' He stared at the vast empty spaces on the surface of Tucker's executive desk.

'By no means, Percy.' Tucker's face lightened suddenly as inspiration seized it. 'I was just about to check on our overtime budget, as a matter of fact.' It was the nearest thing to a threat that he could muster.

'Very wise, sir, that. We may need to draw upon it extensively in the coming months, if I'm any judge.'

Tucker was drawn unwillingly towards this expertly cast fly. 'And why would that be? As I understand it, things have been relatively quiet recently.'

'As you understand it. Yes, sir.' Percy paused, as if to contemplate for a moment this interesting aspect of his chief's expertise. 'They may not be so quiet in the coming months, sir. My information suggests that we may be attempting to net a very big fish, sir. A very big fish indeed.' He smiled knowingly, as if both the idea and the metaphor gave him great pleasure.

'And why should this involve overtime? I've warned you before that—'

'Surveillance, sir. You and I may know a man is a villain.' He paused to smile conspiratorially at Tucker, whose knowledge of villains and of crime was sketchy at the best of times. 'But the men and women in the Crown Prosecution Service want evidence. Detailed evidence.'

'Bastards.' Tucker nodded fiercely, Peach smiled his approbation of the sentiment, and for just an instant the two men were once more united in their contempt for pusillanimous lawyers, who would not even contemplate a case unless it was presented to them with a watertight guarantee of success.

'He won't be easy to pin down, sir, this big fish. We'll have to go carefully. We'll have to be even cleverer than he is.' He looked at his chief and shook his head sadly at the odds stacked against him.

Tucker sighed. 'And who is this pantomime villain you're presenting to me? This Moriarty of crime?'

Peach laughed, suddenly and without warning: it was a startling sound. 'That's very good, sir, Moriarty. That would make you the Sherlock Holmes of Brunton, pitting your wits against the Napoleon of crime! I like that idea very much indeed, sir. We need a little light relief in this job, don't we, sir?'

Tucker glanced surreptitiously at his watch and glowered. 'The name, Peach!'

Peach glanced around him before he leaned forward, implying that even in this inner temple of security, walls might have ears. 'It's Hayes, sir.'

Tucker's face looked blank for a moment, then filled with horror. It was a process which Percy had often observed before, but it gave him as much pleasure as ever. 'Tim Hayes, of Hayes Electronics?'

'That's the chap, sir.'

'Now look here, Peach, you need to be very sure of your ground here. Mr Hayes is a very prominent local businessman. I would remind you that he has provided much employment in the town over the years.'

'And is now providing it for the Brunton criminal fraternity, sir. In increasing numbers.'

'Tim Hayes is very highly respected by important people in this area. By the people who exercise much influence in our affairs.'

Peach's eyebrows lifted impossibly high beneath the shining bald pate as his face shone with delight. 'Mason, is he, sir?'

'Whether Mr Hayes is a member of the

Brotherhood or not is entirely irrelevant, Peach! I've told you that before.'

'Indeed you have, sir. Well, I'm afraid it looks like I have another Masonic villain to add to my ongoing research into the connections between crime and Freemasonry. As I think I've previously demonstrated to you, the connection between membership of a Lodge and serious crime seems statistically very high in our area. This looks like making the sample even more convincing, but we mustn't count our chickens before they are securely in the coop, must we?'

'You must not, Peach. In case you should be in any doubt, that is an order.' The head of Brunton CID sighed theatrically at this unwelcome destruction of his Friday afternoon. 'I suppose you'd better brief me fully on this.'

Percy did that, patiently but succinctly.

Tucker pursed his lips and looked for a way out. 'This isn't evidence, you know. Not evidence that would stand up in court.'

'No, sir. That's where I started from, if you remember. That's why we shall need surveillance and will need to move carefully. According to what I'm told, Hayes is now employing some pretty violent people. He must not become aware of our interest in him until we are ready to move against him.'

'How reliable is your snout?'

Percy shrugged. He thought for a moment of the thin, crafty, fearful face of Ron Peggs, and of how long it was since Tucker had had any direct contact with such denizens of the under-world. 'How reliable is any snout, sir, when the going gets tough? He might lose his nerve, and frankly I wouldn't blame him if he did. What I can say is that he's been entirely reliable in the past and is confident he can provide us with further valuable information.'

Tucker frowned and sighed again, as if his minion had brought him a heap of trouble rather than valuable information. 'You'd better follow this up, I suppose. But for heaven's sake proceed with caution.'

It might have been the motto over his door, thought Percy Peach, as he went back down the stairs to the real world. But he consoled himself by muttering again that delightful notion, 'Tommy Bloody Tucker, the Sherlock Holmes of Brunton.'

It was quite dark by the time Leroy Moore was able to reach the house where Jane Martin lived with her mother.

Jane opened the door almost immediately when he rang the bell. He could see from a glance at her tear-stained face that something was seriously wrong. She said, 'Mum knows nothing about this. I didn't come home until she'd gone out and her shift at the supermarket doesn't end until ten.'

'What's happened, Jane?'

'I'm sorry, you don't know, do you? I've been living with it all day – it seems to me like everyone should know.'

But still she bit her lip and did not tell him. He sat her down on the sofa, put his arm round her and drew her to him. At twenty-four against her nineteen, he felt immensely protective. He also knew in that moment that he loved her. He had never felt like this about a girl before: her distress brought to him a pain which was almost physical. He spoke soothingly, as his mother used to speak to him as a child; he could not remember ever using this tone before. 'You're all right now, Jane. I'm here to look after you. Nothing else bad is going to happen. No one can get at you here. It's something bad, isn't it?'

'Yes. It's much worse than you think. You're going to think I'm a slag. And perhaps I am!' She burst suddenly and violently into tears, when she had thought an hour ago that she could cry no more.

'You're not a slag! Nothing could make my Jane a slag!' But his words felt inadequate. He wondered what was coming next, whether after all he would be strong enough to take it.

'It was last night. At work.' The words came between shuddering sighs.

'What happened?' He felt suddenly empty, drained of the emotion which had been so strong a moment earlier.

'It was Mr Hayes. I – I didn't know who he was, at first. I'd never seen him before.'

'What did he do?'

Leroy spoke now like an automaton, but she

did not notice. 'He made a fuss of me. Came into the rest room when I was on my own and bought me a coffee. He seemed very nice at first.' She spoke wonderingly, as if trying to describe accurately a thing which had happened to someone else.

'And then he took advantage of you.' That was a phrase which Leroy had not known he knew, which fell almost comically from his lips. He must have picked it up from some film, he thought.

'I don't know quite what did happen. I don't know why I went with him.' For the first time, she looked up into the pained black face, into the brown eyes which had widened with horror. 'I wasn't drunk. I was working, until he came. I didn't have a drink at all.'

'So what happened?' His chest felt very tight.

'I told him I had a boyfriend. He seemed to understand at the time. I thought he was just being nice to me. I thought he was too old and too important to be interested in me.' Her voice broke again on that ridiculous thought. She thrust her face into Leroy's chest, muffling her voice as she said, 'Leroy, how could I ever have been so stupid?'

He plunged his hand into the thick, soft hair at the back of her neck, held her tight against him for a moment, and then pulled her head away. 'He raped you, didn't he?'

That was what he wanted to hear now. She understood that, and it was what she wanted to tell him. But she said dully, 'He took me home with him. He walked me through the casino and out with him, for all to see. I – I don't know what I was doing. I didn't resist that.'

'And where did he take you?' The shining, very black features were set in a stone-like mask, a contrast to the mobility of the light brown face a foot away from him as it sought for some sort of control.

'He took me to his flat. I went to bed with him, Leroy. I'm sorry. I'm so sorry!' Jane's whole frame shook violently in his arms, which held her but this time did not hug her.

It was seconds before he could control himself enough to speak. 'How did you feel at the time?' When her sobbing became even more violent, he added gutturally, 'It's important, my love.'

Perhaps it was the endearment which brought a measure of control back to her. She looked down at his new jeans, at the black leather boots below them, and said dully, 'It seems like a dream now. A nightmare. I can't understand why I didn't see what was going to happen, didn't resist, didn't knee him in the balls and get out. I've done that before, you know! Before I met you.'

'I believe you, love. I'm just trying to get a picture of this. I need you to help me.'

A deep, shuddering sigh as the tears finally ceased and she tried to control her breathing. 'I can only remember it as if it happened to someone else. I don't know why I didn't fling him off. It wasn't because he was the boss and I was afraid for my job. That wouldn't have affected me. I feel now as if I was drunk and unable to resist. But I wasn't, was I?'

'You say he bought you a coffee in the rest room?'

'A second one, yes. I think he said the first one would have gone cold whilst we were talking.'

'Did you see him put anything into it?'

Her brow wrinkled. For the first time in hours, there was a little hope within her. Leroy wasn't calling her a slag, or a tart, or worse. Perhaps he wasn't even going to ditch her. Her brow wrinkled in concentration, in that reflection of thought which Leroy Moore had always found so beguiling. 'I didn't see anything, no. But he had his back to me when he was at the machine. I didn't see the coffee until he put it down on the table in front of me.'

The mask of stone cracked for the first time in minutes as Leroy too frowned in thought. 'There's a date-rape drug. I can't remember the name of it, or how it makes people feel. I reckon he gave you that.'

She looked up at him, realized that for the first time in minutes he was looking down into her face and not unseeingly into the distance. 'It could have been that, Leroy. That would explain why I felt drunk, why I didn't see the signs, why I behaved out of character. Because

I did do that, honestly I did.'

He gave her a small, sad smile. 'I believe you, Jane. I think it's the only possible explanation.'

She felt that those simple words were the most extravagant declaration of love and trust that she had ever heard. 'Thank you. I don't know how I could have been so stupid, though. He seemed so nice at first. And he must be nearly thirty years older than me. I couldn't believe he'd be interested in me, I suppose.'

'Believe me, he'd be interested. You're the prettiest thing on two legs, little Jane Martin.' It was a recurring expression of his, and it made them giggle a little, even now.

'And after the first few minutes of chat, he must have given me the drug.'

'Rohypnol.' The name had come back to him. His brain was working again, he noticed, but a cold, dangerous anger was yearning for an outlet within him.

Jane reached her face up to his and kissed him gently on the lips. 'What do I do? Do I challenge him about it? I told you, I'm not worried about my job.'

'It's a matter of what *we* do about it, not you, love. You aren't on your own any more.'

'I still think I should confront him and accuse him.'

'No. He would never admit it, and you'd have no witnesses. He'd say you were there for the taking and he took you. He's a dangerous man, Jane. He employs me to do bad things for him.

110

I'm planning to get out as soon as I can.'

It was the first time he had ever hinted at what sort of work he did within the Hayes business empire. Jane realized that she hadn't questioned him because she hadn't really wanted to know. 'I'll leave. I like the croupier job and it was going well, but I can't stay there now.'

Leroy Moore thought for a moment. 'You shouldn't leave. Don't give him that satisfaction. He won't come near you again. He'll probably make certain you don't even set eyes on him, for a week or two. He doesn't know I'm your boyfriend. Let's leave it that way.'

'I don't want you getting yourself into trouble, Leroy.'

He gave a grim smile as he stood up. 'That won't happen. I can bide my time until I get the right opportunity. But Mr Tim Hayes is going to pay for this.'

Tamsin Hayes felt that she did not even need to visit the doctor. The appointment had been made three weeks earlier, and she felt completely different now. But the doctor had been good to her through her depression and the problems of the 'change', and she felt she should thank her for her care and report how much better she was feeling.

Dr Davies gave her the usual welcoming smile as she sat down in front of the desk. 'And how are you feeling now, Mrs Hayes?'

'Much better, thank you. I've knocked off the

antidepressants. I shan't be needing them any more.'

The doctor smiled and tried not to look surprised. 'That's good news. I'm always happy when I hear a patient telling me they no longer need medication – as you know, I think people in this country look to drugs for a solution when often they should be looking elsewhere. But you've been on them for quite some time. Are you sure you feel confident enough to knock them off completely? What about trying half the dose and then moving on from there if things go well?'

'No. I don't need them. I've been off them for the last week and I feel no ill effects. In fact, I feel better than I've done for years!'

'That's good news. You certainly look well.' She looked at her patient's positively radiant face, at the eyes which shone and the mouth which carried the wide smile she could not remember seeing before. Tamsin Hayes looked almost too well, she thought. 'I don't want to be a Jonah, but I feel that I should warn you that sudden mood swings can be a feature of the "change". It's one of the ways in which physical changes in the body affect the mind: in that sense, it's perfectly natural and you should almost expect it.'

'I expect I shall feel more cheerful at some times than others. That's only natural, isn't it? But I'm sure I'm not going to lapse into the deep depressions I've been prey to over the last

112

year or two.'

'Well, I'm delighted. And I'm certainly not going to counsel you against giving up the anti-depressants. All that I will say is that if you do find yourself feeling low again, don't hesitate to come in and see me. Don't be too proud to ask for help if you need it, will you?'

'That's good of you. And thank you for all your help, doctor. But I feel confident that you won't be seeing much of me over the next few years.'

Dr Davies thought for a moment that Mrs Hayes was going to shake her hand as a gesture of farewell before she left. She eventually contented herself with another expression of her gratitude and a final beaming smile from the door. It was a smile which lingered in the medic's consciousness for minutes afterwards, like that of an animal in a cartoon. It was so wide and knowing that it was almost disturbing. Not many of her patients were as ebullient or as glowing as that.

Dr Davies wondered what new interest could have brought about such a change in Tamsin Hayes's life.

# Nine

Jason Thompson was talking to his sixth-formers about the geomorphology of the Lake District.

It was a formidable word, and the subject sounded dry and uninteresting, especially on a Monday morning. But as usual, his own enthusiasm for both the subject and the area communicated itself to his students. In this very compact area, he explained, were some of the oldest rocks in the world and a potted history of the planet's development, as well as immense variations in the local microclimates.

With his vivid red hair flopping out of control as usual as his head nodded and shook with his enthusiasm, his brown eyes alert and sparkling behind the thick glasses, his gangly frame lurching unpredictably, his thin hands moving swiftly as he wrote and drew on the overhead projector, his whole physical appearance demanded attention. Jason got that attention, even from those who had been determined to be bored when they came into the room.

He drew lots of questions. And he in turn put questions of his own, leading them into new areas of knowledge, new speculations, new discussions. He sat on the edge of the table at the front of the room, swinging his legs, bringing as many youngsters as possible into the debate, stretching his arms wide as if encircling them all in this exciting process, occasionally clasping those arms tight around his thin chest, as he seemed to hug himself with pleasure at his success.

There were eight girls and six boys in this group. There were no real rules about uniform in the sixth form, and the girls wore clothes which transformed them from children into young women. As his teaching succeeded and the atmosphere grew more friendly and informal between educator and learners, Jason Thompson grew intensely conscious of these females who seemed to have bypassed adolescence; of their scent, of their dancing hair, of their laughter, of the curves of breasts and the stretching of thighs.

Until three years ago, he had taught in an all-boys' school. It made him now more aware of these distractions. None of the girls would take him seriously as a lover, of course. He was conscious of his gawky, uncoordinated frame, of his boyish, unruly, carrot-coloured hair, of his thick spectacles and the way his myopia sometimes made him peer at people. That was just as well; there was no danger of him getting himself into trouble through unprofessional conduct. But there was nothing wrong with watching and appreciating beauty, was there? It was a good thing in a man, so long as the teaching was going well, which it was doing today. Nothing wrong with the odd male fantasy, nothing wrong with a happily married man being highly sexed.

It was not until later, when he was marking homework in the staff room, that Jason's thoughts reverted to the situation which he wished only too heartily was a fantasy. He almost regretted now that he'd found Clare out. It was almost comic, the way he had found her badminton kit unworn, when she had supposedly been playing every Thursday night for weeks – comic if it had been someone else, and not him in the situation. He felt the blood pounding in his temples at the thought of Clare in bed with someone else, of the things they might have done, of the sounds she might have made.

That way madness lies, he told himself firmly. It did not prevent him from planning retribution.

\* \* \*

*Mrs Agnes Blake requests the pleasure of your company at her daughter's wedding to Denis Charles Scott Peach on Saturday the 3rd of May.*

*A short ceremony at Goosnargh Parish Church at 11 a.m. will be followed by a reception and lunch at Marton Towers at approximately 12.30.*

*RSVP*

Lucy Blake studied the gilt-edged card with some distaste. It was going to happen, then. She had never really believed that the unlikely concordat between Peach and her mother would bring her to this, but it had. She wanted to marry him, of course she did, but there was no need for such haste. She said sourly, 'We can't have a church ceremony. Percy's been divorced.'

'You're out of date, our Lucy. Not as much on the ball in these things as you thought you were, you see. So long as the divorce is all official and concluded, you can get married in the Church of England nowadays. I've checked with the vicar and he says he'll be glad to officiate himself. He wants to know exactly what vows you're going to make. Apparently there are different formats available nowadays.' Agnes Blake sniffed her disapproval of such laxity in standards.

'Percy won't want all that "Denis Charles Scott" nonsense you've put on the cards. He tries to keep his names secret in the police service.'

'You have to sign the register with your real names, the names you have on your birth certificates,' said Agnes firmly. 'And he's proud of those names really. They're the same as Denis Compton's. And I believe that Percy batted a little like Denis, when he was at his best.' Agnes, who had only read of Percy's exploits in the Lancashire League and never seen him play, spoke with invincible confidence. 'He should never have given up the game so early.'

Lucy knew that the comparison with Denis Compton was the highest compliment her mother could give; she felt a little jealous of her husband-to-be. 'He felt his eye was going a little at thirty-six, Mum. That's why he plays golf now. The people in CID tell me he's quite good.'

'*Golf!*'

Lucy had never heard anyone condense so much contempt into a single monosyllable. It was a prodigy of compression she loved to hear and could not forbear provoking. 'Golf's a good game, Mum, and one you can go on playing for a long time. I might even take it up myself.'

'It's a game for cissies of both sexes! A game which has to have a handicap system, because the people who play it are such wimps that they can't face competing on level terms.' Agnes had been researching the mysteries of this game which in her mind had always been one for effete toffs. She was proud of the knowledge shown by this new form of denunciation.

'Lots of people play golf now, Mum, from all social classes. You need to move with the times.'

The eternal, last-resort advice of children to parents. Agnes sniffed derisively and moved on from the particular to the general. 'You might be able to think about golf in a few years, when I'm gone, our Lucy. Until then, you'll be too busy with your children to bother about such silly things.'

'I don't suppose we'll be in any hurry to have a family. People leave it later, these days.'

'These days! Lots of things happen "these days". It doesn't mean they're right. Your biological clock's ticking, our Lucy.' Agnes produced the phrase she remembered from a magazine in the doctor's surgery with studied nonchalance, then hastened to build upon it. 'In any case, Percy's nearly forty. He's going to want children pretty quickly, if you ask me!'

'It's not as simple as you make out, Mum. There are all kinds of things to take into account.'

'It seems simple enough to me. I suppose you mean your precious career. Well, your fiancé says there are all sorts of perks built into the system to safeguard that, nowadays. You can safeguard your rank whilst you take years off, Percy tells me.'

Not for the first time, Lucy found herself cursing the unlikely and unholy alliance between the man's man Percy Peach and the woman who was shortly to become his mother-in-law. 'I'm doing well, Mum, and learning a lot. You don't give up work easily when it's going well.'

Agnes Blake was silent for a moment,

rejoicing in her daughter's success and in the opportunities which had not been available to her in her own youth. Then her desire to be a grandmother overcame those feelings. 'I'm seventy years old, our Lucy. I want to enjoy my grandchildren whilst I still have the energy. I want to see them going to school, to watch them growing up.'

'You're good for a lot of years yet, Mum. I can see you being a sprightly ninety-year-old.'

'And I can see you still putting off having my grandchildren, then, the way you're going on.'

Lucy was smitten with a sudden guilt over her mother's perfectly understandable yearnings. Was she being selfish? 'I suppose I could have children and just take maternity leave.'

'I don't like that idea. Babies and infants need their mums until they go to school.' Agnes Blake was struck by a new and triumphant thought. 'I'm sure Percy Peach agrees with that!'

'Percy will consult with me and go along with my wishes!' Lucy said loftily. She suspected Percy would support Agnes. But secretly, and unfashionably in one of her generation, Lucy suspected that she herself agreed. 'Anyway, this is all in the future and all hypothetical.'

'Children aren't hypothetical.' Agnes shook her head at such nonsense and addressed herself to more immediate concerns. 'Anyway, we'd better get on with the guest list. It's high time these invitations were sent out.'

Lucy Blake turned her attention reluctantly to whittling down the number of people her mother had on her list. She'd have to start thinking about a dress soon; this marriage was really going to happen. It was just as well that things looked like being quiet on the serious crime front in the next two or three months.

She should have known by now that in CID work, you could never really predict the future.

The woman was very beautiful. She was twenty-four, slim and willowy, which made her look a little taller than her five feet seven. She had long and lustrous black hair and the smooth, unwrinkled olive complexion which was characteristic of her North Pakistani origins. She spoke in a low, soft, educated voice with only the faintest trace of a northern accent.

Matthew Ballack could hardly believe that she was a prostitute.

He said a little awkwardly, 'I'm visiting the people who work for me. I like to keep in touch with my staff.'

She raised her eyebrows. 'Isn't that rather dangerous? Would your wife approve of your visiting me at home?'

'I haven't got a wife. I'm divorced.' He saw her face clouding. 'And I've no ulterior motive. I've been put in charge of this section of our activities and—'

'In charge of the toms?' Her tone as well as her surprise said that surely that couldn't be much of a job. 'I've never met anyone in charge before. I've occasionally met some bruiser who said he was protecting me and wanted payment in kind.'

'I think we might call this our escort agency. I know that we've always referred to it as our cleaning services arm, but I can't quite think of you as a cleaner.' He smiled when she did; the description sounded as ridiculous in his ears as it obviously did in hers. 'We haven't had anyone officially in charge before. We're trying to formalize things a little.'

She glanced at the clock on the mantelpiece. 'I haven't got long. I have to collect the children.'

'It won't take long. It's just that I've always liked to know my staff personally.'

'Even when they were tarts?'

He forced a smile. 'I haven't been in charge of people like you before.'

'No. I should think it must be a shitty job.'

He was used to much worse words, but this mild obscenity falling from lips like hers was somehow very shocking. 'How – how did you get into this job?'

She shrugged, allowed herself a wry smile. 'The clientele's changing, so like almost every other public service they're trying to recruit a certain number of Pakis. I've never seen the country, never been out of Britain, but my skin and my race conform.'

'I didn't mean that. I meant how does anyone

with looks as stunning as yours end up – well, not exactly on the streets, but...'

'In a brothel? Oh, that was quite easy, Mr Ballack.'

She had remembered his name, when he had already forgotten hers. And what Matthew had essayed as a compliment had fallen very flat. 'I didn't mean that. I'm sorry if I don't express myself very well, but this is a new job for me. What I really meant to say was that you look quite stunning and I'm frankly amazed that someone with your looks and intelligence and education couldn't find some other sort of work.' He'd managed to say what he meant at last, but the words had come out all in a rush and spoiled the effect.

She smiled at him, wondering how the man who had said he was in charge of her could know so little of this trade. 'My parents are Pakistanis. When I was taking A-levels at the comprehensive, I got myself an English boy-friend. They didn't like that. When I refused to give him up, they threw me out.'

'What happened to the boyfriend?'

Another shrug; another pitying look for one so ignorant of her world. 'He went off to university when I couldn't. He found himself someone else there.'

'I'm sorry.'

'You shouldn't be. It was inevitable. And I was stupid. When one is eighteen, principles seem important, but within two or three years, one learns that there are more important things. Like survival.'

'But you're married.'

Another quiet smile of contempt for the man who thought that could be a solution. 'I married on the rebound. An English boy, of course, which made any possibility of reconciliation with my family impossible. He was as young as I was. Three months after the second baby, he took off. I've no idea where he is now.' It was flat, matter-of-fact, and totally without self-pity.

That made it much worse, in Matthew Ballack's sentimental view. 'So you took to prostitution to pay the bills.'

'Among other things. It pays well, for the few years whilst you have your looks. It leaves me with a little to spare, even when you lot have taken your forty per cent. Now that the children are at school, I even have time to read a little, during the day.'

He was wondering now how he could terminate what he was finding a very embarrassing exchange. 'Well, I mustn't keep you, as you said. It's good to find an employee who seems in such good health and to be happy with her lot.'

'Happy?' She weighed the word, then dismissed it without comment. 'I don't waste my time and I don't waste my money, Mr Ballack. I even manage to save a little. When the children are old enough, I shall resume my education and get myself a degree. If I can't study full-time, there's always the Open University.'

If someone had retold this story to him, he would never have given it credence. Watching and hearing this woman, he believed every word of it. And it upset him far more than if he had met the kind of woman he had been expecting to meet here. Prostitutes should be different from this, should be grateful for attention from the man who had their welfare in his hands. Except that he hadn't. This wasn't a job at all. It was the final stage in Tim Hayes's degradation of him. When it suited the man, he would cast him out altogether.

As he left, her face lit up with that ravishing smile and she said to him, 'You don't seem to me a bad man, Mr Ballack. I have no idea how you came to be in charge of brothels, but I think you too should have aspirations. The first one should be to get out of this shitty job.'

Tim Hayes didn't often eat with his wife nowadays. When he said he would be home for dinner on this Monday evening, he had half-expected her to tell him in her usual surly way to look after himself. Instead, she had prepared a full meal.

It was a reminder to him of what Tamsin could do when she turned her mind to it. There was beef Wellington and new potatoes, fresh sprouts and new carrots. The meat was tender and succulent; the bottle of Châteauneuf du Pape which accompanied the dish complemented it perfectly. The cutlery and cut glass spark-led on the white linen in the subdued lighting.

It looked like a romantic setting, but there was no danger of romance developing between this pair.

Indeed, Tim became more uncomfortable as the meal progressed. It wasn't that his wife was sullen, or even indulging in the cutting sarcasm which was her other vein in recent months. On the contrary, she was more friendly than she had been for years. She asked him if he was enjoying the meal, even questioned him briefly about his day at work and how the business was going. But he was aware that she was not listening to his replies. She had an abstracted air: she looked at him several times across the table almost as if she was surprised to see him there.

He said stiffly, 'You seem much happier, dear. Have you found yourself a new interest?'

She didn't answer him directly. But she look-ed him full in the face and said with a discon-certingly bright smile, 'The doctor's knocked me off the antidepressants.'

'That's good, isn't it? Are you sure you're quite ready for it?'

'I told her myself that I didn't need them any more.'

He found himself desperately seeking for something to say. She seemed inclined to pur-sue her own stream of thought, whatever he chose to say to her. 'It's the firm's annual dinner in a fortnight. More people than ever will be there, as our range of interests expands. Do you want to come, or shall I make your excuses as I have for the last couple of years?'

Tamsin looked him full in the face again, and this time she answered his question directly. 'This year I'll come. I'll sit beside my husband and support him.' She was trying not to show her excitement. This might be the occasion she had been waiting for. She had no idea yet how she would kill him, but there was plenty of time left for planning.

'Are you sure you want to be there, dear? I know you don't like big formal gatherings. I'm quite prepared to tell them you don't feel up to it.'

'No, you won't have to do that. I'll come and put on my glad rags for you. After all, I'm not depressed any more, am I? That's medical and official.'

That was an odd phrase, he thought, typical of the strange mood of muted excitement which seemed to have taken her over tonight. 'All right. I'll make sure we take account of that in the table plans.'

She served him the blackcurrant cheesecake she had made herself. It was his favourite and he had a second helping before she brought in the coffee in the cafetière. He even went and poured them both a brandy, swirling the cognac thoughtfully round his glass, trying to engage her in a conversation which remained brittle and spasmodic, even now when they should have been relaxed after the excellent meal and the alcohol.

Tamsin remained in the sitting room after Tim had given up the effort and said he was going to have an early night. She stared unseeingly at the television and sipped at the brandy she had not touched whilst he was there. She was glad she had given Tim his favourite food tonight, glad that she had taken the care to see that it was cooked to perfection. It was a nice variation on the old cliché from the days of capital punishment, she thought with her secret smile.

The condemned man had eaten not a hearty breakfast but a hearty dinner.

# Ten

Leroy Moore's mind was in turmoil. He had never had a girlfriend who made him feel like this before. He had never had an employer who paid him so much for so little before. He had scarcely expected the two to come into serious contact with each other, and certainly never contemplated the employer provoking a conflict like this.

He was surprised how strongly he felt. He had been running the streets since he was twelve, initially at nights, then increasingly by day as well, as his truanting from school became increasingly bold and increasingly unchecked. Moss Side, Manchester, was one of the most violent and dangerous places in Britain to grow to manhood: even the police trod carefully there, when they entered the area at all. If you survived, you learned to look out for yourself pretty quickly. There were few moral values, and might was increasingly the only right.

From the age of fourteen, Leroy Moore had carried a knife wherever he went. By the time he was sixteen, he was a member of one of the gangs of feral black youths who were feared but for the most part secretly admired by their contemporaries. There were white gangs, too, and they fought for dominance wherever their territories overlapped. By the time he was eighteen, Moore had killed a man. It had been in self-defence, but it had been swift, violent and efficient. He had never been charged, though he had been extensively questioned by police about the crime. He had neither gloated nor boasted about the deed.

The seething underworld of the city knew the killer, of course, but there was no retribution from there. The general feeling was that the victim had had it coming to him: if it had not come from Leroy Moore, it would have come swiftly enough from someone else. It enhanced Moore's reputation with some of the bigger fish who cruised in these dark pools. He began to get offers of jobs. He drank very little and he kept his mouth firmly shut. He was ruthless, but no more ruthless than was necessary. These qualities brought him employment and promotion.

Leroy was intelligent but uneducated – he had dodged too much schooling to acquire any qualifications. He knew that sooner or later those who lived by the sword were probably going to die by it. Violence was the only thing he knew, but sooner rather than later he was going to learn to do something else and to earn his living in some less desperate and less dangerous way.

His transition from Moss Side to Brunton was the first part of this plan. To threaten people and occasionally rough them up for Tim Hayes was a Sunday School picnic compared with the gang warfare of Moss Side. He could do it standing on his head, or at least without much thinking and without much danger to himself. And there was countryside around Brunton, something he had not met before. A few years ago, Leroy would have considered the very idea of walking for pleasure not only ludicrous but risible. Now he enjoyed exploring the Ribble Valley; he and his friends might get a little noisy in the pub at the end of the day, but it was usually after fifteen miles or so in the open air. He was beginning to acquire an increasing number of non-criminal friends.

The greatest influence in his life now was Jane Martin. The initial attraction had been her looks. There was no mystery about that. The smooth skin, enormous brown eyes, and lithe, gracefully moving figure would have captivated much less susceptible people than Leroy Moore. The second attraction had been her innocence. She was just over four and a half years younger than him, but the gap seemed much larger.

In a single-parent family on a housing estate, Jane Martin had hardly had a sheltered childhood. But she had been a bright girl and had never missed a day at school; her teachers had been disappointed to find that she was not going on to university. She had fought her corner on the town's toughest estate, had even been given a suspended sentence after a fracas between rival groups in which four teenagers had been hospitalized, but she had come through all that.

To Leroy Moore, the young-old veteran of fierce, dog-eat-dog violence in the darkest area of a great city, Jane seemed the epitome of innocence and naivety. These were qualities which had great appeal for him: Jane Martin became the tangible representation of his vision of the better life he aspired to. Soon he would give up even the relatively minor violence which his work for Hayes Electronics demanded, and find himself a new and better career. He and Jane would move forward into the brighter future which her innocence demanded.

Leroy Moore had read very few books, and not a word of romantic fiction. But in the days when he had lived at home, his mother had ensured that he had a steady diet of Hollywood's more dubious and sentimental products. Jane Martin would have been astonished and disconcerted to know that in Leroy's surprisingly vivid imagination she often gambolled through the Alps in *The Sound of Music*.

Moore's instinctive reaction to the news of what had happened to Jane at the hands of Hayes was to turn to violence. It was what he could do, what he was good at. Moreover, it had been the way he had reacted to any setback since the age of eleven, and in his view he had generally been successful. But he had been successful because he had not taken blind, unthinking, immediate action, but had thought first about what he would do. Now he knew that it was more necessary than ever to think about exactly what revenge he could take.

Hayes was a powerful man, with more resources at his command than any enemy Leroy had tackled before. His immediate reaction was to rush to him immediately and beat him senseless. A little thought told him that this was not the right strategy. He would have to make sure that he had the right occasion. And he might need to do something more serious than beat him up, if he was not to suffer retribution from the seriously violent men Hayes could summon so easily to the task.

Leroy realized that he must make his retribution anonymous, must arrange it so that no one could be sure that it was he who had brought it about. That meant he would have to engineer the right sort of opportunity. He would need to get to know the man's movements – then perhaps he would be able to trap him without protection in some alley, where he could mete out his justice swiftly and decisively. He had no idea yet when this opportunity would occur.

That was the state of his thinking when his mobile phone rang and an impersonal voice he did not know said that Mr Hayes wished to see him at ten o'clock on Wednesday morning.

* * *

Matthew Ballack got the name of the lawyer from the Citizens' Advice Bureau. It wasn't that he didn't know any legal men. It was rather that he wanted anonymity: he didn't want someone recalling this meeting inconveniently at a later date. He asked for and was given a source of advice not in Brunton but in the neighbouring town of Bolton, where he thought there was little chance of his name being known.

The man was old. Not the silver-haired, distinguished-looking old which gave confidence, but a little down-at-heel, with hair which drooped over the back of his collar and hands which shook a little as they talked. He looked to Ballack like a man with a drink problem, but perhaps he had dried out now. Matthew regarded him suspiciously, but knew he must be properly qualified, to be used by an organization like the CAB. And this was surely a simple enough legal quandary to put to even a struggling lawyer.

He produced the two now rather dog-eared pages which he had kept through all his vicissitudes of recent years. They made a simple enough document. His fear was that it was possibly too simple to have any legal standing. It was twenty-four years old now, and it was the only written agreement which he and Timothy Hayes had ever made.

They had had so little money when they started their modest electrical components enterprise that they had not employed a lawyer. Instead, they had painstakingly copied out a legal agreement from a manual borrowed from the library. Matthew remembered the laborious process of tapping it into his early and very rudimentary Amstrad computer, then printing out copies for himself and Tim. In that very different world, they had felt immensely sophisticated and at the forefront of technology.

The document simply outlined a partnership, an agreement to bear joint responsibility for the repayment of the loan they had wrung from the bank to get their enterprise under way and to share any future profits which might accrue from this enterprise. Each of the men had signed their assent to these conditions at the foot of the very simple document. Matthew looked for a moment at those bold, young men's flourishes and recalled the excitement and happiness of those days almost a quarter of a century ago, when two friends had thought they needed nothing but the most basic of legalities.

The old man read unhurriedly through the two short pages of the document. He seemed to the anxious Matthew Ballack to take an inordinately long time over it, but he told himself that careful attention to detail could only be a good thing in a lawyer.

The old eyes were watery but keenly observant as the man finally laid the sheets down and looked at his visitor. 'Which clause is it that you

135

wish me to advise you on, Mr Ballack?'

'I simply need to know whether this agreement would still have legal standing.'

'In the absence of any subsequent agreement which overrides it, I think it would, yes.'

'What about subsequent verbal agreements?'

The old head shook quickly and the thin mouth allowed itself a small, sad smile. 'Courts do not like oral agreements. People tend to remember what they and other people have said very differently.' He shook his head again at the frailties and venalities of the human condition. 'Unless both parties were in absolute agreement that these conditions had been changed with the assent of both parties, the original written document would almost certainly prevail.'

'And if the firm has changed its name and extended its activities, would that invalidate the terms of this agreement?'

'Not unless a new partnership or other form of agreement was made at that time, which would of course override this document.'

Matthew tried not to show his elation. There had been no new written agreement, and there was nil chance of any verbal assent between him and Timothy Hayes: he would deny anything the man said, if necessary – except that Tim wouldn't be around to say anything, of course.

The heavily lined face opposite him was looking down with some distaste at the shabby pages in front of him. 'My advice would be to have a new and more modern agreement drawn up immediately, if this enterprise has prospered.'

'Thank you. I shall pass on this view to the parties concerned.'

Matthew Ballack got out as quickly as he could, then drove swiftly back over the moors towards Brunton. A sudden impulse made him pull into a lay-by as he reached the highest part of his route. He looked not at the stark winter countryside but at the high metal wall of the rear of the pantechnicon in front of him, unable now to stop smiling in his private world, which an hour or two had seemed as bleak as the landscape around him.

He took out the precious, grubby document again and looked for the hundredth time at the final clause, which stated that simply that, in the event of the death of either party, all assets of the firm would pass to the survivor.

Jane Martin was very nervous when she next went into the casino. Leroy had persuaded her that it was what she must do, that to resign would merely be playing into the hands of Hayes, who would happily accept her departure and hope never to see her again. If they bided their time, he said, the opportunity of revenge upon him for what he had done to her would surely arise.

After the first hour, she found that she adjusted surprisingly quickly. Once the public came in and she was busy at the tables, the patterns of work took over and she was too active to be perpetually glancing over her shoulder for any sign of the man who owned all this. He did not appear, and everyone else around her behaved exactly as they had done before the events of the previous Thursday night. Even the staff who had seen her leave with Hayes seemed now as if they had not registered that departure.

It seemed that what Leroy had told her was right. People kept their noses clean and got on with their work. In this place, they didn't speculate openly about the actions of the boss, didn't even gossip happily, as girls had done when she had worked in other places. It paid here not to comment on things you had noticed. Perhaps it was expected that the boss would demand sexual favours of attractive female employees, and even that they should willingly accept his attentions for the privileges it might bring to them.

Jane wanted to tell anyone who would listen that it hadn't been like that, that she wasn't some cheap tart who sold her body for the advancement of her career, that drugs had been involved and she hadn't known what was happening. But she was intelligent enough to realize within an hour that her declarations would not be welcome and she kept her mouth shut. Revenge if it came would not come from the law or from the support of her fellow workers.

Jane Martin was growing up fast. Her education in the ways of a dangerous world was proceeding apace.

It was on Tuesday evening, four days after her night with Tim Hayes, that she was given the stiff white envelope. She turned it over several times in her hand, wondering if this was her notice and what she should do if it was. She did not open it until she was in a cubicle in the ladies' cloakroom an hour later. There she read its simple, one-sentence message a dozen times over, searching for some subtext or some hidden code, which it did not contain. She even considered the possibility that this was not meant for her but for someone else entirely, but that was plainly silly. Her name was there in bold black letters.

Ms Jane Martin was invited to the annual dinner of the senior employees of Hayes Electronics and its allied businesses.

Clare Thompson knew about the list of guests for the annual dinner. She had compiled the basic list as usual, submitting it to her employer for deletions and omissions. She had seen him hesitate for a moment over the name of Jane Martin, then sanction that the young woman was to be invited to the function, along with the other three permanent croupiers from the casino.

It was a longer list than usual this time, almost twice the length it had been last year. Clare supposed that represented the successful expansion of the business in other spheres than the original electronics factory, but she did not know that. She had added the names he told her to add without any query. She had ceased all communication with the man whose personal assistant she was, apart from the most formal exchanges. She did not even look at him now, lest he saw in her eyes the cold, abiding hatred she felt for him.

She was glad that her husband was coming to the dinner this year. She had been used to making her apologies for Jason, explaining that this was not really his kind of thing, whilst exchanging knowing winks with Tim in private about his welcome absence. Now she was glad that she would be able to show Hayes that her life was not shattered after all, that it was continuing with Jason and without him. She was aware that Hayes might welcome the sight as evidence that he had successfully shrugged her off and set her back where she had been before their affair, but that would leave him off his guard.

Because the real situation would in fact be quite different. She was merely demonstrating that she was perfectly able to get on with her own concerns whilst she planned her revenge. Clare Thompson said nothing to Tim Hayes about her husband's attendance; that would have showed weakness. She merely added Jason's name to hers in the lists for the table seating plans.

Leroy Moore was waiting in Clare Thompson's office at ten minutes before the appointed time of ten o'clock on Wednesday morning. He had not been here before. Clare eyed him with surreptitious curiosity as she pretended to get on with the work at her computer.

He was very black and rather good-looking, she thought, with smooth features and a ready smile. He wore a good suit in which he looked a little uncomfortable; that was probably because he was not used to wearing suits, she decided. He was a squat and powerful young man, but he looked decidedly nervous; that was no doubt because he was meeting the boss.

She could not know that Leroy Moore was nervous for entirely different reasons. This would be the first time he had seen Hayes since the man had raped the girl he loved. He was telling himself to keep his hands in his pockets, to restrain the tide of violence he felt welling within him as he was forced to remain sitting quietly on the upright chair, knowing that the man he now hated was on the other side of the wall behind him. He wanted to know what Hayes would have to say for himself, how he would explain away his treachery.

When Hayes came through the door of his office to call him in, he was his urbane, commanding self, and somehow his control annoyed Moore far more than some more defensive attitude. Hayes said airily, 'See that we're not disturbed for twenty minutes or so, please, Mrs Thompson,' then ushered Leroy through the doorway in front of him, and shut it firmly upon the world outside.

'You seem to have had the desired effect upon Mr Simpson. He's paid his rent in full since your visit.'

Leroy mumbled something non-committal about bringing people to their senses. He had almost forgotten the name of the wretched betting-shop manager they had beaten up in the doorway of his premises. Then he found himself saying what he had never intended to say. 'I don't like beating people up.'

Tim Hayes concealed his surprise. 'No one likes it, Leroy. I should think the people who get beaten like it considerably less than you who give the beating – that is surely the object of the exercise.'

'Violence can get out of hand.' Then, thinking that made him sound like a wimp, Leroy added gruffly, 'It's all right for the people who give the orders. It's the people like me who take the rap. If something goes wrong, we can end up with a murder rap.'

'Up to you to make sure that it doesn't go wrong, isn't it, Leroy? That's what you're paid so handsomely to do. It should be swift, anonymous and just severe enough to achieve our objectives. As I say, I am so far very satisfied with your efforts. Even pleased with them, in fact.'

'I've done what you asked.' Leroy was sullen, watchful, unsmiling, waiting for the exchange about Jane Martin he had been anticipating when he came here. He was a man not at home with words; almost all of his differences over the last ten years had been settled with fists or knives.

'And you've done it efficiently and discreetly, as I've already indicated. That's why I'm thinking of promoting you. That's why I asked you to come here today. To meet me at the respectable centre of our activities.'

Leroy Moore wondered whether he was being bought off, whether the price of his acquiescence in what had happened to Jane was to be the thirty pieces of silver of advancement in this man's empire. 'What sort of promotion?'

'Come, Leroy, there is no need to be wary. The sort of promotion which brings you a little more prestige and a lot more money. I want what you say you want for yourself. I want you to become respectable. Or at least to appear respectable to the outside viewer. I want you to become Head of Security Services at Hayes Electronics.'

'Head of Security Services?'

Hayes laughed aloud at the bewilderment on those too-revealing dark features. 'That will be the title. Of course, you will not spend much time here: there is little need for your sort of work in this eminently respectable original section of the business. You will oversee the need for security in the other and less predictable areas in which we pursue our profits.'

'Rough up people who don't cooperate, you mean.'

'I suppose I do, yes. But we wouldn't use such terms to the nosy parkers who occasionally question our operations, would we?'

'Would that include responsibility for the casino?'

'It would indeed, very much so. Is that a particular area of interest for you, Leroy? You're not a gambling man, I hope. Employees are strictly forbidden to engage in any of our own gaming activities.'

'My girlfriend works there. Jane Martin.'

A look of astonishment, perhaps even of fear, passed fleetingly across the confident, controlling face. Leroy knew in that instant that Hayes had not known that before, that when he had picked out this ravishing girl he had not known that she was the girlfriend of one of the men he employed. Had not known, in fact, until this moment. It should have put the older man at a disadvantage, but Leroy could not see how he was going to use it. There was a pause when each man stared at the other, as if wondering what came next. Then Hayes said smoothly, 'I didn't know that. I met her briefly last Thursday night, I think. She seemed charming. And she's certainly a looker. I congratulate you on your taste, Mr Moore.'

He hadn't known. Hayes hadn't known until

now that Jane was his girl. And now he was trying to carry it off as if nothing had happened. Leroy's brain reeled as a mass of violent emotions fought for control of it. He felt his fingernails, fierce as needles in his palms, as his fists clenched even tighter. He mustn't attack the man physically, not here and now. That would land him in trouble and Jane would be left alone, without his protection. He eventually heard himself saying, 'Jane wouldn't have gone with you. Not of her own accord.'

Hayes had watched Moore's too-revealing features mirror his fight for self-control. He now smiled the knowing, experienced smile of the man in command. 'You still have a lot still to learn about life, Leroy, though you know your own corner of it well enough. A lot to learn about women. Power and wealth are still very attractive to them. I think that's why in the old days they had what they used to call *droit de seigneur.*'

He threw in the French phrase he was confident this man would never have heard and smiled patronizingly into the frustrated, uncomprehending face. 'Now that I know that the girl has a relationship with you, I shall not assert my rights again. How does that sound?'

He's asking me to thank him, thought Leroy. The bastard wants me to join his rich man's club and say no hard feelings. Beyond leaping across the desk and plunging his fist into that grinning, complacent face, he had no idea what to do. He repeated doggedly, 'She wouldn't have gone with you. You gave her something to make her go with you to your flat.'

Hayes's smile disappeared as his face hardened. 'I wouldn't go round saying things like that, Leroy. You'd need evidence you don't have. Less amenable men than me would take it up now. But because I'm an understanding sort of chap and because I like you, I'm going to ignore it. But I advise you to turn your attention back to business immediately. Do you want to be Head of Security Services at Hayes Electronics or not?'

He rolled out the title and stressed the capitals invitingly. To Moore, it felt more than ever like a bribe, a sop to keep his mouth shut and make no ripples. He told himself that it had been offered before Hayes knew that Jane Martin had any connection with him, but that didn't alter his feeling of being a Judas. He said through lips which felt stiff and unmoving, 'What does this involve?'

Hayes was at ease now. The man was going to take this job – it was a lucrative offer and he'd be silly if he didn't. 'Not a lot that you aren't doing at the moment. You'll be around on public occasions, discreetly in the background but acting as my personal bodyguard. For the rest, it's largely regularizing what you do already. Leaning a little on people who don't come forward with their payments on time, like Simpson. And taking care of people who trespass on our patch, who try to muscle in on our activities.'

It was rather the reverse of that, as Moore knew. Gambling and prostitution are lucrative fields, and Hayes was pushing out onto other people's patches, shoving aside small-time pimps and individual betting-shop owners. He wanted to let such people know that whatever offers he made to them were to be accepted if more violent persuasion was to be avoided.

This was exactly the sort of murky work Leroy had been planning to abandon. But it would get him close to Hayes, would present him in due course with the opportunity he wanted. He said tersely, 'I'll take it.'

'That's good. I'll see that you are formally added to our permanent staff, with that title. You'll have the details of your salary within the next few days. Consider yourself part of the official crew as we sail the ship forward.' Hayes stood up and beamed at the inarticulate man on the other side of his desk. He had more sense than to offer to shake his hand.

Leroy Moore nodded, stood up and turned his back on the man he wanted to kill. He looked back from the doorway, but he still could not force the answering smile which he knew would have been the correct response.

# Eleven

It was one of the new conference hotels that housed the annual dinner of Hayes Electronics and Allied Industries.

Only such places had the large dining room and spacious bar area necessary to accommodate the number of people who were attending this year's function. The numbers now involved, as the carefully prepared handout to the local press pointed out, were evidence of the steadily growing success of the business. This company was of course, as the columns dutifully pointed out each year, founded and led by Timothy Hayes, a Brunton man born and bred (the influence of seven years of boarding school was always conveniently ignored). This was a businessman who knew the area intimately and who had brought employment and prosperity to so many of its residents.

When this hotel was built in the early years of the new century, it was opposed by some as a scarring of the Ribble Valley, one of the prettiest and least spoiled areas of the country. It is true that the complex is large and sprawling, but the planners argued that it would provide much-needed jobs for the area. The hotel faces west, looking across the valley towards the Trough of Bowland and the coast thirty miles away. It has to be large, to contain over a hundred bedrooms and conference facilities to match, and beside it there is the acreage of tarmac mandatory for car parking for residents and day visitors.

But the hotel is set as discreetly as possible into the lower slopes of the fell, and the rawness of its orange-red bricks will no doubt mellow with the passing years. It fulfils the twin requirements of such a place, in being both spacious and accessible, for it is within half a mile of the modernized A59, which now bypasses the ancient old towns of Whalley and Clitheroe and snakes away over the northern Pennines into the Yorkshire Dales.

Because there were no other buildings within half a mile of the hotel, it stood out like some fairy palace as the people invited to attend this annual function drove through the darkness towards it on the evening of Friday, the second of March. It was brilliantly lit along the whole of its long, low facade, and the harsher elevations and newness of the design were invisible in the late-winter darkness. The outside temperature was not much above freezing, but the thickly carpeted reception and bar areas were warm and welcoming, and trays of free drinks ensured that the guests soon felt a pleasant inner warmth.

With the men in evening dress and the women

sparkling with jewellery, it was a glittering assembly. The senior staff of all the respectable sections of Hayes Electronics were complemented by a discreet seasoning of the town's great and good. These comprised three or four of Brunton's councillors who needed to be cultivated or kept sweet, the most respectable and blameless of the town's solicitors, who had been with Hayes Electronics since its early days, the chairman of the Brunton Cricket Club and a couple of other prominent local industrialists.

Tim Hayes's membership of his local Masonic Lodge had enabled him to complete this collection of local luminaries by the addition this year of the head of Brunton's CID. Chief Superintendent Thomas Bulstrode Tucker, with well-trimmed silvering hair and handsome, experienced face, was an impressive figure for anyone wishing to add gravitas to a gathering. The woman at his side was impressive in a rather different way. Barbara Tucker sailed like a lurid galleon into the low-ceilinged room, her ample proportions emphasized rather than disguised by an orange off-the-shoulder dress, which displayed her Wagnerian physique in awesome detail. But in her own thankfully individual way, Brünnhilde Barbara completed the aura of propriety. It would have taken a braver person that any in that sparkling assembly to question the respectability of Barbara Tucker.

Beneath the modern chandeliers of the main

dining room, the glasses and cutlery sparkled on white linen, the food was good, and the wine was plentiful. The sound of conversation at the tables rose from a polite murmuring, as people felt their way with new acquaintances, through a pleasant hubbub, as relaxation took over, to an eventually tumultuous cacophony, as voices occasionally rose to a shout and frequent laughter punctuated the exchanges.

When Tim Hayes rose to his feet at the top table, the moment necessitated considerable rapping of glasses and shushing of neighbours before enough silence could be established for him to speak. He won early applause by announcing that the general idea was to keep things as informal as possible and that this short address would be the only speech of the evening. There were, however, a few observations and a few thanks he would like to make.

He would be brief and to the point, not least because this was the biggest audience he had ever addressed. With eighty-eight people present, this was the largest attendance so far at the firm's annual dinner. That in itself was tangible evidence of how far the company had advanced from the modest little electronics enterprise he had initiated some quarter of a century earlier. (Ragged applause, a little table tapping, and a few slightly inebriated 'Hear! Hears!')

He wanted to thank the distinguished guests who had honoured him and the firm with their presence tonight. The councillors looked at the table in front of them and smiled modestly. Over the heads of the people sitting opposite him, Chief Superintendent Tucker beamed a congratulatory smile at the speaker. The impressive exposed shoulders of Barbara Tucker seemed to turn an even deeper pink with pleasure.

For the rest, his thanks were entirely due to the people who had driven the success of the firm, the employees who were sitting here tonight as a physical recognition of that success. They came in all shapes and sizes (outbursts of laughter, an attempt at applause for this witty sally). And they had been with him on this exciting journey for varying lengths of time.

He hoped that later and very welcome arrivals would understand that he felt a special affection for those who had been with him since the beginning of this odyssey. He glanced down at his wife beside him. Tamsin Hayes was staring at her coffee cup with a strange, abstracted smile, which had not altered since her husband stood up and did not do so now. Probably she was a little embarrassed at this unaccustomed exposure to the public gaze, thought those around her, who did not know her and had mostly never seen her before.

Tim Hayes was glad to see Matt Ballack here tonight, a man who had been with him from the start, who had supported him through thick and thin and through the ups and downs of his own private life. Matthew's smile three tables away was more calculated, a mask consciously adopted to reveal nothing to those around him. He noted that Hayes had drawn attention to his private troubles to diminish him, that he had spoken throughout of this enterprise as being wholly his own. He had been shocked to hear his name mentioned, had thought at first that it was no more than a taunt. Now he realized that it was part of the carapace Hayes was developing around him, the shell of respectability designed to protect him from any gossip about those darker areas of his prosperity, such as the one in which Matthew himself was now involved.

Hayes now went on to speak about one of the new areas he could safely publicize. The new casino and allied areas were going well, he reported. It seemed that the present government had a rather ambivalent view of gambling, at one moment encouraging its entirely legal development in the country, at the next drawing in its horns a little and seeming to have doubts. But it seemed that was the way of modern governments. (Derisive laughter, an enthusiastic 'Hear! Hear!' from an Opposition supporter on one of the lower tables.) It was his view that governments of whatever persuasion were going to see the revenue from gambling as highly important in the next few years, as they strove to replace the income they were going to lose from cigarettes as smoking declined.

Hayes Electronics was in a prime position to

exploit future developments in this field. The new casino enterprise, which some people had opposed – he beamed benevolently over the heads of his council guests, all of whom were in fact here tonight because they had supported him – was now an asset not only of the company but of the town itself. It was bringing people from other Lancashire towns into Brunton to spend their money and enjoy their evenings. The casino was well run and without any of the seediness which the dismal Jimmies had predicted when it was opened. That was due in very large measure to the staff who operated it. He nodded gratefully at the table where the casino manager and its senior staff sat. Jane Martin, the youngest person in the room, sat beside Leroy Moore and noted that, whilst her fellow croupiers were pleased to have this recognition, he like her was staring stonily ahead of him.

Tim Hayes assured his receptive audience that he was almost finished now, bringing forth a couple of groans from dedicated sycophants. But it would not be right to conclude this little review without expressing his gratitude to those unseen and unpaid but nevertheless essential props of all this success and development. He referred, of course, to the wives and partners of his dedicated workforce. In the early days, money had been tight and what profit had been made had been ploughed back into new developments. There had been no more than a dozen people at the first of these dinners, in Brunton's White Bull Hotel, and they had all been colleagues.

It was clear proof of how far the company ship had sailed since then that there was this glittering array of talent and beauty here to-night, and that these vital other halves of his employees were here to share in the success and in the hopes for the future. He glanced down fondly at the head of his own wife beside him, fastened his eye for a moment on Clare Thompson and the scrubbed boyish face and bright red hair of Jason beside her, and asked the company to raise its glasses to the toast of 'Spouses and partners!'

There was a shuffling of feet, a ragged and irregular repetition of the toast down the tables, a clinking of glasses. Then people sat down rapidly as they saw their leader happily subsiding into his chair. The applause for his speech began at his own table and spread rapidly around the large, brilliantly lit room, with people remarking to their neighbours upon its excellence, and a few of the more inebriated men beginning to thump their tables to spread the rumble of approval.

There was a general exodus to the cloakrooms as the formal part of the evening was thus concluded. It was now half past ten and over half of the attendance took this opportunity to depart. But a substantial number repaired to the big bar where the evening had begun. Husbands drank brandies or liqueurs, wives detailed to drive them home stared glumly at glasses of tonic or bitter lemon; Brunton was as conservative as any other town when it came to the allocation of such duties.

There was a little loudness, a ritual repeating of well-worn anecdotes, surprisingly little outright drunkenness. Those guests who had no direct connection with the company had public personae to preserve. Employees and their spouses or partners had more sense and experience than to disgrace themselves in the presence of their affable but ruthless leader. People melted away from the concourse around the bar either when they thought they could or when they thought they should, according to their own inclinations. By midnight, the last revellers were taking their leave of the man who had hosted the evening.

Tim Hayes, after making his final gracious acknowledgements and bidding his last polite farewells, was troubled by the feelings of anti-climax and isolation which often beset him after the euphoria of evenings like this one. He sat for a reflective moment on his own at the bar, revolving his cognac in the bulbous glass, savouring its aroma and its warmth as he sipped it, as he had not been able to savour things earlier in this evening of public exposure.

The evening had gone well, better than he had ever expected. It had been costly, but it would go down as expenses on the entertainment budget. From the public-relations point of view, it was surely a success: he had impressed some important people, whilst diverting attention away from those newer areas of his activities which were risky but highly profitable. He had taken good care to ensure that the official photographs would see him smiling confidently with some important and highly influential people.

On a more personal note, he had been glad to see Clare Thompson sitting with that rather absurd husband of hers. It seemed to him an assurance that she had finally accepted that their affair was over and settled down to be no more than a highly efficient personal assistant. The presence for the first time in years of his own wife at his side must surely have reinforced that judgement for Clare, however abstracted Tamsin had seemed tonight. And he had given that loser Matt Ballack a mention, whilst keeping him firmly in his place in the more obscure part of the empire. He wasn't stupid, Matt. He'd have picked up the message behind the kind words: think yourself lucky to have what you've got and get on with it without complaint. Some time in the next year or two, when he'd served his purpose and it was safe to do so, he would get rid of Ballack altogether.

That girl he had picked up in the casino, Jane Martin, had been the centre of a lot of male attention tonight. With her youth and her dazzling eyes, she was certainly a stunner. There was no doubting his own good taste in women! Nevertheless, if he had known that she had a connection with a member of his staff, and a violent member at that, he would never have selected her. No unnecessary complications was one of his watchword phrases when he was looking to get his leg over. But it seemed to have passed over all right. It had been quite fortuitous that he had decided to promote Leroy Moore before he even knew about their relationship, but it had worked well. The pair had looked quite relaxed together tonight. They had each come up the hard way, and they obviously realized which side their bread was buttered on, those two.

Once everyone but the staff of the hotel had gone, Tim Hayes felt suddenly very tired. They were a strain, these occasions. Whilst you were on show, the tension of the moment and the elation of carrying it off kept you going, but these things took their toll, he supposed. At a quarter past midnight, Tim Hayes said good night to the uniformed man behind the bar. He heard the shutters coming down before he was out of the big room.

The mercy of not being able to drink was that you could drive yourself home; he did not feel in the mood for any taxi-driver's banalities tonight. He had not drunk at all between the glass of white wine he had sipped in welcoming his guests and the double brandy he had just allowed himself at the end of proceedings.

When you were making an important speech, you needed to have all your wits about you, whereas it was a positive advantage if your audience was mellowed and uncritical through alcohol. He would drive himself home slowly and enjoy the journey.

His head swam for a few seconds as he moved abruptly from the warmth of the hotel into the freezing night air. He was glad he had brought the thick car coat he had almost left at home. He paused for a moment to look up at the stars, assuring himself as his head cleared that after a heavy meal and so little drink, he was indeed within breathalyser limits if the police should stop him. He pulled out his car keys and pressed the tag: the orange lights of the BMW winked appealingly at him from thirty yards away.

The big blue car was isolated now, where an hour before it had been one in the serried rows of a hundred or so carefully parked cars. He took a last look up at the sky and the bright, unwinking stars and slid himself onto the leather driving seat. There was frost on both the windscreen and rear window, but that was no problem to a man who was not in a hurry. He started the engine, pressed the switches which heated the windscreen and rear window, shivered for a second as the powerful fan blew air that was initially cold into the interior. It wouldn't be long before it was transformed into a comforting warmth. He watched the frost at the base of the windscreen ahead of him begin to melt, telling himself that tonight he would not drive away until the vision fore and aft was perfect. In a moment, when the noise of the fan abated, he would put on the radio, then ease the big machine out of the hotel car park and back onto the road for the short journey home.

It was then that he felt the mouth of the pistol at his temple. That was Tim Hayes's last mortal sensation. He was mercifully unaware of the explosion which blew away half of his well-groomed head.

# Twelve

Percy Peach was looking forward to his weekend. Crime, one of the guaranteed growth industries of the twenty-first century, was flourishing in Lancashire as elsewhere, but at the moment it was reassuringly low-key in Brunton. There was plenty of it, but little that the press or even the police service would nowadays deem 'serious'.

At the beginning of March, the worst of winter was surely over; indeed, an anti-cyclone over the country and a clear bright day proclaimed the approach of spring. When Peach arose at eight and peered between the cotton curtains of his bedroom at the world outside, there was a white frost on the nondescript lawn at the back of his ageing semi-detached. But there was enough warmth in the rising sun for it to have already disappeared where the grass was not in the shade.

Percy's spirits rose. The golf course would be open and the frost was not severe enough for the course manager to switch the players to temporary greens. He would join his friends at lunchtime for an afternoon round, friendly banter, and the noisy exchanges of the nineteenth hole. The North Lancs course, which was the best in the area, was on high ground north of the town, stretching the cultivated arms of its fairways out into the moorland heather at its highest point. On a sunny, windless day like this, the golf would be good – or if it was not, there would be no excuses possible. And even if performance fell short of expectation, as it usually did for most golfers, there would be the consolation of the splendid views of Ingleborough and Pen-Y-Ghent away to the north, their impressive outlines looking deceptively close on a day as clear as this.

Tomorrow, buoyed by this afternoon's less serious golf, he would undertake the monthly medal and try to lower his handicap of eight a little further. Everyone said that he had done exceptionally well to get it so low in the three years since he had forsaken cricket, but he knew that with a little application and the practice he did not have time for, it could be lower still. Percy Peach had already acquired the unreasoning optimism which is a characteristic of all serious practitioners of this most infuriating of games.

He had no worries about his evening meal. He was dining with Lucy Blake in the neat, bright modern flat which was such a contrast to his nineteen-fifties semi. He would take a bottle of wine to accompany the meal and afterwards drift towards a pleasant somnolence on her

162

sofa. A resting which would be but a preparation for the glorious exchanges of her bed, where his lust would run riot and his most energetic sallies would be welcomed and reciprocated. A wide, uncalculating smile of boyish bliss spread across Percy's round face at the prospect.

He shivered a little as he shaved in the bathroom which Lucy Blake swore was kept at fridge temperature. He would have bacon and egg and tomatoes this morning, he decided. Possibly, with no one there to tut-tut at him about cholesterol, he would even allow himself the ultimate hedonism of fried bread. A weekend of relaxation stretched appealingly before him. A weekend without the depressing shadow of Tommy Bloody Tucker. The chief superintendent's golf had never risen above the aspirational, so that his handicap confined him to the lesser tests of Brunton Golf Club. It was a source of enduring resentment for Tucker that his handicap had meant repeated rejections of his applications to join the North Lancs, where his hated junior had been accepted at the first time of asking.

The phone shrilled as Peach went downstairs, its note like a death-knell in his imaginative ears. It wouldn't be Lucy Blake, and he didn't want to hear from anyone else, with his weekend stretching itself like a friendly Labrador before him. He hesitated, letting the instrument ring for a moment, hoping that it would stop after a few bleeps. It went on. He picked it up with a sigh which anticipated his impending doom.

The voice from the station sergeant was not even apologetic: uniformed men rather enjoyed ruining the weekends of senior CID officers. A suspicious death at the Gisburn Hotel. A corpse in the car park. A death which required immediate CID attention.

Bugger it.

Eight miles away in her mother's cottage, Lucy Blake was not anticipating the morning with as much pleasure as her fiancé.

When she had said on the previous evening that she was too tired to concentrate on the final invitation list of guests for her wedding, her mother had closed her folder reluctantly and said, 'We shall have to get on with it early in the morning, then, our Lucy. I want to get the letters off this weekend.'

At quarter to eight, Lucy's mother appeared like Lady Macbeth in her darkened bedroom. She looked just as determined as that formidable matriarch, but she carried not daggers but a breakfast tray. 'You spoil me, Mum!' said Lucy feebly.

Agnes Blake was not to be diverted. 'I've been spoiling you for twenty-nine years, my girl. Get this lot down you and get yourself up and dressed. It's a grand morning and we've work to do.'

'Yes, Miss Moss!' Lucy pulled herself upright in the bed, straightened her back against the headboard, and imitated the tone she had used as a six-year-old to her favourite primary-school teacher.

She was rewarded with one of her mother's dismissive sniffs. 'Work first, then you can fool about, our Lucy. The water's hot for your shower and it's time you were moving.'

Lucy looked at the tray. There were cereals, a boiled egg which she knew would be just as runny as she liked it, two slices of wholemeal toast, a tiny pot of tea with a knitted woollen cover to keep it hot. She was filled with a familiar rush of affection for this mother whose world she dominated. 'It's lovely, Mum. I promise I'll be fed, washed and ready for action in half an hour.'

'Make sure you are, then. I'll be watching the clock. I don't want to have to tell Percy you've been dragging your feet again.'

With this final friendly threat, she was gone and Lucy settled down to enjoy her breakfast. It was brilliant really, this unexpected bond between the two people she loved most in the world. Where most men moaned about their mothers-in-law, Percy would not hear a word against his. Where most mothers could not find a spouse worthy of their only child, Agnes Blake had found an unexpected kindred spirit and been wholly, almost girlishly, delighted. Lucy knew she was enormously lucky really, even though she had no chance against the two of them when they ganged up on her. She enjoyed her breakfast, but did not linger over it.

Her mother had the table strewn with papers already when she descended the narrow old staircase. Lucy sighed in mock horror. 'I'll wash the dishes and be with you in two minutes.'

Agnes did not look up. 'It shouldn't take too long, once you put your mind to it. I've already separated them into certainties, probables and possibles. If you concentrate, we can have the list completed and the cards written out in a few hours. If you behave properly, I might even let you take me to the pub for lunch.'

Respectable women hadn't gone to pubs when Agnes Blake was a young woman; indeed, they had rarely eaten out at all. She had needed a lot of persuasion from her daughter before she went to eat at the Red Lion. Now, although publicly she disapproved of the extravagance, she found it a delightful treat to go out and eat pub food with Lucy.

Lucy noted that the certainties pile was by far the deepest. 'We wanted a quiet wedding, you know. Just immediate family and friends.'

'That's what you're getting, girl. I'm keeping this to a minimum, just to oblige you. We'll end up by offending people.'

'Percy hasn't got many people to invite,' Lucy called defensively from the kitchen.

'He must have some of his old cricketing pals.

166

I shall have to speak to him about that.'

It sounded like a threat. Lucy grinned over the washing-up bowl and called defensively, 'I expect he'd like to have one or two of his golfing pals, too.'

'*Golf!*' The familiar derisive monosyllable exploded most gratifyingly from the low-ceilinged sitting room.

It was at this point that the phone shrilled. Lucy heard her mother muttering her irritation as she went to answer it. She was drying her hands when Agnes Blake appeared in the doorway of her kitchen. She said dolefully, 'It's Percy. He wants to speak to you.'

Agnes knew just what was going to happen. She could almost have written the dialogue. Within two minutes she was back in the sitting room, looking apologetically at the papers on the table, and saying, 'I have to go, Mum. I'm sorry.'

To her credit, she sounded regretful. And she was sorry – not to get away from that wretched list, but to disappoint her mother. 'There's a suspicious death, Mum, at the Gisburn Hotel. I need to be there.'

'Even on a Saturday morning?'

'Crime doesn't take weekends off, Mum. This sounds as if it might be a serious one. I'm meeting Percy at the scene.'

Agnes accepted the inevitable with a nod and what grace she could muster. 'Be as quick as you can, love.'

'I will, Mum. I might even be back for lunch.' They smiled at each other, knowing that was not going to happen.

It was only a few miles to the Gisburn Hotel. As she waved to her mother and drove the blue Corsa swiftly away, Lucy felt the guilt of the familiar paradox: sympathy, for a victim she did not know as yet, and excitement, at the prospect of the hunt. The thrill of anticipation which the most serious crime of all always brought to the CID officer.

A suspicious death, Peach had said. Police jargon for something much worse.

The woman was from Eastern Europe. The manager had kept her in his office beside the entrance to the building, as if he wished to isolate her and this awful event as far as possible from the operation of his hotel.

'Just tell Chief Inspector Peach what you saw,' said the manager. 'Don't be frightened of him because he's a police officer. There really is nothing to be afraid of.' The manager looked at Peach and raised his eyes heavenwards: you needed to assure such people that they would not be imprisoned and tortured without trial.

Peach fancied that this was merely a woman very shaken by what she had seen. She was ten years younger than he had thought her at first sight. Her long face was very white and her wavy, unruly black hair kept dropping across her face. He smiled at her and said, 'Mr Pearson is right. There's nothing to be afraid of. But it is important to tell us clearly exactly what you saw.' He turned to the manager. 'I think it would be better if you left us alone for this. It won't take long.'

The woman was probably no more than twenty-four years old, he decided. She watched the door close upon Pearson with some relief. When Peach motioned towards one of the armchairs and took the other one himself, she sat on the very edge of the seat, with her arms held out awkwardly in front of her and her hands upon her thin, blue-jeaned thighs.

Peach smiled at her. 'What is your name?'

'Natasha. The people here call me Tash.'

'I shall call you Natasha. Will you tell me what you do here, please?'

'I work in kitchen. I come here from Clitheroe. I have old car. Old Ford Fiesta.'

'I see. And you came to work this morning. What time would that be?'

'Six fifteen. I come at six fifteen. Maybe I was five minutes after that.' She glanced fearfully at the door, as if fearing the wrath of Pearson if she admitted to being a little late.

'Maybe ten?' Peach smiled at her conspiratorially.

'Maybe. Car not start well when cold morning.' She did not return his smile.

'So you arrived here about twenty-five past six and parked your car. Was it light then?'

'Yes. Sun was not up but it was daylight.'

'There wouldn't be many other cars here at that time. I expect you can usually park quite near the hotel when you arrive.'

'Yes. I do breakfasts. Help chef in kitchen.'

'So you parked your Ford Fiesta near the hotel. Natasha, please tell me as clearly as you can remember it what happened next.'

The young forehead furrowed in concentration, as if to be trapped into a mistake of recollection could be costly to her. 'I park in staff area, but I have to pass big car. Big blue car. I not know the make.'

'That doesn't matter. What did you see?'

A sudden, involuntary shiver shook her whole frame. Her hair fell across her face and she brushed it angrily aside, as if it were an outside agency which was deliberately making this difficult for her. 'I see that there is someone inside this big blue car.'

'In the driving seat?'

'Yes. In the driving seat. From the other side he looks as if he is asleep. Then I think is too cold for anyone to be asleep here. So I go round to driver's side, to see if I can help. There is much blood there.' She thrust her small right fist against her mouth, unable for the moment to speak further as the horror of her recollection swept over her.

'You realized that the man was dead, didn't you, Natasha?'

'Yes. His head – his head was—' She lifted her hands hopelessly, then let them drop heavily back onto her thighs.

'His head was badly damaged, wasn't it?'

'Damaged, yes. It was not there, not that side of it. There was much blood. On windows. On windscreen.'

'Yes. This must have been very distressing for you, I know, Natasha. But it's important: did you see anyone else around the car?'

'No. No one else.' She said suddenly, as if searching desperately for some detail which would make her story more believable, 'There is still frost on most of car. Is all white. That is why I could not see blood from other side.'

'I understand. You didn't see anyone going back into the hotel, or watching you from there?'

'No. Is no one about when I find. Only me there.'

'I understand. It looks as if the body had been there all night, doesn't it?'

She nodded eagerly. 'Since last night, I think.'

'I think you're probably right about that, Natasha. Did you open the car door?'

'No. I see man dead. Nothing I can do.' She looked as if she thought she was being accused of callousness.

'Of course not. And it's good that you didn't open the door, from our point of view. Did you touch the car at all?'

Again that intense concentration, as if she feared that a mistake might cost her her liberty. 'I think I may have leant on it for a moment.

171

For a minute, I think I am going to faint. I'm sorry.'

'Don't be sorry. It's quite a natural thing to do. We shall need to take your fingerprints. There may be other fingerprints there, you see, from people who might not be as innocent as you. Do you understand that?'

'I think so, yes.'

'Well, I think that's all, then. One of my officers will come and take your fingerprints, later in the morning. It's nothing to be frightened of.' He stood up, gave her a final reassuring smile. 'Thank you for your help.'

'There is something else. Something else I need to tell you.'

'Yes?'

'I not sure of the words. I – I – do you say, "throw up"? I'm very sorry.'

'You vomited? Well, that's nothing to be ashamed of. Some of our toughest policemen vomit, when they see horrible things like that. Was it on the car?'

'No. On my way into the hotel. I very sorry about it.'

'There's no need to be sorry, Natasha. It's a very natural reaction. I'm sure I did it myself, the first time I saw anything like that. It sounds as if it's outside the crime scene – that's the area we tape off around the car itself. If it is, it's probably already been cleaned up. In any case, you mustn't worry about it. I don't think there's any reason for you to mention it to Mr Pearson.'

She gave him a wan smile as she left. Her dark eyes were round with wonderment that a policeman could be so understanding.

In the car park outside the Gisburn Hotel, the tapes and screens delineating a scene-of-crime area were already in place around the big blue BMW.

Sergeant Jack Chadwick, a former colleague of Peach's who had been shot and seriously injured in a bank raid, was one of the few serving police officers who still supervised scene-of-crime teams. DS Blake's blue Corsa nosed up beside the tapes as Percy was talking to him.

'The pathologist's been and gone, Percy,' said Chadwick. He smiled a greeting at Lucy Blake, whose pretty face and striking red-brown hair always lightened a sombre scene. 'He says we can have the meat wagon in and remove the corpse to his lab for the post-mortem as soon as we've finished. Which we almost have. I'm sure that will please Mr Pearson.'

Percy grinned, guessing that an anxious hotel manager had been hovering around the crime scene since Chadwick had arrived. 'We all have our own concerns, Jack. It can't stimulate bookings for weddings and conferences, having blood and gore all over your car park.'

Chadwick answered him with a sourer smile. 'No such thing as bad publicity, Percy. Given a gruesome murder, a high-profile investigation and a sensational trial, people will be making special journeys to stand on this spot in awed silence within the year.'

'You're probably right. Murder, you said.'

'I think so. Murder dressed up to look like suicide, but too clumsily to deceive old hands like you.' His smile took in Lucy Blake, whom he now included in this flattering category.

Peach said very quietly, 'Who is it, Jack?'

A grim smile, acknowledging that there wasn't too much left that was recognizable. 'Timothy Hayes.'

'Of Hayes Electronics?'

'That's your man.' He glanced at the chief inspector, knowing that a high-profile victim was always less welcome for CID than a simple domestic killing. Such deaths were usually more complex and certainly brought the press attention which was always intrusive and rarely favourable.

Peach glanced at the dark crimson film on the inside of the windscreen and the side windows, then went slowly, almost reluctantly round to the open driver's door and all was left of what yesterday had been human. Every experienced police officer has seen dreadful sights, usually when attending serious road accidents in the early years of their career, but Percy winced a little when he saw this one, as if registering an unconscious concession to his own humanity.

Half the head and three-quarters of the face had disappeared completely. Bits of bone and what he presumed was brain speckled the blood on the fascia and windscreen. He was conscious after a second or two of Lucy Blake at his side, deliberately calm, deliberately displaying to Chadwick as she had done on previous occasions that squeamishness had nothing to do with gender.

Chadwick's voice seemed at first to come from a long way away as he said, 'At least you've got a murder weapon.' He gestured to where a civilian officer was labelling the plastic container in which he had carefully bagged a bloodstained pistol.

'A Smith and Wesson.'

'Yes. They don't leave any chance of survival, when they're fired at close quarters, do they?' Chadwick retreated for a moment into a professional admiration of the weapon's efficiency.

'You said there'd been an attempt to simulate suicide.'

Chadwick nodded. 'The pistol had been placed in the corpse's right hand. In my view, after someone else had blown him away. You'll make your own mind up about that, but the grip was all wrong. Whoever did this wore gloves, though. I think you'll find the only prints we've lifted from the weapon are those of this poor bugger.'

'When?' The other automatic CID question. 'Where' was obvious. 'How' had just been suggested by the SOCO. 'Why' was just beginning and was going to take much longer.

Chadwick smiled grimly. 'You can be pretty

certain that this happened last night. The pathologist was as cagey as those sods always are about exact times, but it was obvious to both of us that the corpse had been here all night. Hayes Electronics held their annual dinner here last night. Pearson said Hayes was pretty well the last visitor to leave the hotel.'

Peach looked at the expensive, blood-spattered suit of the dead man. 'Have you picked up anything useful?'

'Nothing that looks likely from around the car. If anyone came here straight from the hotel, or from another car, he isn't likely to have had mud on his shoes.' Serious criminals were always male in police parlance, a simple recognition of the statistics of villainy. 'We've got various fibres from the back seat of the car. We'll take the vehicle into forensics when we've finished here. Those boys will take it apart and have their usual fun, but whether they'll pick up anything more than my boys and girls here have remains to be seen.'

Chadwick, Peach and Blake looked at the open door and the rivulets of moisture from the melting frost running off the BMW. The sun was rising higher, and at that moment the first insect arrived and settled on the shattered head. They did not need to express the common thought each of them was revolving: someone might well have sat in the back of this car and waited for his or her victim. Had they left any tiny traces of their presence behind them?

The van the police call the meat wagon had arrived by the time Peach and Blake were leaving and the plastic body shell was being prepared for the reception of the mortal remains of Timothy Hayes.

By the time today's visitors arrived for lunch at the Gisburn Hotel, all traces of the most grisly event in its short history would have disappeared.

# Thirteen

The curtains were drawn. Even at midday on this bright day, even with the yellow and white crocuses bright beside the long drive, there was a sombre look about the big detached house.

Peach glanced at the impressive view across the valley and gave the bell a single ring. It seemed a long time before the big oak front door swung half open and a white face peered at them. He said apologetically, 'I'm Chief Inspector Peach and this is Detective Sergeant Blake. We're sorry to intrude at a time like this, but there are a few questions we need to ask you.'

For a second or two, she looked at them as if she did not comprehend. Then Tamsin Hayes said quietly, 'I understand. You'd better come inside.'

She led them into a comfortable small room next to the main sitting room of the house and said unnecessarily, 'This was designed as a breakfast room, but we've never needed to use it as that.' She gave them a wan smile as they sat in the armchairs she indicated. 'But you don't need to know that, do you?'

She was already clad completely in mourning: a long-sleeved black dress was complemented by dark tights and court shoes in fine black leather. There was even a black slide in her brown hair. She looked very smart, even without any sign of make-up on her drawn white face. Peach said, 'We probably won't need to take much of your time at all, Mrs Hayes. Can you tell us what time you left the Gisburn Hotel last night, please?'

'Well before – well before this happened. As soon as Tim had finished his speech, there was a general exodus to bars and cloakrooms. I took the opportunity to leave unobtrusively then.' She watched the young woman she had been told was a detective sergeant beginning to make notes with a small gold ball-pen. 'Quite a lot of other people did the same.'

'You took a taxi back here?'

For a moment, the wan face looked puzzled. Then understanding dawned and a small smile lightened her features. 'I had my own car. I didn't go to the function with my husband. We had agreed that beforehand. He had to be there early, to greet and entertain his guests.'

'But didn't he want you at his side to assist him with that?'

There was perhaps a vestige of irritation at the question before she answered, 'Entertaining isn't my strength. Especially with business contacts and councillors whom I don't even know. As a matter of fact, it was the first time I'd been to this function for several years. I'm quite a shy person, and Tim understands that.' There was a little gasp from her and her small hand flew up to her mouth. 'I'm sorry – I should have said "understood that", shouldn't I?'

'That's a mistake almost everyone makes in these distressing circumstances, Mrs Hayes. Can you tell us what time it would be when you left the hotel?'

'Half past ten. Perhaps a quarter to eleven. There was quite a lot of activity in the car park – a lot of people left at around that time.' She seemed for some reason very satisfied about that.

'And you drove yourself home.'

'Yes. I never drink very much nowadays, so I wasn't worried about driving. I was back here at eleven o'clock.'

Lucy Blake looked up from her notes. This composed, black-clad figure looked like a figure in mourning in an old-fashioned play. She only needed a black hat and veil and long black gloves and she would be ready to stand at the graveside. And the woman within the clothes, unnaturally calm and measured, seeming to anticipate their every question, appeared as if she was indeed playing a part, perhaps one she had designed for herself. Lucy said, 'There was no one with you in the car and no one here but yourself when you got home.'

A small smile, a tiny pause whilst she estimated this new questioner, whose light blue sweater and darker blue trousers seemed almost garish by comparison with her own attire. 'No. I have no witnesses to what I am telling you, I'm afraid.'

'And we have no reason to doubt it, Mrs Hayes. But we need to record these things. Tell us what happened next, please.'

A knowing smile. 'Very little. I made myself a cup of tea and put on the radio whilst I unwound a little after the evening. As I said, I find these occasions quite stressful. But I was in bed before midnight.'

'Weren't you alarmed when your husband didn't come home?'

She gave the fresh young face a sad look, as if she was reluctant to disillusion Blake about the realities of life. 'I didn't expect him. I knew he would have to stay until the last of his guests for the evening departed.'

'But you must have been alarmed when you found later in the night that he still hadn't returned.'

'But I didn't, you see. We have separate bedrooms. Sometimes Tim slept in the big bed in my room and sometimes he slept alone. There's no great mystery about that. There are only two of us and we rather rattle around in this big house. It seemed sensible to make the best use of the accommodation and give each other our own space. There's nothing complicated about the arrangement – I believe many more people would do it if they were lucky enough to have

181

as much space as we have here. I'm told royalty do something similar.'

The explanation fell trippingly off the tongue, as if it had been either used before or prepared in advance for this meeting. Lucy tried not to sound sceptical as she said, 'So when did you find that your husband hadn't returned home?'

'Not until I got up this morning. I called something to him about breakfast and got no reply. When I looked into his room at about eight o'clock, I saw that his bed hadn't been slept in.'

'But you didn't ring in to police or hospitals.'

A pause, a small, sad sigh. 'No. I had no reason to be alarmed, had I?'

'Even when he was still missing many hours after you'd expected him home?'

'Even then. Tim was often away overnight. I gave up wondering where he was a long time ago.'

There was something here to be followed up, an obvious suggestion about the husband–wife relationship. But you could not push a grieving widow too hard only a few hours after her husband had been so brutally dispatched. Grief took many forms; you could not automatically assume that a calm exterior meant that there was not real suffering beneath. Peach said suddenly, 'So when exactly did you begin to feel worried about what might have happened, Mrs Hayes?'

She transferred her attention back to the man,

as if determined to meet his renewed challenge successfully. 'I don't think I ever did, DCI Peach. Not until I saw your policewoman at my door. I feel now that I knew before she told me that Tim was dead. But perhaps that is fanciful.' She nodded very slightly to herself, as if weighing the proposition.

'And until our officer gave you the sad news, you had no inkling of what might have happened?'

'None whatsoever. She told me initially that there had been some sort of accident. When I pressed her, she said that Tim had been shot. She offered to come in and make me a cup of tea. I said that there was no need for that. I asked her for more details, but she said she couldn't tell me anything more.'

Peach pictured an inexperienced woman in a new uniform, prepared for hysterics, then trying to cope with this disconcertingly organized widow. 'She probably didn't know any details, Mrs Hayes. DS Blake and I have actually visited the scene, but as yet we know little more ourselves. You may be able to help us a little with that, if you feel up to it.'

'I shall certainly do whatever I can. That would be my duty, wouldn't it?'

'It's everyone's duty, but not everyone seems as clear-sighted about it as you do.' He was content that it should sound like an accusation rather than a compliment: this abnormal calm in a widow was getting to him more than he would have thought possible. 'Did your husband possess a firearm, Mrs Hayes?'

A small, possibly calculated, pause. 'I believe he had a pistol of some kind, yes. I presume he had a licence for it, if one was needed. I'm afraid I have no interest in such things. Is that what killed him?'

'We don't know, yet. Had he shown any signs of depression in the last few days?'

A longer pause this time, as if she wished to weigh up the implications of her reply before she made it. 'You're asking me if Tim was in a mood to take his own life, aren't you? Well, I'd say no. This wasn't suicide. Someone killed him. Take it from me.'

'Why do you say that?'

She gave a little shrug of those impeccably groomed black shoulders. 'He wasn't a man to take his own life. When you've lived with someone for a quarter of a century, you can say that with a certain conviction.'

'That's interesting. I can tell you that the episode looked at first sight like a suicide, but we're already thinking that someone set it up to look like that.'

She nodded, said with something like satisfaction, 'I presume Tim had enemies. I imagine it's difficult to be as successful as he was in business without making enemies.'

'Can you think of anyone in particular, Mrs Hayes?'

'No. It wouldn't be fair for me to speculate. I

know very little about the way he had conducted his business in recent years.'

'If this turns out to be a murder inquiry, as I now very much fear it will, we shall need to encourage speculation, especially among those who knew the victim best. Your views will be treated in confidence.'

She looked from one to the other of the contrasting faces, almost teasing them, letting them wonder for a moment if she was going to give them anything. Then she said abruptly, 'I think his old partner has had rather a raw deal in recent years. I don't know why.'

'And this old partner's name?'

'Matthew Ballack. He and Tim started what is now Hayes Electronics a long time ago. He's still with the firm, but Tim seemed to me to shrug him off in recent years. I suspect Mr Ballack's been treated rather badly.' She watched Blake make a note of the name and said, 'It's rather unfair of me to single out Mr Ballack. I'm sure Tim had lots of other enemies. But no doubt Matthew Ballack will be able to give you a convincing account of his movements last night.'

It was an odd thing to say. It wasn't clear from her tone whether she believed that or not, or even whether she wanted it to be true or not. Very little was clear about this strangely composed widow, who had dressed herself so carefully to meet them. Peach said with a hint of impatience, 'Do you think Mr Hayes was anticipating an attack? Do you think he had any sort of premonition about what happened last night?'

She thought for a moment, then leant forward a little, as if parting with a secret. 'He had men to look after him. The sort of men he wouldn't have had around him in the old days.'

'Can you give us names, please?'

'No, I can't do that.' She seemed genuinely regretful. 'But they were on the payroll, I expect. I should think his secretary would be able to tell you more about them.'

Peach stood up, threw in his last question almost casually, hoping to catch her off guard. 'Who do you think did this, Mrs Hayes?'

'I don't know ... Wives and husbands of murder victims are always the first suspects, aren't they?'

Peach allowed himself a little smile, carefully concealing his irritation with this enigmatic woman. 'We prefer to look upon them as the first people to be eliminated from the inquiry. Mrs Hayes, no doubt you are still in shock. If any further thoughts occur to you about your husband's death, please contact me at Brunton CID immediately. We shall no doubt need to speak to you again in a day or two, when we have more information to hand. In the meantime, you have our sympathy.'

She stood in the doorway with the curtained windows on each side of her, presenting the perfect exterior of the bereaved widow, whilst they slid into the police Mondeo and drove down the long, curving drive and off her property. Both of them wondered whether when she shut the big oak door the mask would be immediately discarded.

It gave Percy Peach a very nasty shock. He wasn't expecting anything like this on a Saturday afternoon. Indeed, he couldn't remember the last time when this had happened.

Tommy Bloody Tucker's head had appeared without warning around the door of Peach's office. Tucker rarely ventured outside the rarefied atmosphere of his own penthouse quarters at the top of the huge new police building, and had certainly never been sighted before in the middle of a Saturday afternoon.

The head was tilted at an angle of forty-five degrees. The expression on the head resembled that of a rather backward heron. It looked at Peach apprehensively for a moment, after which it straightened and the full glory of the weekend Tucker was revealed. He wore a light green sweater above plus-twos in a virulent brown and orange tartan, which had assuredly no Caledonian connection. The yellow socks and tan shoes on his lower limbs enhanced rather than diminished the startling impact of his ensemble.

He said unnecessarily, 'I've come straight here from the golf course.'

As though it were a virtue, thought Percy

187

darkly. He looked at his chief from top to toe and blinked a little. He had never been able to work out why Tucker swung so far away from the sober, well-cut suits he wore for work to this garish golfing gear; his latest theory was that Tucker tried to compensate for his deficiencies in playing the game by the violently aggressive hues of his attire. Peach said modestly, 'I had to cancel my golf, sir.'

'Of course you did, Peach. A murder on your patch needs your immediate attention.'

Percy noticed that as usual the work ethic the head of Brunton CID expected apparently had no application to himself. He restrained himself from asking the man what the bloody hell he was doing here now. No doubt that would emerge in the next few minutes. He said carefully, 'The death was dressed up to look like suicide. It is in fact murder.'

'And the murder of one of our most prominent citizens. This is high-profile, Peach. The sooner it is solved, the better it will be for all of us.'

'I quite agree, sir. I see why you're here now. I'm glad you've come in to take charge of this investigation yourself.'

The look of panic on Tucker's face gave his junior the first moment of pleasure in a trying day. 'I shan't interfere with your handling of the case, Peach. I shall of course remain in overall direction, but you know that it is my policy to trust my staff and interfere with their work as little as possible.'

'Yes, sir. I often have to assure our more junior officers that you won't interfere with them.'

'There were a lot of people at the Gisburn Hotel last night, Peach. This may not be an easy investigation.'

Percy noted how his chief never lost his talent for the incisive observation and held his peace.

'There were almost a hundred people in the dining room. At the moment, you must treat everyone there as a suspect. Everyone, Peach. If they object, tell them that they mustn't be thin-skinned in a murder investigation.'

Percy said heavily, 'Right, sir. Your overview is as usual invaluable.'

'However, you will need to handle things carefully. There were a lot of very important people there last night.' Tucker moved uneasily from gaudy foot to gaudy foot. 'I was there myself.'

So that's why you're here on a Saturday afternoon. A confession made. Mystery solved. 'That's most fortunate for us, isn't it, sir? A lucky break, you might say, having a senior detective on the spot. Did you see anything suspicious?'

'What? No, of course I didn't!'

Peach slid open the top drawer of his desk and produced the notebook he never used. 'What time did you leave, sir?'

'What? About eleven fifteen, I should think.'

Peach recorded the time carefully and slowly, the tip of his tongue protruding from the corner of his mouth as he wrote. 'Is there anyone who can confirm this for us, sir?'

'I was with my wife. There are lots of people who could confirm that I left at – Peach, what on earth are you on about?'

'You just said I should treat everyone who was in that room as a suspect, sir. I'm merely following your direction.'

'Don't be stupid, Peach! The idea that I could be a suspect is quite preposterous!'

'You mustn't be thin-skinned in a murder investigation, sir.'

'Peach, if you pursue this line of questioning, I shall lose my temper!'

Percy had a nightmare vision of a huge, hysterical parrot and desisted. 'Just trying to eliminate you from the inquiry, sir. You may recall that I told you a few days ago that we were finding out that Mr Hayes was indulging in some unsavoury activities with some dubious companions. It looks as if his chickens may have come home to roost.'

'I find that very difficult to believe, Peach. Last night was a highly respectable assembly. There were many of the town's great and good present.'

'Including yourself and your good lady, sir. I appreciate that they don't come any greater or gooder than that. But you will be aware that the bigger and cleverer villains often surround themselves with the trappings of respectability to mask their darker activities.'

'I still believe you'll find that Tim Hayes was a gentleman and a great loss to the Brunton community.'

'Member of your Lodge, wasn't he, sir?'

'I've told you before that Freemasonry has no influence on my views. I simply think that you'll find me a better judge of the man's character than your dubious informants, that's all.'

'Well, we shall see, sir, won't we? This could be more valuable material for my research thesis on the connection between Freemasonry and crime in north-west England.'

Tucker regarded his DCI with undisguised distaste. 'Just make sure you handle this carefully, Peach. Some important people in the town are likely to be involved in this investigation.'

'Will do, sir. Oh, and don't worry on your own account: I'm sure the admirable Mrs Tucker will vouch for you. We all know how suspect wives' alibis for husbands are, but they're difficult to break, aren't they?'

# Fourteen

By Sunday morning, the tension between them was almost unbearable.

Both Clare and Jason Thompson knew that the normal thing for them to do was to talk to each other about the melodrama which had exploded so suddenly into their lives. The way they had been behaving since they had heard about the shooting was quite unnatural. They should be discussing this startling, brutal disruption of their routine.

Yet it was as if each of them feared to do so. They were two intelligent people. Through a long Saturday, the fact that they were deliberately avoiding any discussion of this death had become more and more apparent to them.

Now they sat at the breakfast table, each with toast and marmalade, each staring at the table and the kitchen appliances around them in turn, seeking for innocent, general subjects of conversation. Each topic they settled on proved futile, since it invariably petered out after a sentence or two.

In the heavy silence which dominated the house, the sound of the bulky Sunday newspaper crashing through the letter box and into the hall made both of them jump. There was a comic moment when both of them started up from their chairs to fetch the journal with a bright announcement of its arrival. With a wan smile at herself, Clare sank back onto her chair and let Jason collect it.

It was the *Sunday Times*, with its multiple sections. He spread it out on the table between them and they made a show of discarding the parts they were not going to read. They had the discussion they had conducted before about the uselessness of some sections, about the fact that everyone who bought the journal must discard approximately half of it, about the number of trees which must be wasted nowadays in surplus newsprint.

Then the phone rang and both of them sprang towards it. This time it was Clare who got there first. She gave their number, listened for a moment, then mouthed at him, 'It's the police.'

Jason could not take his eyes off his wife as she spoke. Because it was so quiet, he heard most of what the woman on the other end of the line was saying.

'My name is Detective Sergeant Blake. No doubt by now you will have heard about the death of Mr Tim Hayes.'

'Yes.' Clare did not trust herself with more than the monosyllable.

'I'm afraid we are having to treat this as a suspicious death, as you probably heard on the radio. We now have the seating plan from Friday night. You were both sitting quite near to Mr Hayes during the evening.'

'Yes. Quite near but not immediately adjacent. I did the seating plan myself.'

'I see. Well, DCI Peach, who is in charge of the investigation, would like to speak to both of you.'

Clare glanced at Jason, saw the alarm in his eyes which she had no doubt was in her own. She forced a smile, looked back at the breakfast she had still not touched on the table. 'Well, if you could come round here in an hour or so, you'd be able to see both of us together.'

A short pause. 'We'd prefer to see you separately, Mrs Thompson. There's nothing sinister in that, it's standard procedure. We need to build up a detailed picture both of the evening and of the victim, you see, and people sometimes remember different things.'

'That really seems rather a waste of your time in this case. I was Mr Hayes's personal assistant and I kept his business diary, so I can see that I could be useful to you. My husband, on the other hand, hardly knew him. I don't see that he's going to be able to contribute much that you—'

'Nevertheless, we shall need to see him on his own. It's standard procedure, as I said. It probably won't take very long.'

Clare felt the phone being removed from her hand. Jason said tersely into the mouthpiece, 'I understand. I'll come into the station to see you.' Then he added belatedly, 'It's Jason Thompson speaking.'

'Thank you, Mr Thompson. When can you come here?'

'Right away. I can be with you in quarter of an hour or so. Might as well get it out of the way.' A high, nervous giggle reminded him how on edge he was.

Matthew Ballack struggled to open the sash window in what had once been an elegant Edwardian room but was now the only decent space in his frowsty flat. He hadn't had this window open since the previous summer, but on this Sunday morning he felt a need for fresh air.

Eventually he managed to wrench the swollen, reluctant frame six inches upwards, allowing cool, clear air and a brave March sun into the stale room. He had drunk more than he should have and stayed up longer than he should have on the previous night, listening to successive news bulletins on Radio Lancashire and revelling in his release from the tyranny of Timothy Hayes.

Now he had to cease rejoicing and decide upon his strategy. Should he keep a low profile or assert himself immediately? It would have to be the latter, he soon decided. There were not many people around now at the original Hayes Electronics factory who would remember him from the early days. Tim Hayes had ensured that he was more and more marginalized and moved him further and further away from the respectable front of the firm.

But Clare Thompson might still remember him, even though he hadn't seen her for years. He would go into the main office tomorrow and let them know the position. More than that, he would fill the vacuum left by Hayes's death before any other person tried to push himself into it. Even when you had the law and natural rights on your side, it was better to declare your position from the first than to come in later and thus have to unseat and discomfort other claimants.

He was thinking like a leader again, asserting sound business principles. Matthew Ballack felt long-dormant ability stirring within him and exulted. He might even clean up this firm and restore its original integrity, once he had retaken the reins of power.

The CID section was not busy on a Sunday morning, even with a murder hunt now initiated. Most of the team were out checking on the less important of the many people who had been present at Timothy Hayes' last meal on Friday night.

Percy Peach could easily have taken the visitor into his own office, where they would not have been disturbed. Nevertheless, he led him into interview room two, marginally the smallest of these facilities. The DCI liked an environment where he was thoroughly at home and strangers were wholly uncomfortable, and this windowless, cell-like box, with its sage-green walls and harsh artificial lighting, filled the bill admirably.

He watched Jason Thompson come in and sit down nervously on the other side of the small, square table, noted with satisfaction how often his hand rose unnecessarily to brush away the carrot-coloured hair which was his most individual feature. Peach gave him the smile a cat might give to a cornered mouse and said pleasantly, 'Good of you to come in here to help us with our enquiries, sir. Nasty business, this.'

'Yes. But I expect you have to deal with them all the time.'

'Not all the time, sir, no. Murder is still quite an event in our lives, isn't it, DS Blake? Still quite an exciting crime for us, if we're honest.' He leaned forward and switched on the cassette recorder. 'I think we'll just keep a record of our chat, if you don't mind, Mr Thompson. Not strictly necessary, of course – you've not been charged or anything like that. But it's useful to us to have a tape: you would be surprised how often people remember things quite differently from us.' He smiled sadly at the omissions of humanity and contrived to give Thompson the impression that he was already a suspect.

'I'm sure I shan't be able to give you anything useful.'

'Probably not, sir. But you never know. In due course, we shall be able to fit your story into the picture given to us by everyone else. Or not fit it in, of course, which would be much more interesting!' He beamed his delight at that prospect. 'How long had you known the victim?'

'Well, I suppose we'd been acquainted for seven or eight years.'

'Acquainted?' Peach's eyebrows rose high towards the white dome of his head. Lucy Blake, silent and studiously expressionless over her notebook, was impressed yet again by the way Percy could pick up the most innocent of words and make it sound like an accusation.

'Our paths didn't cross. He was an industrialist. I am a schoolteacher.' Jason Thompson's brown eyes blinked twice behind his thick-lensed glasses, as if to emphasize how out of touch with Hayes's world he had been.

'But your wife obviously knew Mr Hayes very well indeed.'

He looked startled, and his hand flew up again to the straight red hair and brushed it away, though it was not in fact over his eye. 'In a professional character, yes. She has been on the staff of Hayes Electronics for many years, and has been acting as Mr Hayes's personal assistant for something like four years.'

'And no doubt has given complete satisfaction.' Peach noted the man folding his arms and looking hostile. He said reasonably, 'The business has gone from strength to strength, we're told, and no director of such an enterprise can be successful without a highly efficient personal assistant.'

'Yes. I'm sure that is so.'

'We shall get a fuller picture when we question her about that in due course. In the meantime, do you know of any enemies Mr Hayes might have made?'

'No.' The denial came a little too loud and a little too promptly. As if he realized that and needed to fill the silence, Thompson added, 'I hardly knew him, as I said.'

'Did he seem at all disturbed during the dinner?'

'No. Not as far as I could see. I wasn't near enough to speak to him or to hear what he was saying during the meal. He made a speech at the end of it. He seemed all right then.'

'And what about after that?'

Thompson blinked rapidly again behind the thick glasses. 'I don't know. I didn't see him after that.'

'You weren't in his group at the bar?'

'I left the hotel. Quite a few others did the same.'

'So Mrs Hayes told us.' He watched him stiffen at the mention of the widow's name. 'What time would this be?'

'Around eleven, I think.'

Lucy Blake made a note of the time and looked up at him. 'So you and Mrs Thompson drove straight home from the hotel.'

'My wife wasn't with me. I told you, she's – she was – Hayes's PA. She had to stay around. I'd had enough by eleven. I'd had a long day at school before we went out that evening.'

'So you drove there in separate cars?'

'No. We went together. I'd anticipated that we'd be going home together.' For a moment, his thin face twisted with pain. 'But it didn't matter that we weren't. The Johnsons were there – he's a supervisor in the factory. They live within two hundred yards of us. They gave me a lift home. I must have been in the house by quarter past eleven.' His explanation came in staccato bursts.

'And you didn't go out again?'

He looked into her calm young face and said aggressively, 'No, of course I didn't. What would I want to go out again for?'

'I've no idea. We have to record these things, Mr Thompson. What time did your wife get home?'

'I'm not sure. I'd gone to bed.'

'So you don't recall her coming home at all?'

'Of course I do! I wasn't asleep. I'm just not sure what time it was. Around midnight, I expect, but I couldn't be sure.'

'And we don't want you to guess at times if you can't be sure.' Peach came back in smoothly, making it sound to Thompson as if the whole case might depend on what time Clare had come into the house. 'I expect your wife was quite a long time after you. I think things went on for at least an hour or so after you'd left.'

For some reason, that thought seemed to give him pain. He eventually said, 'I didn't know that. Perhaps Clare didn't stay until the end.'

'Perhaps not. We'd obviously be very interested in anyone who stayed there as long as Mr Hayes did. But we shall be able to speak to your wife in due course, and get a more accurate time, won't we?'

'Yes, I suppose so. If she can remember these things any better than me. No one knew Hayes was going to be killed, did they?'

'Someone did, Mr Thompson. Someone who waited for him in or near his car and shot him in cold blood.'

'That wasn't me. And it certainly wasn't Clare!' Thompson seemed by his vehemence to be trying to convince himself of that.

Peach let the man's intensity hang for a few seconds in the cramped, airless little room. 'You'd known Mr Hayes for several years. A man in that position makes enemies, and you must be aware of some of them. Of the people at that meal on Friday, who do you think wanted Hayes off the scene?'

Thompson looked for a moment as if he was going to volunteer something. Then he said, 'I told you earlier that Hayes and I inhabited totally different worlds. He wouldn't know mine and I certainly wouldn't know his. I'd hardly met the man.'

201

Peach nodded thoughtfully. 'Whereas your wife would obviously know quite a lot about him. I expect we shall get more useful suggestions from her.'

'I don't think she'll know much more than I do.'

'Really? When she's been his personal assistant for the last few years? By your own criteria, she's going to know an awful lot about Timothy Hayes.' Peach, eyebrows raised in innocent surprise, was a model of reasonableness.

'Professionally. She'll know about his professional movements and the people he met in the course of business. Nothing more than that.'

'Did I suggest anything more than that, Mr Thompson? Business colleagues and rivals are bound to come within the scope of our investigation, and the more we can learn about them the better. Or are you suggesting that this may be what our beloved press love to categorize as a crime of passion?'

'No!' Again the word rang out a little too loud and too quickly. As if he too understood that, Thompson said, 'I'm not suggesting anything, am I? I told you, I hardly knew the man.'

'Good position to be in, that, Mr Thompson, when we're talking about a murder victim. But then, I shouldn't be at all surprised if we find the person who did this adopting exactly the same pose.' He shut the file in front of him, looked interrogatively at DS Blake, then said with apparent reluctance, 'Well, that's it, for the moment, then. Thank you for coming in here to help us, Mr Thompson. Your assistance is much appreciated.'

Jason was halfway home in the car before he could put his finger on what was worrying him about an exchange in which he thought he had held his own. It was that simple phrase of Peach's: 'for the moment'.

It was several hours later, in the comfortable warmth of the living room in her small modern flat, that Lucy Blake said, 'He was holding something back, I'm sure, that Jason Thompson.'

'They all hold something back,' said Percy Peach with the cynical assurance of the long-time CID officer. Twenty-four hours later than he had planned, he stretched his legs and lounged a little further back on the sofa, contemplating the gleaming brown toes of his leather shoes and wondering if this was the moment to slip them off.

'Thompson's highly sexed,' said Lucy unexpectedly.

Percy pricked up his male ears at this contribution. 'He's a four-eyed git with carroty hair and a body that needs feeding up,' he said reasonably.

'Doesn't alter the fact that he's highly sexed,' said Lucy with a smile. 'Women can tell. You are lucky to have me assisting you.'

'I've never disputed that!' said Percy, moving

a little closer to her on the sofa and slipping his right arm round her shoulder. He then caressed her breast thoughtfully and added, 'You must allow for the fact that you have the kind of bosom which drives strong men wild.'

'I didn't mean he fancied me, you idiot! I don't think he did. But he wasn't just nervous; he had those quick movements of his limbs which were almost out of his control at times. He kept folding his arms to try to prevent his hands moving. I'm not saying that always means people are highly sexed, but in his case it does. And I wish some other people would also try to control their movements!' She detached her fiancé's hand from her breast and held it firmly as she reiterated, 'Take it from me, Jason Thompson is highly sexed. It probably has nothing at all to do with the case, but he is!'

'Your psychological insights continue to amaze me,' said Percy reverently, setting his head comfortably on her shoulder.

Lucy Blake straightened suddenly. 'Anyway, what do you mean, saying he can't be attractive because of his carroty hair! May I remind you that my own hair is red, Mr Peach!'

'Ah, but not carroty, my dearest. Titian, I'd call it, not common red. A unique shade of hair. And uniquely arousing!' He stroked her hair enthusiastically, then transferred his attention to other areas to show just how uniquely aroused he was.

She controlled his hands with what was by now practised ease, then offered him the promise which would allay his ardour until she had finished the discussion. 'All in good time, dear.'

'Ahhhhh!' A low moan of pleasure which became a long monotone of admiration. Then, unexpectedly, he too sat up straight. 'If you must bring work home to what should be a couch of unmitigated physical pleasure, apply these psychological insights to the puzzling Mrs Hayes, please.'

Lucy was aware that any reference to her psychological knowledge was a concealed insult. You didn't need to be a police officer long to be dragged into the service's habitual distrust of professional psychologists and everything they represented. Much worse, in her view, were social workers who learned a very little psychology and then were beguiled into applying it without full understanding. She had seen this happen in both the most complex and the most straightforward of criminal situations, with equally disastrous results.

Although she knew that Percy Peach was more open to ideas than most beneath his hard-man veneer – he had even been known to invite forensic psychologists into complex cases – she had more sense than to move out of her depth. She said cautiously, 'I thought that Tamsin Hayes, like Jason Thompson, was holding something back.'

'You didn't simply accept that she was a woman in shock and deep mourning?'

She thought for a moment before shaking her head. 'Shock, maybe. I didn't buy the deep mourning. It was laid on too thick.'

'I agree. I think she'd dressed for the part very deliberately. Overdressed, perhaps. And she had all that black gear out very quickly. Within two or three hours of hearing her old man was dead.'

'Her beloved old man.'

'So she said.'

'Maybe she wasn't as attached to him as she'd like us to think. Maybe she went back to the Gisburn Hotel and disposed of him.'

'Maybe. Or maybe she never left – so far we only have her word that she drove home when she left the party.'

'Or maybe she was exactly where she said she was, knowing that someone else was seeing him off.'

'Or maybe highly sexed carroty-bonce was seeing him off. The world is full of possibilities, my darling.' With an abrupt change of course, Percy Peach addressed himself energetically to one of them.

It was some thirty minutes later, when they were lying contentedly tired between the sheets, that Lucy Blake said drowsily, 'I told you I could recognize when a man was highly sexed.'

# Fifteen

Leroy Moore thought he would have heard from the police by now. It was Monday morning and he felt he should be going into work, but he did not know quite where to go: the duties of the Head of Security Services at Hayes Electronics had not been defined at the time of the proprietor's death.

'They'll want to know where you were when he died,' said Jane Martin.

'They'll want to know where all of us were. That's the way they work. Unless they already have a prime suspect for the case. In which case they might well be grilling the poor sod at this minute.' He looked at his watch. It was still not nine o'clock, but they had been up for hours. They'd had coffee and what they could manage to eat some time ago now, and done what tidying up was necessary in his small flat. When you didn't know exactly what you should be doing and where you should be, the time dragged by very slowly.

'You think they'll want to speak to me?'

He caught the alarm in Jane's voice, was moved again by the tenderness which still surprised him. 'I think they'll want to speak to everyone, unless they think they already know who did it.' He wondered how Jane would behave under questioning, whether she would panic like some other girls he had known. He even wondered for a moment whether she had anything to hide from them.

As if she followed his thoughts, she gave him the familiar smile and said, 'I've been grilled by the pigs before, you know. It's a few years ago, but I think I remember the rules.'

'Don't tell them anything you don't have to.' Leroy spoke automatically, almost as a reflex reaction. 'Don't give them anything and they can't use it to trip you up.'

Jane nodded thoughtfully. 'You think that's true, even in a murder inquiry?'

He didn't want to go into the sessions he had had with the fuzz six years ago when he had killed a man. He hadn't told Jane about that, though in due course he would do; he didn't want to have any secrets from her, did he? It had been self-defence, anyway, and eventually he'd convinced the cops of that. Or they hadn't been able to get enough evidence in the murky pools where he had swum in those days to bring a case. He said, 'You want to keep yourself as far away from the victim as you can. Make out you hardly knew him and they won't be interested in you.'

'You don't think I should tell them about – about what happened on that Thursday night?'

Jane still found it difficult to speak of that night, even with Leroy.

'No one else knows about it, do they?'

'No. You're the only person I've told.'

'Leave it that way. Keep yourself as far away from the victim as possible, if you don't want the pigs to get interested in you.'

She nodded. It seemed logical enough, but she was troubled, both by what had happened that night and the way she had felt about the man who had done it.

At that moment, the phone rang and Leroy spoke briefly into it. He forced a smile into his normally cheerful black face as he turned back to her. 'That was some CID bloke. He and his DCI want to speak to me this morning. It's all right, love. I was expecting it, wasn't I?'

Clare Thompson was at her desk at her usual time on the Monday morning. After the cat-and-mouse games with Jason at the weekend, she found the routine of work a relief.

There was certainly no time for private reflection. The telephone calls came in thick and fast. She dealt with them swiftly and efficiently, every inch the proficient personal assistant she had always been. The fact that strictly speaking she was at this moment personal assistant to no one was irrelevant. She kept the day-to-day work of the firm moving along as smoothly as ever. She discouraged gossip about the sensational events of the weekend among the younger women in the outer office, answered the myriad small queries which came in from the factory workforce with a grave smile, repeated at every opportunity the maxim that production should proceed exactly as normal.

Clare accepted the external messages of condolence with grave thanks; her telephone manner had always been one of her strengths. When she sensed unspoken questions beneath the routine sympathy, she reassured both customers and suppliers that business would be proceeding much as usual. She was not herself in control of policy, of course. But she was sure that the death of even as prominent a leader as Mr Hayes would not diminish either efficiency or service, that deadlines would continue to be met and prices would remain as keen as ever.

Clare set the phone down with a little sigh of pleasure and satisfaction after the latest of these calls. Only then did she become aware of the figure who had arrived without her noticing him and was sitting quietly waiting for her to finish the call. Her initial reaction was of irritation that someone should be listening, almost eavesdropping, upon her performance. Only belatedly did she realize that she knew the man.

'It's Mr Ballack, isn't it?' she said, as he shuffled awkwardly to his feet.

'You're good at names. That's a skill I never had and envy in you.' He smiled, wondering how he was going to assert himself as an authority figure with this very efficient bureaucrat.

She saw a man in a well-cut suit which was just a little too tight over a developing belly, a man with earnest, watery, slightly bloodshot eyes, who was probably not much older than Tim had been, but who didn't look very healthy. She wondered just what he was here for this morning, but sensed also that she didn't need to ask him about that, that he had come to tell her about it.

She gave him a little smile in recognition of his compliment. She was good at names: it was one of the necessary skills which she had acquired early. 'I'm Clare Thompson, Mr Hayes's personal assistant. We've spoken on the phone a couple of times, but it's a long time since I saw you.' That was when I was in the general office, she was thinking, before I took on this job and got myself involved with Tim Hayes. I think you used to be quite important, but I'm damned if I can remember what you do now.

He sat down in the chair at the other side of her desk, forcing himself to relax, telling himself that he was here to control this formidable, informed presence, that it was up to him to tell her what was going to happen, not discuss it with her. But he must do that tactfully: he needed this efficient, all-knowing woman on his side, not leading the opposition to his coup. 'I was Mr Hayes's partner at the outset, before even you were around, Mrs Thompson. I was still his partner at the time of his death on

Friday. I've been involved in the newer and more peripheral activities of the firm in recent years.'

'That's why I haven't heard much of you lately.'

'That's one reason, yes.' He might tell her later, much later, about the way Hayes had treated him. But he would need to probe how deep-seated her loyalty to the dead man was before he did that, and that would take weeks, maybe months. 'I've had health and family problems as well, so I've been content to adopt a lower profile in the last year or two. But I'm back in the run of things now, and Tim and I were discussing only last week what new management tasks I should take on.' He smiled at her, thinking he had carried that off rather well.

The phone shrilled, but she told the caller she would ring back. That gave Matthew a little more confidence: at least she was treating his visit as an important one. He said firmly, 'Tim's totally unexpected and tragic death is a loss to all of us, but as you have just been indicating so lucidly to our customers, business must go on as usual. I'm here to help that process.'

They smiled at each other whilst their brains worked frantically. Clare was wondering what this man who had emerged from the shadows was proposing, how it would affect her, what if anything she could do about it. She said, 'I'm sure that the firm's going to need everyone's

212

help to survive. Tim was very much a one-man band, wasn't he? His death has left a huge hole here.'

Matthew smiled, trying to fill her with confidence at the same time as he gathered his own. 'He was perhaps a little too much of a one-man band, at times. One shouldn't speak ill of the dead, but I say that affectionately, I hope. I claim the privilege as his oldest business colleague and his partner.'

'You wouldn't expect me to comment on that. I don't make business decisions or have anything to do with business strategies. I see things from the narrower viewpoint of the personal assistant who kept his diary and arranged his appointments. I never told Tim how to run his firm and would never have wanted to.'

She was stone-walling, waiting for him to make his move. Intelligent woman. Matthew wondered exactly what she had made of the man she was conventionally defending. 'As you say, everyone is going to have to pick up the pieces if the success of the firm is to continue. In a day or two, we'll put out an official statement to that effect, to allay any disquiet amongst our workforce. In the meantime, I should be grateful if you'd continue to convey that message informally to the people around you. It will filter out from here, as you know.'

Clare nodded, her mind still working furiously. Had this man really been as close and as friendly with Tim Hayes as he claimed? She realized how little Tim had actually told her, not only about those newer areas of the business, from which it appeared much of its present prosperity stemmed, but about other people who worked for him. She said, 'I'll do that, of course. May I ask exactly what future role you propose to play yourself, Mr Ballack?'

She was cool, quick-thinking, direct. Men often underestimated women who were blonde and blue-eyed, but with her alert, mature face, her trim, long-legged, slightly angular figure, her air of experience and calm authority, only an idiot would not rate this one. Matthew Ballack was pleased to find he liked her already. He needed her to like him, for she would be a valuable person to have as an ally. An indispensable one, in his case, since she knew far more about the day-to-day operation of the original electronics section of the business than any other person alive.

Matthew took a deep breath and said, 'The original partnership still stands, though not many people other than Tim and I have been much aware of it recently. I shall move in here – into Tim's office.' He glanced instinctively at the closed door to that inner sanctum; it was five or six years since he had last been in there.

Then he turned back with a smile to the woman who had controlled access to the head of this enterprise. 'I expect there will be a little talk about dead men's shoes and hasty assumptions of power, but it is in everyone's interest that I do this, that the firm is not left with a vacuum at the top. I shall depend very heavily upon your support, especially in the next few weeks. Mrs Thompson, I hope that you will agree to become my personal assistant and offer me the same efficiency and loyalty you offered Tim Hayes.'

'Of course I shall. It will make my position a little easier, if I can assure people that there will be a seamless transfer of authority.' Behind her smile, Clare was wondering about his right to muscle himself into power like this. But the challenge to that, if it came, must come from people other than her. 'When do you propose to move into the managing director's office?'

'This afternoon, I think. This morning I shall tour other sections of the business and assure as many people as I can that things can and must proceed as normal. I shall see you later, then.' He smiled, finding this time that there was nothing forced about it, that he was speaking with authority rather than pomposity. 'I look forward to working with you. I'm already sure that I shall enjoy it.'

Clare Thompson had hardly a moment to herself for the rest of the morning, with the constant need to apprise both insiders and outsiders of the new situation. Even at lunch time, she had little privacy, as she answered questions about Matthew Ballack, the partner no one seemed to remember, and eavesdropped a little on the excited conversations of others.

She had to lock herself in a cubicle in the cloakroom to get a few minutes to herself and review this tumultuous first morning back at work. She decided cautiously that she liked what little she had seen of Matthew Ballack, that she had been more impressed by the time he had left her than when she had first discovered him in her office.

The other important idea came suddenly to her, almost as an afterthought. In material terms, Matthew Ballack seemed to have gained more by the death of Tim Hayes than anyone else.

When he moved into the room, Detective Constable Brendan Murphy was instantly reminded of one of Percy Peach's precepts, which formed the young detective's ten commandments of behaviour.

When you had to interview a looker, be careful. If you were a young lad with a cock throbbing where your brain should be (Percy's amiable description of this youngest member of his hand-picked CID team), you should be extra-careful. Lust could be a destroyer of all judgement; even a simple recognition that a face was pretty could make you miss other and more important things.

This one was certainly a looker. He hadn't been prepared for anything so stunning in this shabby, run-down section of the town, where clogs had once clattered over the cobbles and ageing, battered cars and vans now dominated the streets. Her wide brown eyes and skin the colour of creamy coffee framed the most open and winning of smiles, as if she were genuinely pleased to see him. The sinuous movement of her body beneath a simple cream shirt and very tight jeans shrilled like a Peach alarm in his ears as she led him into the bedsit. DC Murphy decided that he had better be very careful indeed.

He felt his voice a little high as he said, 'This is a routine enquiry in connection with the death of Mr Timothy Hayes. I'm DC Brendan Murphy.'

'And I'm Jane Martin. Spinster of this parish.' A slight but definite Lancashire accent. Brendan wasn't sure why, but in this exotic creature, he found that reassuring. She said, 'With a name like that you must surely be Irish,' and gave him another of those radiant smiles.

'You'd think so, but I'm a hollow sham, I'm afraid. I'm from Irish stock, but I've never lived outside Lancashire.'

'Like me. People place me anywhere from Morocco to Cuba, with most of the West Indian islands in between, but I'm from Bolton. Where my dad was from is anyone's guess!'

They enjoyed a mutual giggle at her humour and her frankness. Then she said, 'I suppose I should be disappointed to find you here, but I'm not.' When she saw his puzzlement, she hastened to explain. 'My boyfriend, whose flat this is, rated a DCI and a DS, whereas all I qualify for is a simple DC.'

'And I'm disappointed that you're disappointed. And that you have a boyfriend.' Brendan wondered if his face was colouring up; his fresh complexion and fair skin constantly let him down. He was managing the chat a little better than he usually did with girls who attracted him. Perhaps that was because this was strictly a working context; no emotion here, he told himself sternly. He noticed that she knew all about police ranks: perhaps she wasn't as innocent as she looked, perhaps she'd had contact with the police before.

He told her, 'You should be relieved, not offended. It means you're low-profile, not expected to feature in the later stages of the investigation. Everyone who was at Friday night's dinner has to be seen by a member of the team, in case they saw or heard anything useful, but only senior employees and people who knew Mr Hayes personally will get the full treatment from DCI Peach. Believe me, you wouldn't want that.' Brendan Murphy, who had in his time been on the wrong end of a couple of Peach's legendary bollockings, spoke with genuine feeling.

'I wasn't sitting near to Mr Hayes on Friday night. I didn't speak to him at any time during the evening.' She knew that she should have waited for this unusually friendly policeman to ask the questions, but with his mention of the dinner, she had become very tense.

'That's two of the things I wanted to know. Did you see him having any conversations with other people which now seem suspicious? Any arguments, for instance?'

'No. I was busy with my own concerns, with talking to the people around me. I'm afraid I wasn't even very conscious of Mr Hayes, until he spoke.'

That rang true, anyone placed near to this ravishing girl would certainly want to monopolize her attention, Brendan thought. 'Yes. What about this speech Mr Hayes made? Did he seem at all disturbed or on edge?'

'No. A lot of it didn't mean much to me. But it seemed quite polished.' What she could actually remember was her resentment that the man who had raped her should be so urbane and in control of himself. Jane had wanted to shout out what she knew about him, whilst he had been presenting the innocent businessman so effectively on this public occasion. She thrust that memory aside and made herself speak carefully. 'He thanked the people who'd been with him from the start and acknowledged the support he'd had in the town. Said how much he owed to the loyalty of his workforce. That sort of thing. It was all well prepared and he carried it off well. I wouldn't say he was nervous or upset.'

Murphy looked at her for a moment in that close, unembarrassed way which CID men had.

People weren't used to being studied like that in a social context, so that it often disconcerted them. Then he said abruptly, 'How well did you know Mr Hayes?'

'I scarcely knew him at all. He didn't interview me when I was appointed as a croupier at the casino. I expect he hardly knew me.' This was what she had agreed with Leroy that she would say. Best not to give away that she had any sort of motive, they'd decided, so as to keep her out of it altogether. She thought she'd delivered it reasonably well, but she wasn't happy about it.

'Like it at the casino, do you?'

She hadn't expected this. 'I do, yes. More than I thought I would, when I applied for the job. It's interesting work. My mother was worried about me going into a gambling den, as she called it, but I never feel in any danger. You meet a few dodgy characters at the tables, but you don't get involved with them. There are people around who make sure that everything is conducted properly.'

And lots of men who are persuaded to put a few extra quid across the tables, with someone like you smiling at them, I'm sure, thought Brendan. 'What about the company at work? Do you have people to chat with?'

'There are three or four people of my own age or only a little older, yes. And lots of the older people have led interesting lives. We're a good working group, I feel.'

'Interesting. In all the gossip and chat amongst this varied group of people, you must have discussed the boss at times.'

'Yes. It's human nature, isn't it? I expect all of us speculate about the people in power, the people who control our working lives.'

For the last few minutes, since he had moved the questioning to her work at the casino, Jane Martin hadn't been looking at him. This was particularly noticeable because of the frankness he had seen earlier in those large brown eyes. But what she was saying was straightforward enough and made sense. Brendan said, 'You must have picked up snippets of knowledge about the way people felt. Do you recall noticing that anyone felt very strongly about Mr Hayes?'

'No. There were the usual bits of speculation about how much he was making out of the casino, the usual bits of jealousy of his success. Nothing serious enough to suggest that someone might be planning to kill him, if that's what you mean.'

He grinned at her, willing her to look him in the face again. 'That's what I mean, yes. Wherever there is any evidence of strong feeling, we shall have to follow it up. What did you hear about his personal life?'

She did look him full in the face again now, and Brendan thought he glimpsed a flash of alarm. 'That's too vague. I'm not sure what you mean.'

'Well, we need to know what weaknesses he had. Weaknesses lead a man into trouble, if they're serious enough. Was he a big boozer, a big betting man? Had he a fiery temper?'

'No, none of those things, as far as I know. You'd need to speak to people who knew him better than I did.'

'And other people will be doing just that, Jane. But at the moment I'm asking you. What about women? Or men, for that matter? Was he too fond of either?'

She was staring at the carpet between them again. 'Not men. You heard bits of gossip about women. But I didn't pay much attention. I told you, I hardly knew the man.' She had asserted this too often, but she couldn't think of anything else to say.

'Well, if there were any serious liaisons, we shall no doubt learn all about them in the next few days. If you hear anything that you think might interest us, please contact me at this number.' He gave her his most friendly smile as he left, and earnestly hoped that she would.

Jane Martin looked at the small, neat card, with 'DC Brendan Murphy, Brunton CID Section' neatly printed above the telephone number. He hadn't been at all frightening, but she'd found it more taxing than she'd hoped it would be. Nevertheless, she'd done rather well, she thought. Men were simple creatures, most of them. But she was glad that it was over. She made herself a cup of tea and thought about work in the evening, wondering what the others would have to report about the police questionings.

She would have been surprised and disturbed if she had known what Brendan Murphy was thinking. Driving his car back towards the station, he was deciding that he must relay things to DCI Peach about this routine interview. He would need to tell Percy that in his opinion the ravishing Jane Martin knew a little more about Timothy Hayes than she had been prepared to volunteer.

# Sixteen

Leroy Moore was having a less easy ride than his girlfriend. DCI Peach was giving him the sort of interview which Brendan Murphy said Jane Martin had done well to avoid.

Leroy was surprised to find another black man lined up against him. He was used to hard men, to handling himself, and he wasn't usually upset by appearances. But he feared this was a leaner, harder and tougher black man than himself. DC Clyde Northcott was six feet three, without an ounce of surplus fat upon his rangy frame. With his narrowed eyes, his smooth skin over the prominent bones of his face, he looked, to Leroy, as hard as ebony. Northcott sat beside Peach, watching their quarry and waiting his moment, looking like the muscle who silently waited to enforce the views of a gangster boss.

Leroy Moore had met men like this before, had operated both with and against them in his Moss Side days, but he had never seen one on the law-enforcement side of the table. Leroy had kept the idea of playing the race card as his fall-back position, the one which gave you time and made the fuzz cautious if all else failed; now he gave up this idea, even before Northcott had spoken a word to him.

Peach looked round the flat coolly, taking in its tidiness and the faint vestiges of perfume which told him that there had been a woman here recently. He looked unhurriedly at the pictures of animals on the walls which had been hung there by unknown hands long before Moore came here, the enlarged photograph of a stream running through trees in the Trough of Bowland which was his single, unlikely addition to the furnishings. Peach looked at the drawers in the shabby oak dresser which dominated one wall, as if he was wondering whether to open them and inspect the contents. Leroy was glad that he had no drugs in the flat, that Jane Martin and his determination to reform had seen the last of coke and horse for him.

This short, bald-headed man with the smart grey suit and eyes like black coal seemed to know all of this as he turned his attention back to the occupant. It was almost a relief to Leroy when he finally spoke. What he said soon dismissed that reaction. 'You've got form, Mr Moore. You should know that we are aware of that form. You should take that into account when answering our questions. Any attempt to deceive us will not be well received.' Peach smiled grimly, relishing his understatement. 'What was your function in this grubby little empire?'

This shook Leroy even more than the reminder about his past. He'd expected them to accept all the stuff Hayes had put out about the respectable businessman, to accept the wall of respectability he had set about himself. He sought for words which Hayes might have used himself. 'I don't know what you mean by "grubby". Hayes Electronics is a reputable concern, much appreciated in Brunton for the work it provides. Ask any of the people who were at the Gisburn Hotel on Friday night.'

'Oh, we shall, Mr Moore, we shall do that. But we know certain things already, you see. We know certain things about the new and profitable parts of the business, the ones that Mr Hayes did not care to publicize, don't we, DC Northcott?' The policeman at his side nodded, without ceasing his scrutiny of Moore's too-mobile face. 'You would do well to remember that when you make your replies to our questions, Mr Moore.'

'I don't know anything about that sort of thing.' It sounded woefully inadequate, even in the ears of the man who framed it.

'Really?' Peach's dark eyebrows arched impossibly high towards his bald pate. His small black moustache seemed to Leroy to bristle with disbelief. 'I think you're trying to deceive us already. I don't like that, and I shouldn't think DC Northcott does either. Now, how about answering my first and very simple question, Mr Moore? I'll put it to you again, even more simply, if you like. What is your function in this shitheap?'

'I'm the Head of Security Services.' Leroy tried to roll out the title impressively. He failed.

'And what exactly does that involve?'

The question he had feared. The question to which he really didn't have an answer. He swallowed and launched himself into the sentences he'd prepared before they came. 'It was a new appointment. It reflected the growth of the firm. The exact terms of the post hadn't been formally defined. I was due to discuss that with Mr Hayes today.'

Peach allowed a slow smile of scepticism to steal across his round face. It was a facial exercise he had practised much over the years and it was an unnerving sight for Leroy Moore. 'Reading from the sheet, are you, Mr Moore? If you can't tell us what you are planning to do, give us an account of what you've done for the firm in the past, will you?'

'A variety of jobs. Whatever Mr Hayes asked me to do. Mainly in places like the casino and the betting shops, but also round the electronics factory from time to time. Anywhere he found a use for me.' Leroy heard the desperation level rising in his voice as he stumbled from phrase to phrase.

'A variety, eh? And what would you say your particular skills were, Mr Moore?'

'I wouldn't say I had particular skills. Mr Hayes gave me a chance and I took it. He must have been quite pleased with me, or he would not have offered me this major new post, would he?'

Peach gave him a broad smile, as if it was pleasant to be hearing the things he had expected. 'Makes sense, that, Mr Moore. It's almost the first thing that does in what you've been saying. DC Northcott and I were in danger of losing our footing among the bullshit. So we all agree that Mr Hayes must have been well pleased with the skills you had been employing on his behalf. Trouble is, you still haven't come clean about what those skills are.'

'I told you, I was employed in a variety—'

'So I'm going to help you out, Mr Moore. I'm going to ask DC Northcott here to suggest what he thinks these mysterious skills of yours might be.'

Clyde Northcott looked for three long seconds at Leroy Moore as if he might be something unmentionable he had just scraped off his shoe. You didn't work regularly with Percy Peach without learning how to exploit a silence. Then he said, 'You brought your skills with you from where you learned them, Moore. From gang warfare in Moss Side, Manchester. You haven't got qualifications. You haven't got experience, except in beating up people. That's what Hayes employed you for. To make sure small people did what he wanted them to do. To make sure loans were repaid punctually and with interest. To make sure rent and protection money came in on time. To make sure the users who become

228

small-time drug dealers kept in line. To make sure the toms came up with their forty per cent without question and didn't try to moonlight on their own behalf.'

'That's not fair. I came to Brunton to get away from that sort of life.' To his horror, Leroy caught in his voice the familiar old lags' whine which he had heard so often in his youth and had been determined he would never use.

Clyde Northcott went on as if there had been no interruption, as if he had not even heard Moore's protest. 'Hayes employed you to keep his own hands clean. To enforce what he was doing to make serious money whilst he pretended to be the enlightened capitalist, bringing employment and new industries to the town.'

Leroy Moore hadn't been prepared for any of this. He had known his own position would be dodgy, that he would be expected to provide some account of himself. But he had thought that Hayes's position as a pillar of local society and a valued provider of employment would be unquestioned. They had cut the ground from under his feet by telling him that Hayes was a villain and then asking what particular branch of his roguery he himself had been involved in. He said sullenly, 'I told you, I left Moss Side to get away from all that. I like it here. I'm making a new life. I'm planning to get married and make something of myself. All the things you pigs told me that I should do.'

Perhaps because for the first time he had

spoken spontaneously, this wasn't treated with the cynicism which coppers would normally have afforded it. They heard similar protestations far too often not to treat them as either evasions or pious hopes. But this time Peach growled, then said as though pandering to a weakness in himself, 'I'm almost prepared to believe that, Mr Moore. If it's true, it shows more sense of reality than I see in most men of your background.' He sighed like a fond father over an errant child. 'The trouble is, you still haven't provided us with any proper details of the work you were doing for this whited sepulchre Tim Hayes, have you?'

Leroy felt a little thrill of unexpected pleasure at that phrase. It took him back to his brief period in a Sunday School with a dozen other black seven-year-olds, where a young West Indian he had thought the most beautiful woman on the face of the earth had told them Bible tales and taught them gospel songs. Whited sepulchre was the sort of phrase he had been seeking for to describe Tim Hayes, ever since the bastard had done that thing to Jane Martin. He wanted to repeat the words, to shout them out, to agree with them that yes, that was what Hayes had been, a whited sepulchre who deserved exactly what had happened to him.

He couldn't do anything of the sort, of course. But he said with a dull air of confession, 'All right. Hayes did use me to do his dirty work, to put the frighteners on people who weren't meeting their deadlines. But that was mainly what it was. Frightening people was usually enough. If you could give them an idea of what might happen to them, get them shit-scared, they usually came up with the money. Or they got out and let someone else take over – someone Hayes wanted to put into place and control.'

Clyde Northcott nodded at him, almost conspiratorially, as if he could now acknowledge an honest description of the situation. 'And if they didn't conform, you applied just enough violence to make them see reason. Gave them a beating without putting them into hospital. Let the news of what had happened to them filter around to others so that they would be expected to come up with the goods on time.'

It was much too accurate a description of his work over the last year for Leroy's taste. This man seemed to know all the workings of that underground world which the public did not see. Moore could not know of course that Peach had recruited Clyde Northcott from exactly such a background to become first a policeman and a couple of years later a member of his CID team. Leroy said rather dazedly, 'It was a bit like that, yes.'

'Those are your skills, Leroy. There's quite an art in knowing just how thoroughly you can beat a man without putting him into hospital, isn't there? How you can put the fear of God into people without breaking bones.'

Leroy looked into the very dark face, at once so near to his in hue and so unlike it in form. This man from whom he had hoped for a little sympathy was utterly unflinching. There seemed more hope now in the round white face beside him. 'It was a bit like that. But violence was all I had to offer, when I crawled out of Moss Side. I was serious in what I said just now about wanting something better. I was hoping this new job which Hayes was offering me would be the first step towards that.'

Peach said, 'I'm a sentimental old fool and I'm relying on DC Northcott to keep shtum about it, but I almost believe you, Mr Moore. But to convince me for more than thirty seconds, you've got to come clean about everything you know.'

'And let you throw the book at me for what I tell you?'

Percy smiled. 'We're not here to do deals, Mr Moore. But no one so far has laid a complaint against you. You and I know that that is because the people you've been threatening and thumping aren't in a position to go to the police. But this is a murder inquiry and I'm only interested at the moment in arresting a murderer. If you give us all the help you can, if you're sincere about wanting to mend your ways, we may be able to regard your Brunton career to this point as a closed book.'

'I'll tell you whatever I can.'

'All this assumes of course that you're not the

murderer yourself. I don't want you to think that we've written off that possibility.'

'I didn't kill Hayes.'

'Good to hear it. However, as that comes from a man who's killed before, you'll understand when we treat it with a degree of cynicism.'

Leroy told himself not to panic, that he'd always expected the pigs to throw his record at him. 'It was self-defence. It wasn't premeditated, like this killing.'

'Know all about this death, do you, Mr Moore? Now that *is* interesting. Isn't it, DC Northcott?'

'Very interesting indeed, sir. I'd even say significant.'

'Would you indeed? Well, I'd probably have to agree with you on that. This might be the first break we've had so far.'

Leroy fought for words which would interrupt the torment. 'I don't know anything about the death. I just thought—'

'We're keeping an open mind, you see. We haven't even had the post-mortem report yet. You know more than us, if you know for certain that it was premeditated. The question for us now is *how* did you come to know?' Peach's brow wrinkled in puzzlement at this fascinating development.

'I – I thought the bulletins on the radio said someone had waited for him and shot him in his car.'

'Death in suspicious circumstances was all

they said. Body found on Saturday morning with a gunshot wound to the head. I sanctioned them myself. Nothing about premeditation.'

'I must have assumed that happened. Must have thought that sounded the likeliest way for him to have died.'

'Must you really?' Peach shook his head sadly. 'We try to prevent our CID officers from making assumptions, Mr Moore. But then you're not a CID officer, and unlikely to become one.'

'I don't see how else he could have died.'

'Really? Oh, there are certainly other possibilities.' Peach leaned forward, staring into the apprehensive face, fixing the mobile brown eyes with his own unwavering black pupils. 'There could have been an argument. Mr Hayes might have pulled out his own gun to defend himself, then had it turned upon him in the ensuing struggle.'

'I suppose it's a possibility, yes.'

'Quite an interesting one, really. Because it would replicate the killing carried out by a certain Leroy James Moore in Moss Side, Manchester, six years ago.'

'I didn't kill Hayes.' Leroy found his fists clenched tightly against his thighs. Like most men who had come to use violence as a tool, he felt helpless when it was not an option.

'If that's true, the best way to convince us of it is to point us towards the person who did.'

'I'd do that if I could. I just want this over

with.'

'Tell us where you were in the hour after Mr Hayes had finished his speech on Friday night.'

'I stayed around the hotel. Not in the same room as Hayes. In a different bar, a smaller one off the main one.'

'Where you could keep your eye on the man you were protecting, without being obtrusive.'

Moore nodded. 'He hadn't told me to do that. I thought as Head of Security Services, it must be part of my job to see that he was safe.'

'An interesting interpretation of your role. One in which you conspicuously failed, of course. But I don't suppose anyone is going to bollock you about that now. Carry on.'

'Well, I waited until there were only two or three people left with Hayes. I didn't know them – one was a councillor, I think.'

'We know them. They've been interviewed. From your point of view, it makes it more important that you get this right, doesn't it?'

Leroy tried to ignore that, to concentrate under the unflinching gaze of these two experienced, cynical men. 'Hayes saw me checking on things from the doorway. He gave me the nod to go and I went.'

'What time did you leave the car park?'

'I can't say exactly. After midnight, but beyond that I can't be definite.'

'Witnesses?'

'No.' He wanted to mention Jane Martin. But he had been determined before they came to make no mention of her, to keep her out of this, and his resolution held. Just held. 'There weren't many cars left in the car park when I drove out.'

They took the details of his Ford Focus, told him to let them know of anyone who could corroborate his statement, left him with the uncomfortable idea that he was more suspect than anyone else because of his previous record.

He told himself when they had gone that he'd kept Jane out of it. There was no motive for either Jane or himself, unless they found out about what Hayes had done to her. He'd found himself wanting to shout at those pigs what kind of man Hayes had been, how much he had deserved to die. But he hadn't done that, and he knew now as he had known before they came that it had been right to keep quiet about it.

He must go in to work soon, tell people there that he was the Head of Security, pretend that he had been given a job brief by Hayes before he died. He must get on with the new life he planned for himself. In a little while, he would be able to do it.

At the moment, he was too drained for any sort of action.

# Seventeen

The post-mortem report was available by midday on Monday. The pathologist had been as good as his word; he had made it a priority and opened up the lab over the weekend. Brendan Murphy, who had been the police officer in attendance, had controlled his stomach with difficulty as the organs were paraded before him and assured himself that he was now taking such things as routine.

The report provided Peach and his team with little that was new and nothing that was unexpected.

There was a moderate amount of alcohol in the body, but this man would have been just within the limits for driving. It was possible, however, that his awareness of what was happening around him would have been minimally impaired. In other words, that anyone waiting for Hayes, inside or outside the car, might have got fatally close before his or her presence was detected.

Death had resulted from a single discharge of the powerful Smith and Wesson pistol at point-blank range. Powder marks on what was left of the head indicated that the weapon had been held against the right temple of the deceased. Indications were that the weapon had been placed in the corpse's hand after, not before, the shooting. Time of death had been several hours before the discovery of the corpse at shortly before six thirty on Saturday morning. Analysis of the stomach contents and the partial digestion of the meal eaten between eight fifteen and ten fifteen on Friday night made it possible to give an unusually accurate estimate of the time of death, which was almost certainly between twelve midnight and one o'clock on Saturday morning.

'Thanks for nothing!' muttered Percy Peach sourly as he scanned the contents of the five-page report.

A call to forensics revealed that the scientists there held out little more hope of providing significant assistance. There were no prints other than the deceased's on the murder weapon. Various fibres had been taken from the seats and carpets of the BMW for analysis and retention against an arrest. But indications were that the interior of the car had not been cleaned for at least a month. This was the official way of suggesting that most of these samples probably predated the night of the killing and were therefore likely to obscure rather than illuminate what had happened in those few vital minutes.

There was a single definite and vital piece of

information, and in Peach's view even that was confirmation rather than anything new. The pistol had been registered and licensed to the deceased. Timothy Hayes had owned the Smith and Wesson which had blasted away his life.

Clare Thompson was pleased to receive the CID visitors in her office at Hayes Electronics. It was an impersonal environment and one where she felt in control. Had they come to her home, she felt that they might have picked up something of the febrile atmosphere that had dominated her exchanges with her husband since the murder of Tim Hayes, even without Jason being present.

Lucy Blake always got a little extra frisson of excitement when they interviewed a woman in connection with any serious crime. She found herself more easily able to feel what the person must be feeling, to put herself into the interviewee's shoes.

These particular shoes were elegant leather court ones, with a sensible height of heel. The woman within them also impressed her as both elegant and capable, as she welcomed them into her office with a practised, professional smile and assured them that they would not be disturbed here. She was alert and blue-eyed, with the slim build and easy movement which made her look a little taller than she actually was. They already knew that she was thirty-eight, but Lucy would have taken her at first glance as younger than that: her blonde hair was expertly cut, and her face was carefully though lightly made up to conceal the incipient wrinkles round her eyes.

DCI Peach introduced them and Clare Thompson nodded a neutral welcome to DS Blake, no doubt conducting her own assessment of this woman who was intruding into her world. Peach said, 'Murder is the one crime where the victim cannot be questioned. We have to build up a picture of a man we never knew through the impressions and judgements of others. I'm sure that you can be more help to us in this than any other single person, Mrs Thompson.'

Clare had a moment of panic which she hoped didn't show on her face. For an instant, she thought these intruders must know already that she had been Tim's mistress, that he had ditched her and left her feeling vitriolic about him – angry enough to kill him, by implication. Then she realized the man was probably only referring to her position of knowledge and trust as his personal assistant. She said carefully, 'I obviously know a lot about Mr Hayes's professional life – it's part of my job to do so. But I would remind you that he has – had – a wife.'

She managed that rather well, and even managed to tack a little ironic, rebuking smile onto the end of it. All that Peach said was, 'Yes, we've seen Mrs Hayes. She wasn't able to offer us much. We were hoping you might be able to

240

enlighten us rather more.'

'I'll obviously help you as much as I can. We all want the man who killed Mr Hayes arrested as soon as possible.'

He smiled at her, and for a moment she thought he was going to challenge these conventional sentiments. Then he said, 'Except one person, Mrs Thompson. Or more than one, if it should prove that there is a conspiracy involved here. What makes you assume Mr Hayes's killer was a man?'

'Nothing. I never even thought of it being a woman.'

'And thus at a stroke excluded almost half of Friday night's attendance from consideration. Including, of course, your good self. It would be useful to us if we could make such assumptions, but we have to consider all possibilities, Mrs Thompson.' He stretched his legs out in front of him for a moment, looking very relaxed, reminding Clare of how tense she felt herself. 'I understand that you compiled the guest list for this fatal function.'

He made it sound like an accusation. Clare said defensively, 'In consultation with Mr Hayes I did, yes.'

'I see. Were there any additions to the usual annual list? Any names you were rather startled to find there?'

She paused, showed them that she was giving the question proper consideration. There was a legitimate chance here to divert suspicion away from herself and towards others, without any need to tell obvious lies. 'The list was the longest it's ever been. Mr Hayes was anxious both to recognize the efforts which had contributed to the firm's success and to do a measure of discreet public-relations work. She smiled. 'I think you could probably include the invitation to your Detective Chief Superintendent Tucker and his wife in that category.'

Peach would have loved to ask her what she had made of Tommy Bloody Tucker and Brünnhilde Barbara. He did no such thing, of course. 'We are collecting statements from everyone who was at that dinner. But it is the employees who interest us most at this stage. What I asked you was whether there were any names which stood out and surprised you on this extended list.'

'There were some I scarcely knew, but that is in the nature of things. My job is mainly concerned with the original core work of the firm, with the factory and office staff in the electronics division here. Outside that circle, I do not know people well. I have never even met some quite senior staff in the newer sections of the firm's development. One of the advantages for me of the annual dinner has always been to meet these newer faces.'

She was playing with him, Peach thought. Fencing carefully and allowing him to make the running. All right, lady. 'Some of these new areas are pretty murky ones, Mrs Thompson.

Apparently you're claiming that even as Mr Hayes's PA you knew little about them.'

'I've already said that.'

'Just checking that you didn't want to amend or retract that position. Would it surprise you to know that drugs and prostitution figure as very profitable colonies in the Hayes empire?'

'It would indeed. It would surprise and shock me. Perhaps it is because of that that my employer made sure I knew nothing about them. I knew about the expansion of our gambling arm, in the betting shops and the new casino, though I had no direct involvement, but nothing of any illegal activities.' Clare was sure that she looked shaken in the face of his aggression. She told herself that it was right for her to look shaken.

'I see.' Peach contrived to get an incredible degree of scepticism into the two simple mono-syllables. Even if it's only guilt by implication and association, keep 'em on the back foot, even if that foot was as well turned as this lady's. 'Murky activities involve murky people, Mrs Thompson, take that from us who have to work among them. Perhaps you can now appreciate how names which were unfamiliar to you are going to be of interest to us.'

This stocky little bantam-cock of a chief inspector had shaken her a little, but this was really going rather well, Clare told herself. Suspicion was moving away from her and Jason to these shadowy figures she knew so little about.

For the first time, she was glad that, even in pillow talk, Tim had volunteered so little to her about how he made his real money. 'I can give you the names of employees. I can give you names of people who are operating in the new areas of development, beyond the original electronics division. I shouldn't like to think that I am in any way implicating them in criminal accusations. Still less that I am accusing any one of them of being the murderer of Mr Hayes.'

Peach gave her the grimmest of his smiles. 'If there is any implicating to be done, they will do it themselves, Mrs Thompson. We shall approach each of these people with an open mind, as the law demands that we do.'

She slid open the top drawer of her desk, pretended to fumble for a moment to unearth the list she had in fact been studying immediately before they came here. She proceeded to underline a series of names, frowning with concentration over the paper to show Peach how diligently she was obeying the man's instructions. 'These are the people who are employees of Hayes Electronics but not familiar to me. Without exception, they are Mr Hayes's additions to my core list of invitations. One or two of them have been attending the annual dinner for years, but most of them are recent additions.' She slid the list across to him. He glanced at it for a moment, noting the name of Leroy Moore and Jane Martin among those underlined, then handed it across to DS Blake. Clare said, 'As you will appreciate, things are pretty hectic here at present, but given a few minutes to myself, I could probably turn up last year's list and tell you which ones were attending for the first time.'

'If you could do that in the next day or two, I should be grateful to you. For the present, we shall correlate and cross-reference this with the other information which is coming in all the time from our team. Are there any of these names which you think should have special attention? I need hardly assure you that you will be speaking in confidence.'

One name had been circling in Clare Thompson's mind for the last few minutes. She hadn't known what to do about it; she had thought this man should be challenged, but hadn't been able to see how she could do that herself. Here was a chance to have him looked at, to have his claims checked out by a different kind of authority. She sighed, masking these thoughts under an apparent reluctance. 'One of the people I hardly know is Mr Hayes's original partner in the business. A man called Matthew Ballack. I'd heard the name, even met him years ago, but certainly in the years since I moved into my present post, he has hardly been around. I think he's had health and personal problems, but I don't know any details. But it appears he is still Mr Hayes's partner in the business – as you probably know, the business has never been floated on the stock market and has been in recent years very much a one-man band. But Mr Ballack assures me the original agreement still stands. He is proposing to take over the direction of the business.'

She had gathered confidence as her explanation developed. They had assured her she was speaking in confidence, so she would make sure that they checked out the man and his claims. She had rather liked the little she had seen of Ballack this morning, but he might have all sorts of skeletons in the cupboard which she could not know about and was in no position to investigate. And he had a better motive for murder than anyone else around, hadn't he?

Clare extracted Matthew Ballack's details from her files and gave them to Detective Chief Inspector Peach, who received them with a poker face and gave her no clue as to how important he considered this contribution.

Then he said without preamble, 'What time did you leave the Gisburn Hotel on Friday night?'

She thought back to what Jason had told her: she had quizzed him carefully after he had returned from Brunton police station and his interview with this man. 'Around midnight. I couldn't be sure of the exact time.'

'After your husband, then.'

'I believe he's already told you that.'

Peach gave her a wry, unembarrassed smile. 'Husbands and wives don't always agree. Some of our most significant breakthroughs come from marital discrepancies, Mrs Thompson.'

The man had a disconcerting ability to give you the impression that he knew more than he possibly could, that he knew all about the difficult weekend she had endured with Jason. Clare said firmly, 'Although it was an informal occasion, I was still conscious that I was Mr Hayes's personal assistant. I thought it was my duty to stay at his side, or at least to remain available, until I was unofficially dismissed.'

'Which was at around midnight.'

'Yes. I decided for myself that I was no longer necessary and drove myself home then. As I said, I couldn't be precise to a few minutes.'

Just when she had grown used to her duel with this aggressive, observant man, the female presence she had almost forgotten spoke up. 'Is there anyone who can confirm this departure for us?'

She realized that the younger woman had been making notes on her replies. 'There were one or two other people around, but no one I can instantly recall. It was cold in the car park and there was frost on the windscreens. I think we were all preoccupied with getting visibility from behind the wheel and then getting away as quickly and as safely as we could. There was a little shouting and laughter: I'm sure there were people around who'd drunk a lot more than I had. But they weren't necessarily driving, of course.'

'You didn't see anyone hanging around in the hotel, perhaps waiting for Mr Hayes to leave?'

'No. I suppose anyone planning murder would be careful to conceal himself from casual observation.'

'Or herself, Mrs Thompson. You were sitting on Mr Hayes's table. Did you see or hear anyone behaving suspiciously during the evening? In the light of what we now know happened later, I mean.'

'No. I've thought about it, of course, over the weekend. But I can't remember anything. I was on the table, but several places away from Mr Hayes. I could not at any time hear his conversations, but I didn't see any arguments or any sign of anyone losing his temper. Mr Hayes has always been a good speaker on these occasions, but I've seen him speak before, so I think I might have detected any sign of his being disturbed. He delivered what he wanted to say very effectively, and he seemed to me quite unruffled.'

Peach took his departure as abruptly as he had done everything else, like a man who could scarcely contain his energy. 'You've been very helpful, Mrs Thompson. You may well have further thoughts on this crime, even in the hectic days which undoubtedly lie ahead of you. Please let us know of them.'

He was almost out of the room before the woman with the striking chestnut hair had gathered her belongings. He left Clare Thompson with the uncomfortable feeling that she hadn't seen the last of DCI Peach.

# Eighteen

March hadn't come in like a lion at all. There had been no gales, no wild winds bringing down trees in the Ribble Valley and funnelling down the narrow old streets of Brunton to make the residents scurry for their homes. The month had so far been as unthreatening as the small creatures struggling uncertainly to their feet beside the ewes on the fresh green grass of the valley farms.

Tuesday the sixth dawned as mild as its March predecessors. There was no frost, but also no sun. The cloud was low over the old cotton town and a thin drizzle drifted steadily across the slates of the low terraces and the tiles of the newer suburbs. A grey, depressing morning, thought Percy Peach, as he climbed the stairs to the top floor of the new police station. He paused for a moment to gaze out over town and country and gather his thoughts. An appropriate morning to report to Detective Chief Superintendent Tommy Bloody Tucker.

He found Tucker in his brisk directorial mode. 'I've been holding off queries from all sides about the death of Timothy Hayes, Peach.'

'One of your strengths, that, sir.'

'I can't do so indefinitely. This is a high-profile crime, Peach.'

'Yes, sir. With many high-profile people among the suspects. We've been treading carefully, as you advised.' They had been treading exactly as normal, but there was no reason why this fool should know that.

'You must proceed very carefully indeed. You must also make an arrest very quickly.' Tucker apparently saw no contradiction in these two injunctions. He jutted his jaw in Churchillian mode, wishing fleetingly that he could adopt the boiler suit favoured by the great man in his wartime bunker. 'I shall be keeping an overview of the situation.

'We've cleared a few people of suspicion already, sir.'

'Peach, I'm not interested in whom you've cleared. What I want to hear from you is that—'

'I'm happy to be able to tell you, sir, in confidence of course, that you and Mrs Tucker have been eliminated from the investigation. As suspects, that is – the team will of course welcome your input as our leader.'

Tucker bristled dangerously, a reaction which Percy always studied with interest. 'I warned you last time we spoke about this ridiculous charade of pretending that I was a suspect.'

'You also told me that I must treat everyone present at that dinner as a suspect, sir. The high and the low alike. Anyway, fear not, sir. Your tale tallies with that of Mrs Tucker, sir. It now appears that you drove away from the scene of the crime approximately one hour before murder was committed. We don't like husband–wife alibis any more than any other police division in the country, but I'm happy to say that on this occasion we are convinced. Perhaps you would convey that to your good lady, sir. I'm sure it will be a relief to her to hear it.'

Tucker glowered at his DCI. He did a good glower, Percy had to admit: credit where credit was due. 'Peach, you need to come up with a result here. Mr Hayes was an important and highly respectable businessman.'

'He was a crook, sir.' Percy paused for a moment to savour his chief's outrage. 'And he used some pretty devious characters to further his criminal activities. Present company of course excepted, sir.'

'You had better be able to substantiate these claims.' Tucker's voice was heavy with menace, he hoped.

'Indeed, sir. You are not in any way implicated yourself. That goes without saying.'

'Except that you managed to say it. What is it that you're accusing Tim Hayes of?'

'Pimping. Drug-dealing. Protection rackets. Assault. Intimidation.'

'I cannot believe that a man like Tim Hayes would have soiled his hands with things like this.'

'Not personally, sir. He employed other people to do his dirty work. He kept himself at what he thought was a safe distance.' Percy paused, as if seeking a phrase. Then his round face brightened with inspiration. 'I suppose you could say he kept an overview of the situation, sir.'

Tucker glowered again. It really was quite impressive. 'Where does this information come from?'

Peach gave him a knowing look and tapped the side of his nose. 'Unimpeachable source, sir.'

'A snout, you mean.'

'An unimpeachable snout, sir. Or as I suppose you might say in my case, a "Peachable snout"! Being as he works exclusively for me, you see.' Percy cackled delightedly for a moment.

It was a rare sound, one which would have filled the Brunton criminal fraternity with terror and which now serrated the nerves of Thomas Bulstrode Tucker. Catching the thunder in his master's visage, Percy resumed hastily, 'To be accurate, a snout who has never given me false information.'

'You seem to positively enjoy dealing with the scum of this world.'

A comment sprang immediately into Peach's active mind, but he did not voice it. Instead, he said with apparent concern, 'I'm sorry that Mr Hayes isn't all he seemed to you, sir. Especially as he was a member of your Lodge.'

'The Lodge is quite irrelevant, Peach. And please don't embark on the subject of your research into connections between crime and Freemasonry.'

'No intention of doing that, sir. No time for research at the moment. Know a man called Matthew Ballack, sir?'

Tucker peered at him suspiciously, wondering what trap was being set here. 'No, I don't think I do. Are you about to arrest him for this murder?'

Percy cackled again, suddenly and unexpectedly, rattling the empty teacup in its saucer upon Tucker's desk, causing the man behind it to leap with shock. 'Good to see you still have your impish sense of humour, sir. We're in no position to arrest Mr Ballack, sir.' A thought appeared to strike him and he leant his bald head and his small, perfectly formed ear towards his chief. 'Unless you know something we don't, sir. Unless you've been quietly beavering away at the case whilst we plodders have been finding ourselves dead ends.'

Tucker sighed a heavy, hopeless sigh. 'Who is Matthew Ballack?'

'Partner of the deceased, sir. I thought you might have chatted to him at the dinner on Friday night. Formed an impression, perhaps.'

'I didn't. I've never even met the man. Would not even recognize him if he walked through that door.'

Peach regarded the door in question as if it

might at any moment spring open to admit this mysterious person from Porlock. When it remained firmly shut, he turned back to his chief and said, 'Pity, that, sir. Partners are always of interest, in situations like this. This one has been almost invisible for some years, and has now surfaced to claim control of the firm. It would have been useful if you'd talked to him a little on Friday night and been able to give us your assessment of the man.'

He shook his head sadly and contrived to make this innocent omission of Tucker's sound like a major career blemish. The head of Brunton CID found himself searching frantically for a way to assert his pre-eminence. 'Tim Hayes had a wife, you know.'

'Yes, sir.'

'You should pay close attention to wives. Wives are always leading suspects in a murder case.'

Having delivered this pearl of wisdom, Tucker sat back and nodded sagely. Peach eventually said, 'That had occurred to us, sir. The lady has already been interviewed.'

'And how did she seem to you?'

'A little abstracted, sir. Not quite with it.'

'There you are, you see. Evasive!' Tucker was triumphant. 'You mark my word, wives are always suspect.'

Peach wondered whether to investigate this latest misogyny or to suggest that Tucker in his marital views might be projecting from the particular, in the formidable shape of Brünn-hilde Barbara, to the general. With admirable self-control, he said merely, 'Mrs Hayes did not seem exactly devastated by this death, sir. But grief takes people in different ways. I am planning to see her again when the team has gathered more information from other sources.'

'Do that, Peach.' Tucker gestured with a sweep of his right arm towards the world outside his office. 'And it's high time you got on with interviewing this partner chap.'

'Matthew Ballack, sir. In view of the fact that he seems to be emerging as a prominent industrialist, you wouldn't like to undertake this interview yourself?'

'No, no! You know it is not my policy to interfere with my staff. And it might seem like overkill to this Mr Ballack if he was interviewed by the head of CID himself.'

'I'm sure he would find it a most intimidating experience, sir.'

Always leave the lazy bugger wondering quite what you had meant, thought Percy Peach as he went back down the stairs. He noticed that it had stopped raining.

It was almost a relief to Matthew Ballack when the call came through to him from Brunton CID. He had been expecting it since Saturday morning, and the tension had built in him over three days. But the delay had served a useful purpose. It had given him time to assert his position at Hayes Electronics, to move into the vacuum created by his partner's death.

It seemed to have gone smoothly so far. Hayes's personal assistant, whilst not empowered to make policy decisions or to oppose Matthew's takeover, could have caused him a lot of trouble. Anyone with her knowledge and information about the day-to-day operation of the firm could cause trouble, particularly when he himself knew so little about the detail of the way things had run in the last few years. She could make life very difficult if she chose. But so far she hadn't done that: he would describe her attitude so far as cautiously cooperative, which was fair enough.

Clare Thompson certainly seemed efficient, and he could not detect in her the kind of loyalty to a departed employer which sometimes made things difficult for the new man. The acid test had come early, when he had moved into Hayes's office; he had been prepared for a little resentment, but she had shown none. If he could win her allegiance, he had already learned enough about her efficiency to realize that she would be a valuable ally in the months to come. She had so far given no indication that she would not accept the offer to become his PA. In due course, but not so early that it might seem like a weakness, he would give her a rise in salary.

He inspected the office, swinging himself around in the big swivel chair behind the leather-topped desk, looking at the Lakeland scenes and the prints of Modigliani and Magritte upon the walls. Pretentious sod, Tim Hayes! He might introduce some large Beryl Cook prints, bring a bit of humour and relaxation into the place, when he had settled in. But there was no need to hurry about things like that. Change would be gradual, as he divested the firm of its more questionable activities and set about regenerating the traditional ones.

On this, his second day in the director's room, he was already beginning to feel at home. He told the impersonal voice at Brunton CID that he would receive the senior officer who was conducting the enquiry here at eleven o'clock. It was a much grander setting than his rundown flat. He must think about moving to a different and more appropriate home, when he had the time.

Matthew had half-hoped to be interviewed by that Chief Superintendent Tucker he had observed at the table next to his on Friday night. From what little he had seen and heard there, the man had seemed an affable, unthreatening cove who might give him an easy ride. But he knew enough about police procedures to know that the senior officer in charge of an inquiry rarely moved away from his desk these days.

The man who actually came into his office at precisely eleven o'clock this morning was a different man entirely: a stocky, powerful, bald-headed man with a black fringe of hair and a small black moustache, whose dark eyes seemed to dart everywhere and see everything before they eventually fixed on the visage of Matthew Ballack and stayed there.

He announced himself as Detective Chief Inspector Peach and introduced the young and attractive woman beside him as Detective Sergeant Blake. 'Just moved in here, have you, Mr Ballack?'

The quick survey the man had given the room seemed to have already established in his mind that this office was all Hayes, no Ballack. Matthew said briskly, 'Yes. After Friday night's tragedy, someone had to take control of the ship. I was as shaken as everyone else, but the only appropriate person to move in here was the surviving partner.'

'Been a partner for a long time, have you, sir?'

'Since the very early days. We began all this together twenty-four years ago. It's all quite legal. I've checked it out.'

'Not our business, that. Unless of course it was a motive for murder.'

The DCI spoke breezily, and Matthew responded with a grin, to emphasize that he didn't resent the joke. He felt rather foolish when he realized that Peach was perfectly serious. 'I can assure you it would never have been that. Tim and I had our minor differences over the years, but—'

'When did you have the partnership checked out, sir?'

'What? Oh, a few weeks ago, I suppose. I couldn't be precise.'

'Interesting timing, that. In view of what happened on Friday night.'

'I suppose it is. I hadn't really thought about that. It was just a routine enquiry, in view of the fact that the partnership agreement dated back so far and was so rudimentary. I wanted to assure myself that it still held.'

'I see. Was Mr Hayes aware of this routine enquiry of yours?'

Matthew thought furiously. He couldn't see how this one could be checked out. 'Yes, he was. We didn't have many secrets from each other, Tim and I.'

'Really. So this routine enquiry was a mutual one, was it, conducted through the firm's solicitors?'

Suddenly, Matthew was trying not to panic. He could scarcely believe that one small mistake, his nervous and needless assertion that the partnership was legal, had landed him in so much trouble. 'No. I made an independent enquiry.' He wanted to say he'd used his old family lawyers and asked for informal advice, but if they traced this down, that elderly legal gent in Bolton would tell them that he had been referred by the Citizens' Advice Bureau. 'It seemed best to have an independent opinion, you see. Tim was aware of what I was doing.'

'Was he really, sir? Well, obviously the trouble in a murder enquiry is that the one person we can't question is the victim.'

It was at this point that Clare Thompson brought in the coffee and biscuits Matthew had ordered. He had anticipated that they would have been occupied with the social niceties of introductions and commiserations about Tim's death for the first few minutes, not deep into what were embarrassing areas for him. He dismissed Clare, who studiously avoided any eye-contact with his visitors, then poured the coffee and offered the biscuits himself, taking his time and seeking in vain to dissipate the tension he felt in the room.

'Not been around much lately, have you, Mr Ballack? Mrs Thompson is very professional, but she gave me the impression that your arrival here yesterday was quite a surprise.'

'I've been quite low-key in the last few years as far as the people here are concerned, I suppose. Tim and I agreed that my function would be to explore new areas of business for us. Things like the casino and the betting shops.'

'And other areas as well, no doubt.'

'There aren't any other areas. Not that I'm aware of.'

Peach paused for a moment, savouring the man's discomfort, noting the sweat on the high forehead beneath the balding head. 'And you a partner, Mr Ballack? I don't think it's likely you'd get away with the ignorance defence, do you?'

'I was in charge of one of the betting shops. And I had overall direction of the casino.'

'Not quite what the people who work at the casino have told us in their statements, is it, DS Blake?'

'No, sir. We have a Mr Holden down as manager of the casino. The couriers say they've never seen you there, Mr Ballack.'

The woman had clear, aquamarine eyes of startling beauty. At this moment, they seemed as threatening to Matthew Ballack as the piercing black ones of the man beside her. Neither of these officers apparently needed to blink, whereas he found himself blinking with increasing frequency. 'I was a policy-maker rather than a hands-on manager. I know a lot about the gambling industry.'

Peach nodded, almost sympathetically, it seemed. 'Too much perhaps, Mr Ballack?'

Peach's expression invited confession and Matthew found it a relief to give it. 'All right. I admit I had a gambling problem myself. I lost far more than I could afford to lose with Ladbrokes and William Hill. It – it affected my work. It destroyed my marriage and almost broke my health.'

'And saw you marginalized in the firm.'

Peach's voice now was as persuasive as a priest's, but Matthew realized that he must not give them the details of his feud with Tim Hayes or he would become an even stronger suspect for his murder. 'Yes. Tim was quite good about it. He found me new positions where I wouldn't be under so much pressure. I joined Gamblers Anonymous. I don't bet at all now. We were discussing how I should resume more responsibility for directorial policy just before Tim died.' On this lie, he looked not at that round, all-seeing face but down at his cooling coffee. He picked up the cup and drained it a little too quickly, which resulted in a fit of coughing.

Peach studied his distress for a little while before he said quietly, 'We know quite a lot about the way the firm has been making money away from the electronics arm in the last year or two. I advise you now that it would not be wise for you to conceal what you know about illegal profits from drugs and prostitution, Mr Ballack.'

'I know very little about these things. I told you, I've been out of touch for a year or two.' He looked at the softer, female face, but found those remarkable blue-green eyes almost more disconcerting than the male ones.

Lucy Blake said, 'But not so out of touch that you couldn't take over this office and the direction of the firm at the drop of a hat.'

What happened to 'good cop, bad cop', he thought. They've both come here to hang me out to dry and they're making a pretty good job of it. He said doggedly, 'It was an emergency. Because of the partnership, I was the only one entitled to take this chair. I intend to make a good job of it. If there are fringe profits from the things you mention, I want no part of that.'

He sounded very earnest. The look on Blake's face cheered him, suggesting that she might even believe he meant that. But it was Peach who now renewed the attack. 'A very commendable attitude. Let's hope you're still here next week to put it into practice. What time did you leave the Gisburn Hotel on Friday night?'

His brain reeled before this sudden switch of ground. 'I had one drink after Tim's speech. A bitter lemon. I gave up drink as well as gambling, you see.' He allowed himself an acid smile at his own expense. 'I was away before midnight. Back in my flat in Brunton within quarter of an hour or twenty minutes.'

'Can anyone confirm these times?'

'I don't know. I shouldn't think so. I didn't chat to anyone after the meal and Tim's speech. A lot of people left immediately. Those that stayed on were pretty loud. When you're a non-drinker amongst a lot of drinkers, their conversation can seem a bit puerile, you know. I sat and reviewed the events of the evening before I left.' That at any rate was true. He felt a relief in saying it.

'Who do you think killed Tim Hayes?'

'I don't know. I'd have told you if I did, wouldn't I?'

'Would you, Mr Ballack? I hope so. I want you to reconsider what you've said to us, with a view to revising it. I don't think you've given us everything you know about this firm and its activities. If you didn't kill Mr Hayes yourself, your best policy is to give us as much information as you can. We shall be back when we have compared what you have said to us with the statements of other people involved. Good day to you.'

Matthew Ballack didn't call Clare Thompson in for quite some time after they had left. He needed time to compose himself. He didn't seem to have given them very much, yet he felt both depressed and apprehensive.

# Nineteen

She was normally a confident woman, but she looked round a little nervously in these strange surroundings. Apart from a couple of speeding fines, she had never been a lawbreaker, and it was many years now since she had set foot inside a police station.

She had expected to be kept waiting, like the long-haired youth in torn jeans and the defeated-looking woman who sat on the battered seats in front of the station sergeant, but when she stated the purpose of her visit she was ushered immediately into the CID section. Two minutes later she was sitting in the office of Detective Chief Inspector Peach, the man she had been assured was directing this investigation.

She said diffidently, 'My name is Davies. Dr Marian Davies; I'm a GP in Clitheroe. I'm not at all sure that I should be here at all.'

She was a well-dressed woman in her mid-fifties, with rimless glasses on a square face which had a concerned, anxious look. Peach gave her one of his friendlier smiles. 'Much better to let us be the judge of that, Dr Davies. We speak in confidence. If what you have to say proves to have no bearing on this case, it will go no further than this room and no damage will be done.'

'Thank you. That is important. There are issues of patient confidentiality here.'

'I understand that. But this is a murder investigation, which overrides normal rules. We need to know as much about the people concerned in it as possible. If they are innocent, which quite obviously most of them are, it can only work in their favour, by helping us to eliminate them from suspicion.'

Peach was trying not to show his impatience as he issued this standard reassurance. He might be both busy and baffled, but people like this needed gentle encouragement, if they were going to reveal everything they knew. This woman was also no doubt busy, and it had cost her quite a mental effort to bring her concern do him. He said with a smile, 'I assume you are a GP to one of the people who was close to Mr Hayes.'

'Yes. To the closest one of all, his wife. Tamsin Hayes has been on my patient list for many years.'

'And you have something to tell me about Mrs Hayes which you think may be relevant to this case.'

'It may be quite irrelevant. It probably is, in fact. But in view of the seriousness of this crime, I feel that it is something you should know.'

'If it is irrelevant, Dr Davies, Mrs Hayes need never know that you have spoken to me.'

She nodded, almost absently, concerned now only with how she was going to phrase this. 'For the last three years, I have been treating Tamsin Hayes for clinical depression. She refused to see a psychiatrist, and assured me that the drugs we were using to treat her condition were working, or at least keeping it in check.'

Another Prozac user, thought Peach. Another person in danger of becoming dependent on the 'happy drug' to get through life. He had more sense than to voice any thoughts on the subject to a professional prescriber, or even to enquire about which drugs were being used.

As if she read some of his thoughts, the doctor said, 'I was afraid of the patient becoming drug-dependent. I wanted her to discuss the cause of her illness with a specialist in the area: depression is an illness, once it reaches a certain stage, whatever the "good kick in the pants" school thinks.' She glanced accusingly at Peach but found him inscrutably neutral. 'Tamsin would not take that advice. She talked a little about her problems to me, but I'm no expert in illnesses of the mind. Sometimes the only cure is to get right away from the source of the trouble, but that isn't always possible. Mrs Hayes said it wasn't possible in her case.'

Peach said quietly, 'Her depression was connected with her husband, wasn't it? You'd hardly be here otherwise.'

She looked grateful to him, as though his deduction had made this easier for her. 'She said she'd discussed her concerns with her husband and he hadn't responded. Whether that is true or not, I couldn't tell you – people aren't always honest about these things. At that stage, which was just over a year ago, I suggested that she should consider ending the marriage completely. There were no children and no financial concerns, so that a break-up might be the lesser of two evils, if it safeguarded her health. Tamsin said that her religion wouldn't allow her to contemplate divorce.'

Peach couldn't see any way of making his next question less brutal. 'Are you here this afternoon because you suspect Mrs Hayes may have taken another and more violent way out of the situation?'

'No, I'm not suggesting that at all. I'm here to give you information. To relay to you facts which I think you should have and which I cannot explain.'

'Right. Please do just that.'

'Tamsin Hayes came to see me a little while ago. She announced that she was cured of her depression and no longer needed her drugs. I was pleased, as I always am when someone in danger of becoming drug-dependent decides that they no longer need them. But I warned her that mood swings should be expected in the days and weeks to come. She said that she understood that, but that she was confident she would not need drugs again. She has been as good as her word: I haven't seen her since. She used to have a regular monthly appointment, but she's cancelled that.'

'Did she give any explanation for the change in her health?'

'No. I'm confident that she hasn't had professional help. I tried to discuss the reasons for her recovery, but she didn't want to do that and it wasn't within my remit to push for information.'

'It may be within mine, in the next few days,' said Peach grimly. 'Thank you very much for bringing this to me, Dr Davies.'

'There's more. I'm not sure I'd have come to you to report a recovering patient.' Her rather square face broke into a self-deprecating smile, and Peach realized what an attractive woman she must have been when she was Lucy Blake's age. He liked professionals who didn't project themselves too seriously and didn't claim to know everything in their field. She said, 'I told you, I don't pretend to be anything more than an amateur psychiatrist. But Tamsin Hayes had a very odd bearing when she told me happily that she was cured. She had an abstracted air: the air of someone carrying a secret, a secret she was very happy about.'

'As if she was cocooned in a world she did not want you to know about?'

She looked at him sharply. 'Yes. As if her

270

whole personality and conduct had been taken over by one idea. Almost an obsession, I'd say, though I'm no psychiatrist.'

Peach shook his head with a puzzled frown, wondering what significance, if any, this might have for his murder investigation. 'It's my turn to speak in confidence now, Dr Davies. I saw Mrs Hayes on the day after her husband's murder. She was elaborately dressed in mourning black. Too elaborately: she was in black from top to toe and behaved as if she was acting the part of a newly bereaved widow in a stage play – acting it and quite enjoying it. She behaved as if she knew things which we didn't and felt quite superior about it.'

Dr Davies nodded enthusiastically. 'That's just it. As if she had an obsession disorder which was dominating her thinking, and was quite content to exist in a world outside the one where we live out our lives.'

'The question is, what bearing has this on what happened to her husband on Friday night?'

The smile lit up the intelligent, ageing face. 'That is a problem which I am quite happy to leave here with you, Chief Inspector Peach.'

Most people had left the school by five o'clock. That suited Jason Thompson. He wanted as few people as possible to see him being interviewed in connection with the murder of his wife's boss.

271

He took them into the small geography store-room behind the classroom, hoping that he would feel more relaxed in his own environment than in the cramped little box of an interview room where he had been forced to meet the CID on Sunday. Perhaps it wouldn't be the man in charge today. He hoped not: a visit from a lower-ranking officer would surely suggest that he was regarded as no more than a fringe player in this strange drama.

His hopes were dashed. It was DCI Peach, who arrived with the convivial urgency of a man on a mission. 'So this is where the money poured into education goes!' He flashed a look at the rolled maps upon the table and spun the big new globe of the world in 2008 speculatively, watching the multicoloured continents flash before his vision. Before the globe had ceased to turn, he was sitting on one of the chairs Jason had set out for them.

'A little of it.' Jason forced a smile. 'These are necessary visual aids. You wouldn't expect us to teach geography without them.'

'Certainly wouldn't, would we, DS Blake? But nor would you expect us to be able to do our job when people tell us porkies.'

'Porkies?' Jason kicked himself for repeating the word and playing into the man's hands.

'Porkies, Mr Thompson. To be very charitable – people tell me that's one of my failings – I'll call it concealing information. Either way, it's perverting the course of justice, which is a serious crime, isn't it, DS Blake?'

'It is indeed, sir, very serious.' Lucy didn't mind being a Peach echo, if it took things forward.

'We've now had an opportunity to study and digest information from a whole range of different sources, Mr Thompson. Including all of the guests who attended on Friday evening and all of the staff working at the Gisburn Hotel on that night. Certain interesting contradictions have emerged.' Peach beamed widely.

The grin seemed to Jason to stretch impossibly wide: he wondered if the moustache and the baldness above it accentuated the glee beneath. He brushed his vivid red hair away from his temple and onto the top of his head. 'I hope you're not accusing me of concealing information.'

'Not accusing. Not yet. Merely clarifying the position.' Percy's elaborate delivery of the phrase made that sound much worse. 'You said you left the hotel at eleven o'clock. There is a conflict of evidence here. A serious conflict.'

'I did leave then. I went home with the Johnsons as I told you on Sunday. They'll confirm that for you.'

Percy held up a magisterial hand. 'They have already done that, sir.'

'Then where's the problem?'

'The problem, sir, is that you were seen by one of the barmen in the hotel at just before midnight.'

'Then he's mistaken, isn't he? The Johnsons will confirm that they dropped me off at—'

'He isn't the only one, sir. One of the waitresses who attended to your table earlier in the evening saw you at around the same time. "Slinking", she said you were, unless my memory is at fault.'

He looked interrogatively at DS Blake, who flicked over a page in her notebook and said after a pregnant pause, '"Slinking" was the word she used, sir.'

Jason looked from one to the other of this contrasting and sinister double act, blinking repeatedly behind his thick-lensed glasses. Then he stared down at the grubby rug which some anonymous previous incumbent of this room had imported to try to make it more homely. 'I went out again. Drove my own car back to the hotel.'

'Why did you do that, sir? And why did you choose to conceal this from us?'

'I went to look for Clare. I was worried about her. I don't know why I didn't tell you this on Sunday.'

Peach let five long seconds drag by before he said, apparently almost reluctantly, 'You were worried about your wife's association with Mr Hayes, weren't you, sir?'

Jason wanted to deny it, wanted to tell them to go to hell and get out of his life. Instead, he heard his voice saying dully, 'How did you know about Clare and Hayes?'

274

'I told you, we've talked to a lot of people since Friday night.' Peach was at his most gnomic. When people confirmed one of his imaginative sallies, the last reaction he showed was surprise.

Thompson was too distressed to suspect his mistake. 'I suppose everyone at the factory knew about them. I suppose everyone was talking about their affair. I suppose the husband was the last to know, as usual.'

His tone was one of flat despair. Peach said gently, 'I don't think that is so at all, sir. But that is not what concerns us here. We need a full and accurate account of your actions on Friday night.'

Thompson went on as if he had not heard him. 'I'd only just found out about them. I never thought my Clare would do that to me.' Then he looked up desperately at Lucy Blake. 'I still love her, you know. Still want her. Still need her. There's no one else for me, God help me!'

Peach's calm voice cut harshly through this passionate avowal. 'I seem to remember that God helps those who help themselves, Mr Thompson. So tell us what happened when you drove back to the Gisburn Hotel.'

Jason looked hard into Peach's face, feeling that only by confronting him could he focus on the matter in hand. A slow, mirthless smile crept onto his face. 'Very little happened. I was looking to catch Clare and Hayes together, to have it out with them. I don't know what I'd have done to them if I'd found them together. Killed him, I shouldn't wonder!'

'Which someone did. At around that time.'

'Not me, Chief Inspector. I began in the main bar, where I saw Hayes still drinking with his cronies. There was no sign of Clare. I looked round all the main rooms, even asked the waitress you mentioned to check the ladies' cloakroom for me, but she wasn't there. I suppose the staff who saw me wondered what I was about.'

'As we do, Mr Thompson. Especially since you chose to conceal these actions from us.'

'I had a motive to harm Hayes, didn't I? I didn't want you to know about that.'

'Which we now do, with the fact that you lied to us heaped upon that motive. Did you kill Mr Hayes? Did you not in fact wait for him to come out to his car and then take the opportunity to be rid of him?'

'No! I drove away from the hotel when I couldn't find Clare. I drove back home and went to bed.'

Blake looked up from her notes. 'You have told us that you didn't locate your wife on the premises. Were you convinced that she had left the hotel?'

'Yes. I knew when there was no sign of her with Hayes that she had left the place. I wanted to get home. I wanted to hold her tight against me and take her to bed with me!'

'But how could you be certain that she had left? Did you check whether her car had gone?'

'No, I'd expected her to be in the hotel, you see. When I couldn't find her there, I eventually checked the spot where we had parked earlier in the evening. I was very relieved when I found that the car was gone.' Jason found it easier to talk to this softer, female presence than to the man who seemed to doubt every word he said.

But it was Peach who now asked him, 'And when you returned home for the second time, was Mrs Thompson there?'

This time it was Jason who paused, his mind working furiously on the implications of what he was going to say. 'Yes. We must have got in at almost the same time. She was still in the garage when I drove into the drive.'

'She must have been surprised to see you coming in after her.'

'Yes. Yes, she was. I told her I'd forgotten my coat and had to go back for it.'

He sat in the room alone for a good quarter of an hour after they'd gone. He would need to talk to Clare about this when he got home. It was urgent, now. But they hadn't talked at all, not really talked, since that bastard Hayes had been put out of their lives.

Jane Martin's mother was very proud of her daughter, in the way that successful one-parent mothers always are.

She'd made sacrifices for her daughter – she had mended her own ways to set an example to the girl, for a start. Times had been hard, before

Jane went to school and through most of her primary-school days; the social helped with the rent, but there wasn't much left over for luxuries from what Sally Martin earned in the supermarket. She had sometimes been tempted to go back to her old ways to make easy, quick money, but each time she had looked at her pretty, innocent daughter and her resolution had held firm.

It had all been worthwhile when she got to the comprehensive. She hadn't realized how bright Jane was until the teachers there had told her. The people at the junior school had always said what a nice, helpful kid she was, but now these new teachers insisted that her daughter was intelligent. There was nothing Jane could not do, they said, if she put her mind to it. Even a good university was possible, if she worked hard.

No one in Sally Martin's family had ever been to university, good or otherwise.

Jane justified everything the teachers said. She got a clutch of GCSEs with handsome grades, then two A grades and a B grade in her A-levels. University beckoned, but she would not go. 'You've worked for me for long enough, Mum. I'm not taking on a student loan and giving us more debt. I want to be able to contribute to this household: I've never earned anything except from my paper round years ago and my Saturday mornings in the shoe shop this last year.'

She had taken the croupier's job at the new Brunton casino, though her mother was against it and she knew that her daughter was much more nervous about it than she pretended to be. And being Jane Martin, she had made a success of it. She was reliable as well as intelligent, and her sunny personality had gone down well with both staff and clients. The money was good, and a good portion of it came to Sally, even after Jane had moved into the bedsit in Brunton.

That move had disappointed her mother, but she told herself that the girl had her own life to live and needed her independence. Anyway, the new place was much nearer to the casino, so that Jane didn't need to make the long journey home in the early hours. She could almost pay the rent for the bedsit on what she saved in taxi fares, she assured Sally. And she did as she had promised, and came back to see her mother regularly. At least once a week.

It was almost a week since she had seen her now, so that when the bell of the council flat rang at seven thirty on Tuesday evening, Sally Martin thought that it must be Jane.

Her face fell when she saw who it was. Not only was it not Jane, but it was a copper. The old fears and hostility she thought she had buried long ago rose within her at the sight. This was a pig on her doorstep. A pig who had done his best for her; a pig who had set her on the right path and helped her stick to it. But it was still a pig, and she didn't want pigs in her life any more.

She looked at him for a moment, then said, 'I suppose you'd better come in, Sergeant Peach.'

He waited until he was sitting on the worn sofa and she had switched off the old television set before he said, 'It's Detective Chief Inspector Peach now, Sally. I've gone up in the world.'

'Aye, well. It's been a long time. I've gone straight, so I don't know why you're here.' She didn't know why she couldn't be more gracious. Years ago, when Jane was still at primary school, Peach had got her the job at the supermarket and had a word with the manager. She was pretty sure that the past sell-by-date food she'd got almost for nothing in those hard, far-off days had been down to a suggestion from this man.

But he was still a copper, and she didn't want coppers coming here and the neighbours talking. She said abruptly, as if trying to make amends for her welcome, 'You still Percy, then?'

'Fancy you remembering that, Sally Martin. Aye, I'm still Percy. The fuzz don't let you escape a name once they've pinned it on you.' He looked at the rapidly ageing face, at the blonde hair already streaked with grey and the once-pretty features which were now heavy and furrowed. She couldn't be much more than forty, but she had lived hard in her troubled youth and life couldn't have been easy since then. He looked round at the clean but shabby room and said, 'You've made a go of it. I told you that you could.'

'Aye. You want a brew?'

'I could murder a cup of tea, lass. It's been a long day.'

He transferred a small box of chocolates onto the scratched dresser behind her chair while she was in the kitchen. He divined correctly that it was a long time since a man had brought this woman chocolates. He took an appreciative sip from his beaker before he said with real feeling, 'I'm glad you made it, Sally.'

'It wasn't easy, even after I'd kicked the drugs. But Jane helped. She's a good kid. A good young woman, I should say now.'

'Aye, I'm sure she is, Sally.' He dropped easily into a broad Lancashire accent when he came into places like this and spoke with women like Sally Martin. 'Her dad never came back, then?'

'No, he didn't, thank God! His heart were as black as his skin, that bugger! He only wanted to bed me to show his pals 'e could 'ave me.'

'At least he gave you a beautiful daughter, Sally Martin.'

Her face lit up at the mention of her daughter. 'Aye, he did that, all right. He weren't a bad-looking lad. She's a little belter, isn't she, my Jane?'

'She is that, Sally.' Percy thought that Brendan Murphy had used a very similar phrase in reporting back on his meeting with Jane Martin. 'It's about her that I'm here, Sally.'

'She isn't in any trouble, is she, Mr Peach?' The lined face was suddenly full of anxiety.

'No, I don't think she is, Sally. But one of my officers saw her yesterday, as part of a murder inquiry, and I thought I'd follow that up by having a talk with you. Just so that we're sure we've got everything we need to know.'

Now she was really alarmed. Her mouth set in a stubborn line. 'Jane's a good girl. She's never been in any trouble.'

'Not quite true that, is it, Sally?'

Once a pig always a pig. They never let you forget, pigs. 'That was years ago. She got in with the wrong set.'

'A violent set. There were knives involved.'

'She was with the wrong set. The court knew that. She only got a suspended sentence. She's never been in any trouble since then.'

'I'm glad to hear it. Has there been anything odd in her conduct recently? Anything different from the way she normally behaves with you?'

'No. Nothing. I want you to go now.'

Peach leant forward, waited patiently until she looked up into his face. 'Do you trust me, Sally? Have I ever been anything but straight with you?'

She dropped her eyes to the worn carpet. 'S'pose not.'

'And I'm being straight with you now. At this moment, I don't believe your daughter killed her employer. But I do believe she held something back when she spoke to my officer. That's why I'm here. And whatever the situation is, the best thing you can do now is to be absolutely frank with me. Concealing things won't help anyone, believe me.'

She nodded slowly, knowing that deep down she trusted this copper, however much that went against her old watchwords. 'I don't know anything. She hasn't told me anything. I haven't even seen her since this man Hayes died.'

'But how was she before he died?'

She considered again whether she wanted to tell him even this little thing, when her instincts were so much against it. But she had gone too far now to draw back. And in her heart of hearts, she believed against her code that this man would do his best for her and for Jane. 'There isn't much to tell.'

'So tell it, Sally.'

'The last two times I saw her, she wasn't her usual self. She was – distant, I suppose. A mother knows her daughter, you know.'

'I know, Sally. She was withdrawn, you say.'

'That's it, yes. Withdrawn. She's usually bubbly, wanting to talk about her week at work. Last week and the time before she wouldn't say anything about that.'

'Have you any idea what it was that was disturbing her?'

'No. I tried, but she wouldn't be pressed. I'm sure it had nothing to do with the death of this man Hayes.'

'I'm sure you're right, Sally. Don't worry about it.'

But as he drove thoughtfully back to his cold and unwelcoming house, Percy Peach was not at all sure about it.

# Twenty

Tamsin Hayes was quite pleased to hear that the CID people were coming to see her again. She'd rather expected them to be back before now. The sooner this business was done with and she was rid of Tim Hayes for ever, the better she would like it.

She wondered whether to deck herself out in her widow's weeds again. She'd rather enjoyed that little charade on Saturday. But she was getting bored with the part now. She'd accepted the condolences of her neighbours and of those friends who didn't know the real state of her marriage with scarcely preserved decorum, wanting all the time to let her face crack into a wholly inappropriate smile.

She was tired of deception. She decided to abandon it, even for the police. She dressed herself in the fawn woollen dress and expensive tan leather shoes which she had always liked. She felt very relaxed and quite daring when she looked at herself in the mirror. It was the right appearance for someone embarking on a new life, she thought. She'd already joined the history of art group at the adult-education centre.

One of the men had asked her to go for a drink afterwards. She'd refused, of course: she wasn't going to get into anything at all with men for a while, let alone anything heavy. Still, it was nice to be asked.

Once she had got this CID business out of the way, she'd give her full attention to her exciting new life.

Chief Superintendent Tucker hadn't wanted the television cameras in. But the press and communications officer told him that he couldn't leave it later than Wednesday to issue some sort of statement. Timothy Hayes had been a prominent figure in Lancashire industry, and the press, local and national, were going to turn hostile if they were not given something to bite on quickly.

Tucker always dealt with the media himself. Public relations were his forte, the area which had raised him to his present eminence. He thought he was rather good at handling young television presenters. He was certainly much happier with their limited experience than with the older and more cynical crime journalists, who tended to cut through his suave assurances and ask questions which were altogether too prescient for his resources.

The interview began rather well, he thought. He assured the pretty young woman from Granada that no stone was being left unturned and that much had already been discovered. Then she asked him if anyone in particular was helping police with their enquiries. He gave her a polished, experienced smile. 'It is everyone's duty to assist the police, Grace. And everyone so far has acknowledged that duty. I am satisfied with the progress of the very large team I have allotted to this case.'

'But have you yet isolated a prime suspect?'

He shook his head sadly. 'The prime suspect is a concept beloved of television crime dramas, isn't it? Your medium has a lot to answer for, I'm afraid.' He gave her a benevolent, forgiving smile.

'There has been no arrest, then.'

Tucker tried to remain unruffled. A woman as young as this really should know her place. Perhaps he would have a word with the producer once the cameras were switched off. 'Contrary to some public opinion, we do not rush to arrest innocent people. Justice is our aim, Grace. Our aim and our watchword. When we have reason to think someone should be under arrest, we shall move quickly and decisively.'

'It sounds to me as if you are not even near to an arrest, Chief Superintendent Tucker.'

'We have been working night and day on this baffling case, Grace. I have scarcely left my desk since I was called upon to coordinate this investigation.' Tucker hoped fervently that Percy Peach would be too busy to see this performance.

'You use the word "baffling", Mr Tucker.

Would it be a fair summary of the present position to say that the police are baffled, then?'

The headlines leapt black and huge into Tucker's nightmare vision. He wondered if he was sweating, if the light powdering which the make-up girl had given him was sufficient to cope with this. He resisted the impulse he felt in his thighs to squirm, forced himself to lean forward and jut his chin as he said confidentially, 'We are anything but baffled, Miss Wilkinson. But at this delicate stage, you will understand that enquiries are confidential. Once we have more definite news, I shall be happy to speak to you again.'

'Would you care to hazard a guess as to when that would be, Chief Superintendent Tucker?'

He forced a smile, tried to look his most urbane, and said, 'That would not be a professional thing to do, Grace. I'm sure you know enough about police work to understand that by now.' His patronizing smile said that she actually understood none of the subtle nuances of his delicate mission.

Grace Wilkinson swung round to confront the camera full face. 'It seems that there is as yet little progress in this case. A case which the head of Brunton CID himself admits is baffling. He currently holds out no hope of a swift arrest.'

Ten minutes later, the head of CID fumed in private in his penthouse office. That bugger Peach was out, of course. Interviewing the widow, his DC said. Tucker couldn't even give himself the release of a good bollocking.

On this bright spring morning, the view from the big detached house where Timothy Hayes had lived was at its best. Lucy Blake looked across the valley towards Longridge Fell and the village where she had spent the first twenty-two years of her life. Beside the car as she drove slowly up the long drive, the first daffodils shone boldly in the borders. The gardener had given the lawns their first mowing of the year and cut their edges. The camellias on the south wall of the house were bursting into a fresh and defiant pink, which proclaimed that the hounds of spring were indeed upon winter's traces.

The curtains on the big windows at either side of the oak front door were no longer tightly drawn, the woman who opened the door to them was no longer clad in the elaborate mourning garb she had worn to meet them on the day after her husband's death. Her tan leather shoes, her light brown dress and the sunlight which streamed into the big sitting room where she took them seemed to echo the spring and new growth outside the house.

She gave them a wide smile and said, 'I thought I'd drop the mourning weeds. Not my style, I thought. No point in moping over what can't be changed.'

There was something brittle about her gaiety

– for gaiety it was, Lucy Blake decided. Tamsin Hayes wasn't merely putting a brave face on things, she was genuinely looking forward to the months ahead. And genuinely glad to be rid of her husband? Percy Peach also saw these things and was reminded of Dr Davies's description of her patient's current state: 'She had an abstracted air: the air of someone carrying a secret, a secret that she was very happy about.' It was an exact description of how she now appeared to them.

Peach said, 'We've talked to a lot of people since we saw you last, Mrs Hayes. We've found out a lot more about your husband and the way he lived.'

'That's good. Have you also found out a lot more about the way he died?'

She was edgy but bright, teasing him a little without there being any personal animosity in it. Percy had talked to many newly bereaved widows over the years, including three who had dispatched their husbands. He had never spoken to one like Tamsin Hayes. He said bluntly, discarding any subtlety he had planned, 'Your marriage was on the rocks by the time your husband died, wasn't it?'

She nodded vigorously, then poured the coffee she had prepared for their visit and handed round a plate of shortbread. She made quite a ritual of it, demonstrating to each of them in turn how steady her hands were, how unruffled she was by this revelation. 'I'm well rid of Tim.

If you've found out as much about his life as you say you have, you'll understand why.'

'Other women?'

She frowned a little, concentrating upon her reply, as if it was important to her to explain herself and her hatred. 'That's an oversimplification. Other women were part of it. More radical was the fact that he behaved as if I didn't exist at all. Tim never asked for an opinion from me: if I volunteered one, he ignored it.'

She did not seem to feel at all threatened. Peach said harshly, 'You're telling us that the mourning you put on for us on the day after his death was play-acting.'

An apologetic smile: she became a child who had been caught out in some minor offence but knew she was going to be indulged by a fond father. 'I'm afraid it was, yes. It seemed to be the thing to do at the time. I quite enjoyed it, actually.'

'It was also a deception. An attempt to mislead CID officers beginning a murder enquiry.' It seemed a trivial rebuke: the woman was luring him into her own mysterious, amoral world by the self-confidence she exuded.

'I suppose it was. I apologize, then. But I don't think my little charade did any harm. And I'm being completely honest now, aren't I?'

Lucy Blake sensed an unusual uncertainty in her mentor; she was having to work hard not to smile. She said sternly, 'How honest, Mrs Hayes? You've just told us that you had ceased to have any feelings of affection for your husband.'

'That's rather neutral, dear. Let me be completely honest and say that I detested the man and that I am very happy that he is no longer on the scene. Is that honest enough for you?' She looked at Lucy affectionately, her head a little on one side, transformed for this new interrogator from child to elderly aunt advising a favourite niece.

'Put yourself in our position, Mrs Hayes. You say you detested a man who was shot through the head on Friday night. You furnish us with an excellent motive for murder. You almost invite us to consider you as a murder suspect. In our extensive enquiries among staff and guests at Friday's function, we have as yet found no one who can substantiate your claim that you were not in the car park at the time of this killing.'

Tamsin smiled at her, then at the man beside her. 'You think I wanted to revenge myself on him for the way he'd treated me? "Revenge is a kind of wild justice." Francis Bacon said that, you know. Well, it's an intriguing little scenario for you to work out, when you put it like that. I left after the speeches, along with quite a lot of other people. Quite a long time before Tim was killed, apparently.' She repeated the mantra she had mouthed so happily to herself in the four days since she had seen them last.

Peach came back in impatiently. 'So you tell us. Yet no one saw you leave the hotel at the time you claim and no one saw you arrive here. This morning you've told us that you're delighted to be a widow and that you deliberately deceived us about that on Saturday. It doesn't look good for you, does it?'

She rocked herself backwards and forwards on her chair, as if inwardly debating an intriguing proposition, then calmly refilled their coffee cups. 'As you say, it doesn't look too good, does it? I should have been honest with you from the start, I see that now. But I couldn't resist playing the heartbroken widow for an hour or two. Overplaying her, I fancy.' She grinned and shook her head a little, as if her proficiency in amateur dramatics was at that moment the most important consideration in her life. 'But I don't really want you to catch the person who rid me of Tim, you see. I thought anything which helped to muddy the pool would be a good thing.'

Peach didn't waste time on tedious reminders of the necessity for justice if anarchy was to be avoided. This woman seemed to have successfully suspended all the normal moral canons for herself, and she was in danger of drawing him into her mysterious ethical world. He knew by now that Tim Hayes was a human being whose death possibly represented a moral gain in the world, but policemen could not afford to be beguiled by such dangerous considerations. 'You should consider your position, Mrs Hayes. Consider what you have told us and where that leaves you. Consider the fact that you will make a massive financial gain by this death. If you were in fact the person holding that pistol on Friday night, would it not be better to tell us now?'

She paused before she replied, showing him how calm and unthreatened she felt. 'I'm sure it would, Chief Inspector Peach. I'll even tell you now that I'd considered how I might kill Tim in the weeks before his death. But someone else believed me of that task – I almost said of that pleasure, but that would have been an exaggeration. I didn't kill him and I put my faith in British justice. Innocent until proven guilty.' She beamed at him, an eminently respectable middle-class housewife mouthing the words he usually heard from desperate old lags.

Peach said gruffly, 'You remain in the frame, Mrs Hayes. If you should recall anything which will enable us to determine who committed this crime, it is your duty to get in touch with me immediately.'

He got out as quickly as he could, refusing to wave to the beige-clad, elegant figure who stood smiling on the wide doorstep until their car was out of sight. They had gone a mile before he said irritably, 'Dr Davies was right. That woman isn't of sound mind, if you ask me.'

DS Blake guided the police Mondeo expertly through a long, attractive bend on the deserted road. 'That doesn't mean she didn't see her old man off, though, does it?'

# Twenty-One

Jason Thompson picked up the two glasses of white wine from the bar and took them over to the table in the alcove. 'What would you like to eat?'

'I don't want anything to eat. I don't know why you wanted me to come out for a pub lunch. You must realize that things are hectic at work this week.' Clare knew that she was being churlish, but she had too much on her mind to be generous.

'You're my wife, Clare. There's nothing wrong with us having lunch together occasionally, is there? We should enjoy it.' Jason gave her a weak smile whilst his brain raced towards nowhere, trying to find a way of saying what he had to say. He'd thought it would be easier to speak here than in those silent rooms at home. But he hadn't expected the place to be as crowded as this at lunchtime. That was making it even more difficult to speak privately. Or was this just another excuse he was offering himself? He said desperately, 'It's about the CID interview I had yesterday.'

'You could have talked to me last night about

it. You chose not to.' She made herself take a drink of wine, aware that she wasn't helping him, just as she hadn't helped him last night. She knew now that she was afraid of what he was going to say.

'I know. I wanted to talk at home, but I just didn't know how to begin. I'm a wimp, aren't I? But I love you, Clare.' He took her hand in his, held it firmly, trying to let his passion flow like an electric current between them. He shouldn't be doing this here. He should have her to himself in the privacy of their bedroom, where he could run his hands over that familiar, responsive flesh. He should be able to whisper into her ear that she still excited him as much as she had done all those years ago when they were twenty. No, not as much as that: much more than that. This passion did not stale; it grew with the years.

Instead of any of this, he said limply, 'They know, Clare. You need to be aware of that, when they see you again.'

She let go of his hand abruptly, her eyes widening with horror. 'What do they know?'

'They know about you and Tim Hayes.'

She stared at him for a long, horrified moment before she dropped her eyes to the table and the glasses of wine. 'Who told them?'

'I let it out. But I think they might have already known. They've been questioning a lot of people since—'

'You knew?'

He nodded, unable to find the words for this awful truth.

'How long have you known?'

'Not long.'

'How did you find out?'

'Does it matter?'

'Yes.'

'The badminton story wasn't convincing.' He didn't want to elaborate, to remind her about opening her sports bag, examining her kit, finding it had never been worn. Didn't want to descend into tragic farce and hysteria in this busy, impersonal place, where people chatted over their drinks and broke into the occasional peal of laughter.

'I'm sorry, Jason. I never meant to hurt you.' The old clichés, the phrases she would have flung back contemptuously at anyone who offered them to her. Jason didn't do that. He looked down at his still untouched glass with a small, painful smile. She reached out for his hand and held it tight, waiting for the answering squeeze which would tell her that they were going to get through this.

He said, 'I couldn't tell you that I'd found out. I didn't know how to tackle it. We've never had to talk about anything like that.'

'I know. And we never will again. For what it's worth, it was all over with Tim. It was finished well before he died.'

Still Jason did not look at her. He said dully, 'You gave him up?'

She should have left it at that, should have left him with at least that shred of comfort. But a desire for honesty, a wish to confess which was entirely selfish, made her say, 'No, love, he told me to go. But it couldn't have lasted. It was always a madness. A fling I needed to have because I'm worthless. It wasn't love. You're the one I love.' She yearned to convince him, but the words felt as trite and worthless as her behaviour had been.

Jason gave her hand a belated response and then set it aside. 'It's important that you know what I told the police.'

'Yes. It would be.' Clare was trying to see how this would affect what she should say herself when she saw the CID again, but her mind was racing with too much emotion to reason anything out.

'I left the Gisburn Hotel at about eleven.'

'I know that. I saw you go.' She was suddenly impatient.

Now at last Jason drank from his glass, savoured the sharp taste of the wine in his mouth. Now that he had told Clare that he knew about her and Hayes, he could return to the real world. He felt suddenly calm. 'What you don't know is that I didn't stay in the house when I got home. I was there for perhaps ten minutes after the Johnsons dropped me off. Then I got out my car and went back to the hotel.'

'Why was that?' Her mouth was suddenly dry, wanting water, not wine.

'I went to look for you and Hayes. I didn't know it was finished and I couldn't stand the thought of your being with him.'

'But you didn't find me.'

'No, and when I didn't, I eventually went home again.'

'And you've told the police this?'

'Yes. But only yesterday. I didn't tell them on Sunday that I'd gone out again after I got home.'

'They must have asked you about me.'

'Yes. I told them yesterday that I'd looked for you and not found you at the hotel. That I'd looked in the car park and found that your car was gone, and realized then that you must have gone home. I told them that you'd got home just before I returned, that you were still in the garage when I got there.'

There was silence for many seconds. They emptied their glasses, held them for a moment and stared into their emptiness before putting them down. She reached out her hand again towards his. Clare wanted to tell him again that it had all been over with Hayes, that it had been a tawdry episode which meant nothing, that she would make it up to him in the years which stretched ahead of them.

Instead, she said quietly, 'That's how it was, then.'

Jane Martin took them into the room she had arranged to use at the Brunton Casino. 'We won't be disturbed here. It's quiet in the after-noons.'

Peach looked round this office, wondering who it was who usually occupied it. A variety of people, probably. There were chairs and a desk with a computer on it, filing cabinets, no pictures or ornaments to personalize the room and assert rights here.

He turned his attention to the nervous girl who sat opposite them on the upright chair, as if she was being interviewed for a job. She was a looker all right, the sort of female who could rouse passions and cause trouble without any effort on her part. He didn't waste any time on the preliminaries. 'What is it you've been hiding from us, Jane Martin?'

It was the way schoolteachers used to use your full name when they suspected you'd been up to mischief, and she was disconcerted in the way she had been years ago. 'I haven't been hiding anything.'

'Not what my water tells me, Miss Martin, and my water is reliable nine times out of ten. DC Murphy here thought you were holding something back when he spoke to you on Monday. You may think he's a big daft gobbins, and I'd have to agree with you there most of the time, but he knows when someone's withholding information. Even your mum noticed that you were holding something back, in the days before Timothy Hayes died.'

'You've seen my mum?' The huge dark

brown eyes widened in consternation.

'Last night. We go back a long way, me and your mum. Back to the days when I pinched her for shoplifting and she decided to give up the drugs and go straight.' Peach gave her the understanding, persuasive smile which said that she had much better come clean quickly than waste everyone's time with further prevarication.

'I couldn't tell Mum. She wouldn't have understood. I'm still not sure that I understand it myself.'

'Try us, then. DC Murphy and I understand lots of things. We don't always approve, but it's better that we know.'

'It was Tim Hayes.' She sat perfectly still, watching her fingers twining on her lap. She knew now that she was going to tell them. She had an overwhelming feeling of relief. 'It was on a Thursday night. Four weeks ago.' She nodded slowly, as if she could scarcely believe that it was now that long ago.

Brendan Murphy said softly, 'So tell us about it, Jane.'

She looked into the fresh, open face above his denim shirt and could scarcely believe he was a copper. 'I'd never seen Tim Hayes before. He came in here, into the staff room, and introduced himself to me as my boss. We chatted for a while – we were the only ones in there. He seemed nice at first. Friendly. But I couldn't understand how I went out to his car with him.

Leroy says he gave me drugs.'

'Leroy Moore?' Murphy was studiously low-key, careful to avoid any glance at his chief.

'Yes.'

'He's your boyfriend, isn't he?'

'Yes.' She was so preoccupied with her explanation, with telling them about the monster Hayes, that she didn't realize immediately that the simple monosyllable had given Leroy Moore the motive for this crime which he had lacked until now. 'Leroy said it was a date-rape drug.'

'Rohypnol, probably. You should have come to us immediately, Jane. There are tests, but they have to be done quickly.'

'I didn't know what had happened myself, until I talked to Leroy. Apparently Hayes had done the same thing with other girls.'

'I'm sure he had, from what we know about Timothy Hayes now. Why didn't you tell me about this when I saw you on Monday, Jane?'

'I wanted to. But Leroy said we mustn't say anything. Not in view of what happened on Friday night. He said it would make us both murder suspects.'

'So what did you do about it?'

'Nothing. I told Leroy what had happened the day afterwards. He said to leave it to him.'

'I see. And what did Leroy do about it, Jane?'

'Nothing! I'm sure he did nothing!' But the panic in the huge brown eyes told them that she was not sure at all.

*  *  *

He was a strange combination of old-fashioned gentility and human frailty. His grey hair was slicked back very sternly against his head and he was one of the few men Lucy Blake had interviewed who still wore a three-piece suit. But the hair was now very thin, so that the brown moles on the scalp showed through it, and one of the buttons of the waistcoat was missing.

Lucy Blake said, 'Can I just confirm that you are Mr Robert White?'

'You may indeed. Formerly of Sandersons Solicitors, in King Street, Bolton, where I practised for forty years.' He gave her the smile he had offered to clients across the old leather-covered desk for most of those forty years. She was far too pretty to be a copper, he thought, with her deep chestnut hair, her fair, faintly freckled complexion and her remarkable green-blue eyes. He was glad he'd taken himself off for a haircut after he'd heard the police were coming to see him. In the far-off days of his youth, when he had attended magistrates' courts, coppers had been large, powerful young men with very short hair and the occasional battle scar. This was one of the few developments of modern life to which he could give his unqualified approval.

'And you now work for the Citizens' Advice Bureau.'

'I offer them a few hours a week of my retirement. It is for the most part a rewarding exercise.'

'And it was in this capacity that you met and advised Matthew Ballack.'

'It was.' He coughed discreetly, and Lucy thought she caught the scent of whisky working against the efforts at decorum he had made on her behalf. 'Perhaps I should state at this point that exchanges between clients and CAB staff are entirely confidential.'

'Except where the demands of a murder inquiry override the normal conventions.' Lucy gave him a bright smile to mitigate the firmness of her assertion.

'Except for extraordinary circumstances such as that, yes.' Robert White returned her smile. He found as many others had before him that to be involved in a murder case, even if it was only on the fringes, was bringing a little frisson of excitement. That the agent should come in this charming and curvaceous form was decidedly a bonus. He gave the bonus an affable smile. 'In those circumstances, I am entirely at your service, Detective Sergeant Blake.'

'We need to know exactly why Mr Ballack consulted you, Mr White.'

'That is simple enough. He brought to me a rather tattered but apparently quite viable affirmation of partnership which was apparently very important to him. It was very rudimentary and it did not bear the mark of a competent professional lawyer.'

Lucy was becoming a little impatient with this ageing charmer. 'You mean it wasn't hedged about with gobbledegook.'

White bravely beamed his approval of the word, trying to show this charming young woman that he wasn't out of touch with modern attitudes. 'I mean, my dear, that it didn't contain the clauses which a thoughtful professional man would have inserted to take account of possible changes in circumstances.'

'Would you tell me the details of this document, please?'

'It was a deed of partnership between Matthew Ballack and Timothy John Hayes. I use the word "deed" rather loosely here. After perusing the pages and in response to his queries, I had to advise Mr Ballack that my view was that in the absence of any subsequent written agreements to override it, this document would still hold legal validity.'

Lucy wanted to tell him to cut to the chase, but she divined correctly that he would plead a lofty legal ignorance of any such vulgar phrase. So she said flatteringly, 'I need your judgement here, Mr White. What would you say was the most vital clause of this document? The one which Matthew Ballack was most anxious to have clarified or confirmed for him?'

Her appeal to his expertise pleased Robert White. It combined with the thrill of his belated connection with a murder hunt to make the old man pertinent and succinct. He steepled his

fingers and nodded understandingly. 'I confirmed for Mr Ballack that the document
entitled either party to take over the direction of
the firm and the management of its assets on the
death of the other.'

At Hayes Electronics, Clare Thompson locked
herself in a cubicle in the ladies' cloakroom
after she had returned from lunch with her husband. It was the only place she could give
herself privacy and time to think.

When she emerged after twenty minutes, her
mind was made up. Don't wait for them to
come looking for you: take the fight to the
enemy. It had always been her way to take the
initiative and she wasn't going to change now.
A murder investigation shouldn't alter your
behaviour; that would only invite suspicion.
She picked up the phone, told the impersonal
voice at Brunton CID that she had information
to give them, misunderstandings to clear up.
No, she would rather come to the station than
be interviewed at her place of work. She was
asked to hold the line, then told within thirty
seconds that DCI Peach would see her at four
o'clock that afternoon.

Now, sitting in the windowless interview
room with the cassette turning silently, hypnoti-
cally, in front of her, she was not so sure that it
had been a good idea to come here. This man
Peach, with his dark, gimlet eyes and his shining bald head, seemed even more formidable on

306

his home ground. He looked at her with a slow smile, seeming both to understand how nervous she was and to relish the fact. 'Misunderstandings, I think you told my officer when you rang. Strange word, that. A big word, where a much smaller one like "lie" would seem more appropriate. But I'm at your disposal, Mrs Thompson, for whatever revisions to your statement you now wish to make. I suppose I should warn you that you should be very careful about what you choose to say. Anything less than the truth is likely to land you in the deepest doo-doo. Of course, if you're here to tell us that you killed Timothy John Hayes, that would be very straight forward indeed.'

'I didn't kill him.'

'You're sure about that? It would be best to tell us now if you did. Get a good lawyer and go for the crime-passionnel defence would be my advice. Dress smartly and play the wronged woman and it's surprising what a jury will take.'

'I didn't kill him.'

Peach's smile disappeared abruptly. 'Then why did you lie to us so comprehensively on Monday?'

'I didn't lie. I concealed things.'

He shook his head sadly. 'Impeding the course of justice, we call it. It can lead to very serious charges when you impede a murder investigation.'

'I didn't tell you about my relationship with

Tim Hayes.'

'You didn't tell us about a lot of things.'

This man hadn't a sympathetic fibre in his body: plainly he understood nothing about passion. Clare said plaintively, 'It was over. You can understand me wanting to conceal it, surely?'

'I can understand that you withheld information after a brutal murder.'

'It was all over between Tim and me. Three weeks before he was killed.'

'Interesting. You must have been very resentful about that.'

Clare wanted to scream at this squat little man that she had got rid of Tim, that he had still wanted her when she decided to terminate the affair. But she didn't know what Jason had told them and she couldn't afford to be caught out again. She said dully, 'I hated Tim. Hated him for the manner in which he told me it was over. You say his murder was brutal. So was the way he ditched me. At least it opened my eyes to the sort of man he really was. For two years, I hadn't wanted to contemplate that.'

'What time did you leave the Gisburn Hotel last Friday evening?'

She watched the fresh-faced officer he had introduced as DC Murphy as he prepared to make a note of her reply. Despite the brusqueness of Peach's question, her mind was quite calm. She told herself that she had expected this, that she had Jason as a witness if she

308

played it carefully. 'The majority of people left after Tim's speech, at about eleven o'clock.'

'But you didn't.'

'No. I waited around for a while, until I was sure that my services were no longer required.' She was studiously neutral on the last phrase. 'I was still Tim's personal assistant, and an efficient one. It was a point of honour with me not to let the break-up of our relationship affect my work.'

'Highly commendable. When did you leave?'

'Jason got a lift home with the Johnsons, who live in the road next to ours. I sat at a table at one end of the main bar whilst Tim Hayes talked to people who had been at the dinner. Waited until I was quite sure that my employer would not need me again that evening.'

'No one has reported seeing you there.'

She smiled wanly. 'There weren't many people around by then. And it's part of a PA's job to be unobtrusive at times like that.'

'So when did you leave?'

'It must have been just before midnight, I should think. I wasn't watching the clock at the time.'

'Are there any witnesses to that?'

'No. Except that there is one, in a way. I never saw him, but my husband had gone back to the hotel to look for me. Apparently he didn't know Hayes and I were finished and he had some vague idea of catching us together.'

'But he didn't find you.'

'No. I must have left whilst he was looking round the hotel for me. I drove my own car home slowly and carefully – I was very tired by that time. I'd worked hard all week organizing the function and I suppose I was emotionally exhausted as well. I was still in the garage when Jason came in, so at least he can confirm the time when I arrived home.'

Brendan Murphy looked up from his notes. He was tall and gangling, with a fresh, innocent young face; he could hardly have presented a greater contrast with the intense, watchful man beside him. Because of his name and his appearance, Clare had expected him to speak with an Irish brogue: it was quite a shock when he spoke softly with an accent which was un-mistakably Brunton. 'Would you say your husband is a passionate man, Mrs Thompson?'

'I would, yes.' She was suddenly proud of the feelings she could arouse in Jason, of the way they would now resolve their problems and get on with their lives. But she saw too late where this was going and said with deliberate, almost comic, understatement. 'I believe he is very fond of me.'

'Then it must have occurred to you that he went back to the hotel that night to kill Timothy Hayes.'

'No. He didn't do that.'

'Perhaps he had no clear idea what he was going to do when he went there, but when the opportunity arose he got rid of him once and for all.' DC Murphy's voice was soft and infinitely persuasive.

For an instant, part of Clare exulted. Jason surely couldn't have committed murder, and the fact that they were even considering it meant that they were no longer thinking of her as their culprit. Then she hastened to defend him. 'Jason was back home before Hayes was killed. I was in the garage when he came in and I can account for that.'

'How can you be so sure of the time when Mr Hayes died?'

'I can't. But he was still in the main bar when I left and Jason was home at the same time at me – well, perhaps a couple of minutes later.'

'But you've just told us that you drove home very slowly.'

'Jason isn't a quick driver. He must have left the hotel immediately after me to arrive home when he did.'

They waited to see if she would offer them any further thoughts, but she held her nerve as the silence stretched, feeling instinctively that any more elaborate protestation of her husband's innocence would ring false. Peach eventually said heavily, 'So who was holding Mr Hayes's pistol when it blew half his head away, Mrs Thompson?'

She bit back the reply that the answer to that was surely their business, not hers. But she knew now that the crisis was past, that the real pressure was off. She said calmly, 'I don't know. What I do know is that you've been questioning people like Mrs Hayes and Matthew Ballack and Leroy Moore. You no doubt know quite a lot about people's movements on that night.'

When she had gone, Brendan Murphy said, 'She tried hard to take herself and her husband out of the frame when she mentioned those other three. She never even thought of mentioning Jane Martin.'

Peach himself dearly wanted to rule out the delicious Ms Martin. But he said sternly, 'Perhaps she didn't know that Hayes had been near young Jane or that we're interested in her. As for you, you're still too much affected by a pretty face, lad. You'll need to watch that. Stops you being objective.'

Half an hour later, Leroy Moore was thinking that he hadn't felt so nervous for a long time. He sat on the chair in Clare Thompson's office, waiting to see this man he had never seen before, who it seemed was now in charge of his destiny.

He didn't have long to wait. Matthew Ballack buzzed the intercom. The woman who had accepted that she was now his personal assistant said, 'You can go in now, Mr Moore.'

The room didn't seem to have changed since he had seen Timothy Hayes in here and been offered his promotion two weeks ago, but Leroy was too much on edge to notice any details. The man in the dark suit and red tie didn't get up from his desk. Leroy took the chair towards which he was motioned. Matthew Ballack gave him a guarded smile and said, 'Mr Moore, this is what you might call a "clear the air" interview. I'm having them with several people in the firm. How would you describe your role under Mr Hayes?'

Leroy cleared his throat, trying to remember the words he had rehearsed so carefully with Jane Martin last night. 'I did various things connected with the firm's security. There was more need for security as the range of activities expanded.' The phrases had seemed easy enough when Jane had given them to him, but they felt now like a foreign language upon his tongue. He cut the rest and said too eagerly, 'I'd just been promoted when he died. Made the Head of Security. But you probably know that.'

'I didn't, actually. Things were left in a bit of a mess, to be frank with you. Tell me more about your role in the firm and what you do for us.'

'I was hoping to discuss that with you today, sir. Mr Hayes hadn't had time to define my role when he died.'

Ballack looked at him for a long moment, watching him become more uncomfortable with the silence. Then, as if deciding to put Moore out of his misery, he said, 'You knocked people about, didn't you, Mr Moore? Took Hayes's orders and made people jump into line.

I've read your file. It doesn't tell me much about you and what you did, but I know where you came from.'

'That's a bit unfair, sir. I agree I had to—'

'We're going to have to let you go, Mr Moore. It's nothing personal, but there isn't going to be that sort of work for you here any more.'

'I'm very versatile, Mr Ballack. I've done all sorts of things. Mr Hayes must have been pleased with my work, or he wouldn't have—'

'I'm sure he was. Hayes liked people who could do the dirty stuff and leave him with his hands looking clean. I'm a different sort of chap, Mr Moore. There isn't going to be that sort of work. It's nothing personal.'

'He was a whited sepulchre!' The old biblical phrase from his Sunday School days, the one Peach had used about Hayes, was out before Leroy knew it was coming.

Matthew Ballack looked at him with renewed interest. 'You didn't like him.'

'I didn't like him or the work he gave me. I'd no choice at first. But I've changed since then.' Leroy looked at the watchful eyes in the lined, experienced face on the other side of the desk, sensing that this man too had had no time for the dead Hayes, striving now to convince him of the depth of his own hatred. 'He raped my girl! I'm glad he's dead!'

'Whoa there!' Matthew held up his hand to stop this runaway colt. 'Be careful what you're saying. I hold no brief for Tim Hayes, as you no

314

doubt realize by now. But rape doesn't seem quite his style. He wasn't a man to take risks, for a start.' He released a little of his own bitter contempt into that thought.

'She's a croupier at the casino. He didn't just hold a knife against her throat whilst he shagged her. The bastard used Rohypnol.'

'That's more his style,' said Ballack quietly.

'He was offering me the Head of Security post as a bribe to keep my mouth shut.' There was nothing to be lost now: the post was being taken away from him anyway. 'I was biding my time. I wasn't going to let him get away with it.'

There was a long pause whilst the two men who had hated Hayes stared at each other, Ballack very still and Moore breathing heavily. Then Matthew said, 'What sort of future did you see for yourself here, Leroy?'

It was the first time the man had used his forename. 'Less of the stuff I'd done before. More genuine security work. Checking the bouncers at the casino, making sure we get the right sort of people, not thugs. Tidying up the betting shops. I'm willing to turn my hand to anything, especially if you're going to clean up the firm.'

'You haven't been a regular employee until now. How about a three-month probationary period? To see how you perform and whether there is genuine work for you here. To let you see whether you like the new regime.'

Leroy could not keep a smile off his face. He

said eagerly, 'You'll need personal security, if you're going to clean things up. There are some pretty dodgy characters around the edges, people who won't take kindly to being flung out.'

'I'm sure there are. And you'd know all about that,' said Ballack grimly.

'I won't let you down. And when you've cleaned the place up, you'll find me indispensable!' Leroy had managed to get one of Jane's words in at last.

Matthew Ballack came out of his office with Leroy Moore, was still talking animatedly to him as they went through Clare Thompson's office and out into the car park. The new boss was gathering confidence, Clare thought.

There was quite a contrast between the man of forty-seven who looked much older and the squat young black man of twenty-four who could have passed for twenty. Both of them looked as if they were taking on a new lease of life and looking forward to it. She wondered what part in the future of the firm these two would play, where the firm itself might be in a year's time.

The strange and overriding thought at the moment was both of those smiling men must surely be murder suspects.

# Twenty-Two

Leroy Moore's elation lasted for precisely an hour.

At half past seven that evening, he was taking his supermarket meal out of the microwave when his phone rang. 'DCI Peach here. We need to see you again, Mr Moore. Urgently.'

Leroy didn't like the way he said the last word. And surely a DCI didn't normally phone people himself? He said uncertainly, 'Tonight?'

He could almost see the man's sardonic smile. 'No. Tomorrow morning will do. Give you time to think about things, won't it? You've got rather a lot of explaining to do. Nine thirty at Brunton nick, Mr Moore. I may wish to record what you say this time, you see. To make sure there are no misunderstandings later.'

Leroy Moore slept but fitfully, as Percy Peach had intended.

He presented himself in good time at the raw brick building which was the new Brunton police station. Peach left him waiting in interview room two for ten minutes. Leroy steeled himself to meet his tormentor and his assistant, prepared himself for the formidable, unsmiling black face of DC Northcott.

But nothing seemed to be predictable here. When Peach eventually bounced like a rubber ball into the room, he said, 'This is Detective Sergeant Blake. I thought we'd have a different perspective on what you have to say this morning. We always like to be entirely fair.' He gave Moore the smile of a tiger approaching a tethered goat. 'I think we'll have this recorded, even though there aren't as yet any charges.'

Leroy tried not to watch him as he made an elaborate play of unwrapping a new cassette and inserting it into the machine. Peach turned his anticipatory smile back on to Moore as he announced with relish, 'You've a lot of explaining to do, Mr Moore.'

'I didn't tell you about my girlfriend.'

'You didn't tell us about a lot of things. We're investigating a violent death. You're a man whose trade is violence, a man who was employed by the late Timothy Hayes to use violence. Now we find you've been lying to us. Doesn't look good from your point of view, does it? Of course, from our point of view, with an arrest in mind, it looks very good indeed.'

Leroy licked his lips, telling himself that he'd dealt with pigs often enough before, in his Manchester days, striving to banish the thought that he'd never come across one quite like this. 'I didn't tell you about what Hayes did to Jane because I didn't want to tell you how much she hated him.'

'Because it gave her a motive for murder, you mean? It certainly does that. It also gives you an even stronger motive, when we take into account your attachment to Jane Martin and your previous history of killing.'

Moore's broad, revealing features winced too obviously at the barb. 'That was self-defence. And I've altered since then.'

Peach shrugged his broad shoulders elaborately. 'Actions speak louder than words, Mr Moore. And your latest action is to conceal key facts in a murder inquiry.'

'Jane didn't do it.'

'And how do you know that?'

'I just know it. Not my Jane. She couldn't do something like that.'

Peach shook his head sadly. 'Not good enough, I'm afraid. We need evidence, not opinion.' Then he brightened visibly. 'Unless you're telling us that you know Jane didn't do it because you shot Hayes yourself?'

'No.' Then, belatedly, 'Of course I didn't.'

Peach savoured his discomfort for three, four, five seconds. 'What time did Jane Martin leave the Gisburn Hotel last Friday night?'

'Not till around midnight. She left with me in the Focus. She doesn't have her own car.' His voice was very soft and a tone higher as the tension hit him.

'But she didn't get a lift back into Brunton with anyone else who had been at the dinner, though she must have known people. Pity, that.

It would have given her witnesses and taken her out of the frame.'

'She didn't kill him.'

Blake leaned forward, her fair colouring and dark red hair a startling contrast to that of the man opposite her. 'So where was she between eleven and twelve, Leroy? We've got statements from most people who were around during that time, but no one mentions seeing Jane.'

'I don't know. I think she stayed in the ladies' cloakroom for a while, then went out to wait for me in my car: I'd given her the spare key. I wasn't with her, because I was watching Hayes. As his security man, I wondered whether he wanted me to see him safely off the premises.'

'Which you conspicuously failed to do.'

'I told Mr Peach on Monday, Hayes gave me the nod from the bar to say I could go. Around midnight, that was. I went out quickly then and drove Jane back to her bedsit.'

'Or did you wait for Hayes in his car, extract your revenge for what he'd done to Jane and then drive home?'

'No!'

'I think I'd have been tempted, in your place.'

What happened to 'good cop, bad cop', he thought desperately. This woman who was not much older than he was, with the quiet voice and the persuasive suggestions, was almost worse than the aggressive Peach. He said with all the conviction he could muster. 'It wasn't like that. I drove Jane home and then went back to my own place.'

'Pity you didn't stay the night. Then at least your tales would look a little more convincing.' She made a note with her gold pen in her small, neat handwriting.

Peach stood up abruptly. He announced the time of termination of the interview and stopped the recorder. 'You can go now, Mr Moore. Don't leave the area without letting us know your movements and leaving us an address. But then with your previous record, I expect you know the form.'

Agnes Blake's old stone cottage, with the long mound of Longridge Fell running away behind it, seemed a world away from the interview rooms of Brunton police station. And the lady herself, with her concern for her daughter, her enthusiasm for Percy and the cricket he had relinquished, her automatic and unthinking integrity, seemed to Peach to represent all that was best in that world outside crime. The world which police officers could easily believe had ceased to exist.

They had told her they wanted nothing but a sandwich. Percy surveyed the home-made steak and kidney pie with potatoes, spring cabbage and carrots and said guiltily, 'You should have let us take you out for a pub lunch, Mrs B.'

'And let our Lucy shirk her duty with the wedding lists again? Not Pygmalion likely!' It was a favourite expression of Agnes's: respectable working-class women brought up as she had been did not use even the most modest of bad language.

'I have to admit she has a rather high-handed carelessness about paperwork which even I, her greatest admirer, cannot approve,' agreed Percy sententiously.

Lucy gave him the molten look which this agreement between mother and fiancé often occasioned in her. 'Let's eat before this gets cold. You shouldn't have gone to so much trouble, but thanks, Mum.'

The meal was punctuated only by the diners' approval of the cook's expertise. Then Percy, who had long since mastered the art of pleasing his future mother-in-law and irritating his future wife with an apparently innocent suggestion, said, 'I think we should finalize those wedding lists as quickly as we can. They should really have been posted some time ago.'

Agnes Blake beamed. 'You're absolutely right. May isn't really very far away.'

Lucy, knowing they were right, still felt a need for ritual resistance. There was one sure way to upset Percy's smiling equanimity. She looked at the ceiling and said thoughtfully, 'I still think we have to invite Chief Superintendent Tucker.'

'We don't want Banquo at our bloody feast.'

Lucy smiled primly. 'Thomas Bulstrode Tucker is a living being. Banquo was a murder victim.'

'And so will Tommy Bloody Tucker be if he presents himself at my wedding.'

Lucy went on thoughtfully, as if he had not spoken, 'And surely you must agree that Barbara Tucker would add tone to the occasion.'

'Brünnhilde Barbara would ruin a Barbara Cartland wedding,' said Percy grimly.

'But I'm sure Mum would love to see her wedding hat.' Lucy pouted prettily.

'I'll have the rest of the regular team. I might have Clyde Northcott as my best man.' Percy smiled contentedly, anticipating the stir the tall black man with his shaven head and uncompromising chiselled features would make in the ancient village church. 'I should think he does a good line in wedding speeches, Clyde.'

Agnes brought the list in with the tea which always followed lunch in her disciplined Lancashire mind. 'You'd better add any names you want.'

Instead, Lucy struck a few names firmly out and reasserted the line she had taken for many months, in a phrase her mother might have used herself. 'We want a quiet do, Mum. As few guests as possible. No rubbish like morning dress.'

Agnes looked at Percy for support, but this time he could not give it. 'Your Lucy must wear a posh dress. But she'll be the bonniest lass in church, whatever she wears. I'll make sure the lads wear suits and ties and I'm sure Lucy will tell her pals not to show too much bare bosom.

But we do want it quiet, Mrs B. Nothing formal.'

Agnes Blake knew when she was beaten and she didn't really care, so long as the wedding went ahead and Lucy had what she wanted. She gave a token but still formidable sniff. 'I suppose you're only regularizing what's been going on for months.'

'Don't make me blush, Mrs B. I don't do it as prettily as your daughter.'

'I still think Tucker should be there,' said Lucy, by way of riposte.

'Tucker doesn't even know we have a relationship yet. He couldn't let us work together if he did. I'll need to enlighten him soon, I suppose. And bring him up to date on this Hayes murder investigation.'

It was on that melancholy thought that they concluded their business in this innocent world and turned back to Brunton and the crime face.

Matthew Ballack tidied the seedy flat as thoroughly as he could. He made sure all the crockery was stowed in the single kitchen cupboard and ran the vacuum over the fraying carpet. He couldn't do anything about the dark marks of damp on the ceiling and he hadn't got a shade to cover the bare light bulb, but he moved the scratched dresser along a little to hide the patch of wallpaper torn away by the child of some previous tenant.

He hadn't wanted to meet them here, but the

impersonal voice on the phone had said that DCI Peach would prefer it. It seemed that preference from this quarter amounted to a command. Matthew wondered if the man had divined from their meeting on Tuesday that he had endured hard times in the last few years and was determined to see how he lived.

He was right, of course. Peach had noted the address with interest: it was in an area of Brunton that he knew well, because it housed many people who lived on the fringe of and beyond the law. It was by no means a Dickensian den of thieves, but this rabbit warren of flats and bedsits in what had been a century earlier the best part of the town housed drug-dealers and felons and many of the less successful criminal detritus of the town. After many visits, he knew its streets of high, increasingly decrepit Victorian detached and semi-detached houses intimately.

Clyde Northcott parked the police Mondeo carefully on the concreted forecourt of the house, where it could be seen from the front windows; this was the sort of area where police cars excited juvenile interest, even on an afternoon when teenagers should have been at school. The days when the 'truancy man' had been a feared figure in the streets of the old cotton town had long since departed, along with the gentility of areas like this one.

Peach noted the grimy ceiling and faded wallpaper with interest and without haste. Matthew

Ballack, who had been determined to brazen things out without comment, found that resolution seeping away swiftly with Peach's scrutiny. 'It's just temporary, this. I'm negotiating for a new property. But things have been pretty hectic this week, as you can imagine.'

'I can indeed,' said Peach. 'Been here long, have you, Mr Ballack?'

'Longer than I should have been, I suppose. I moved in here after my marriage broke up, as a temporary measure, and seem to have just stuck here.'

'Just stuck here.' Peach repeated Ballack's nervous, unthinking phrase as if it had some hidden import, which must be teased out. 'I suppose your gambling addiction didn't help. Atrophied any inclination to move, I should think, as the rest of your fortunes went downhill.'

It was so accurate a summary of his state in those years that it unnerved as well as infuriated Matthew Ballack. The watery brown eyes bulged a little and he ran a hand over the sparse hair on his cranium. 'I had a bad time. I admit it became an addiction. An illness, in some people's view. It cost me a lot, but I'm completely cured now.'

'I'm glad to hear that. Your work must have suffered, along with the rest of your life.'

'It did, yes, for a few years. I'm glad that my health was fully restored some time ago. In view of what happened last Friday, I shall need to be at my best in the coming months.'

Peach looked at him for a moment with his head a little on one side, as if inviting further thoughts. When none were forthcoming, he asked almost apologetically, 'Mr Ballack, what exactly was your official job description at the time of Timothy Hayes's death?'

'I am a partner in the firm.'

'A very low-profile one, in recent years. In any case, "partner" is hardly a job description, is it?'

'No. Well, I had what I suppose you might call a roving commission, making sure that the executives handling the various new branches of the firm's activities were operating efficiently.' Matthew tried boldly to stare the man out, hoping that the panic which was raging in his brain was not apparent in his eyes.

DC Northcott now leaned forward, as if to assist in a pincer movement upon their victim. 'Mr Ballack, I think you should know that I spoke yesterday to a woman called Sandra Rhodes.'

For a moment, the name meant nothing to Matthew. Then the memory of a house and the overweight slob who had allowed him access to the lady came back to him and his heart sank. He said as breezily as he could, 'One of our most reliable cleaning operatives. I hope she gave you a good account of us.'

'She said that was the phrase you used for it, Mr Ballack. A euphemism, DCI Peach calls it.

We're more used to calling such ladies prostitutes. And as for your firm, she seemed to think that forty per cent of her earnings from spreading her legs for a string of sad weirdos was a lot for you to take. That's the cleaned-up version, but no doubt you get the point.'

Matthew licked his lips. 'I'd no idea these things were going on.'

Peach said contemptuously, 'And you a partner, Mr Ballack? Come off it!'

'On this scale, I mean.' His head dropped hopelessly.

'Mrs Rhodes said you were in charge of the brothels,' said Northcott quietly. 'She told me you visited her on the seventh of February and announced that you were now her boss. She was a little surprised by that, I think. She said no one from the firm had ever talked to her or the other toms before.'

'Hayes told me I was to take charge of the brothels. It was one more step in his humiliation of me.'

Peach found himself feeling sorry for the man whose distress was now so apparent. He decided that in this instance there was no need to conceal his sympathy. They might have a confession before they left this depressing place, if they played this right. He said gently, 'You didn't like each other very much, did you, you and Mr Hayes?'

'He hated me and I had learned to hate him. I was a fool with my gambling, but he pretended

328

to be sympathetic, when all the while he was depriving me of all control and status in the firm we'd begun together.'

'So he put you in charge of something quite illegal. And you took it over willingly.'

'I had no choice. I didn't plan to do the job for long. Now that I'm in charge, the firm will divest itself of all connection with prostitution and drug-dealing. I've already begun the process.' His voice had risen with the genuine zeal of the evangelist, as he contemplated the crusade he planned.

Peach said quietly, 'So you disposed of Mr Hayes, so that you could take control and implement this righteous mission. It's understandable, from your point of view. It might even excite a degree of sympathy in a jury. It will come to that, because it is also murder, Mr Ballack.'

'I didn't kill Hayes.' There was fear apparent now in those moist, slightly bloodshot eyes, as if Ballack felt the lack of conviction in his own voice. 'God knows, I wished the bastard dead, but I didn't—'

'Why did you visit a lawyer in Bolton on February the thirteenth, Mr Ballack?'

They knew everything. For a moment, Matthew was overwhelmed by the hopelessness of the situation. Then he said in a voice which was so hollow that it seemed to belong to someone else, 'I just wanted professional confirmation of what I knew in my own mind. The only written proof of our partnership dated back over twenty years and I wanted a lawyer to run his eyes over it.'

'Mr White said you were particularly interested in one clause. The one which related to what happened in the event of the death of either partner.'

'I suppose I might have been.' Ballack looked up with what little defiance he could muster. 'It's natural enough, isn't it? That's the only way I was going to get back the position I should have had in the firm.'

'Timothy Hayes was a man of forty-nine, in excellent health. Isn't it odd that you should suddenly decide to check on the situation in the event of his death? And to do so secretly?'

'Secretly? You surely couldn't have found out about my meeting with Mr White if it had been that.' Matthew found himself clutching desperately at straws, delaying them for a moment whilst he tried to marshal his resources for a defence which seemed hopeless.

'You didn't use the company lawyers or your own family solicitor. You deliberately used the anonymity of a Citizens' Advice Bureau enquiry in a different town. If this hadn't been a murder investigation, overriding the normal rules of confidentiality, we'd never have discovered it.'

'I – I didn't want Tim to know I was checking things out.'

'Fair enough. It doesn't explain why you

made the enquiry at this particular time. Put that fact together with the brutal dispatch of Mr Hayes three weeks later, and you can see the implications as clearly as we can.'

Matthew looked at the sentimental Victorian print of children fondling a dog in its battered frame behind them, realizing with a shock that it had been there throughout his tenure of this place, without his ever looking closely at it before. He kept his eyes upon it, not daring to look at Peach as he said, 'A man is allowed to dream. The only way out of my predicament at the time, the only way back for me, seemed to involve the death of Tim Hayes.'

'Which you duly accomplished last Friday night.' Peach's voice was quiet, resigned, that of a therapist encouraging full confession as a prelude to reform.

'No. No, I didn't kill Hayes.' Matthew could not get the vehemence he wanted into the denial. He felt the rising apprehension in his voice. 'I don't say I didn't want him dead, I don't even deny that I thought about killing him after I'd checked out our contract. But it was a delicious dream, nothing more than that. I found when it came to it that I wasn't cut out for murder.' He said it with an acid note of self-disgust, as if he was recognizing not a virtue but yet another failing in himself.

Clyde Northcott's deep voice said quietly, 'If you killed him, it would be much better for you to tell us here and now, Mr Ballack.'

'I didn't kill him. Someone else did me a favour: I don't know who.' Ballack spoke with the defeated, exhausted air of a man who did not expect to be believed.

Peach said, 'Tell us again about your movements after eleven o'clock last Friday night, please.'

'I told you this on Tuesday. Your DS Blake made a note of it.'

'So tell us again.'

Matthew knew now that they were trying to trip him up, to make him contradict himself in his account of the events of that fateful night. He said with wooden concentration, 'The majority of people left after the speeches were over. I ordered a bitter lemon and stayed for a while, thinking about the events of the evening, about the situation within the firm. It was probably half-past eleven or a little later when I left, but I can't be sure of the exact time. I drove straight back here. I didn't go to bed immediately, because I knew I wouldn't sleep. But I didn't go out again. There are no witnesses to that: I slept alone, as I normally do.' There was again that searing flash of self-contempt in his last phrase.

Peach spoke like a man reluctant to abandon an argument he knew he must win. 'You are the man who has gained most by this death, Mr Ballack.'

'I know that. I plan to take full advantage of it. I have my firm back and a job to do.' He smiled wryly at this small, belated touch of defiance.

'I trust you will be allowed to do that. We too have a job to do, Mr Ballack. We shall find the person who killed Timothy Hayes. Murder must be pursued, whoever is the victim and whatever are the consequences. Goodbye for the present.'

# Twenty-Three

'It's Friday, Peach.' Chief Superintendent Tucker tapped his fingers ominously upon his large, empty desk.

'Yes, sir. I had noticed. It was on the news at seven o'clock this morning.'

'This is no time for insolence! I am here to remind you that it will be a week today since the murder of Timothy Hayes – a much maligned man, in my opinion. Are you aware that serious crimes which are not solved within the first seven days are often not solved at all?'

'Yes, sir, I am. I seem to recall you quoting that statistic to me on other occasions.' Percy reflected that his chief's talent for the blindin' bleedin' obvious seemed to have been honed rather than blunted by the passing years.

Tucker jutted his chin and went into Churchillian mode. 'Zero hour is approaching, Peach. If you do not make an arrest today, your chances of making one at all will be minimal.'

Both the philosophy and the statistics of this were debatable. But Tucker was an expert in neither of these disciplines. Peach contented himself with observing, 'We are certain now that Hayes was killed after midnight. That would make his death Saturday morning and give us another day on your theory.'

It was difficult to bollock a man who refused to grovel, who refused to observe the deference normally accorded to rank in the police service. Logic was no more a strength of Tucker's than philosophy or statistics, so he now said with a breathtaking arrogance, 'You should abandon this preoccupation with timescales and get on with your job of detection, Peach. You've already sent me into a television interview deplorably ill-equipped with information.'

'On the contrary, sir, I warned you that it was not the moment to call in the media. If you wish me to brief the chief constable on the facts of matter, I shall be able to do so as soon as the case is concluded.'

Tucker decided reluctantly to abandon the bollocking which would have enlivened a cloudy Brunton Friday morning. He was Churchill in his boiler suit as he leaned forward and said sternly, 'You had better give me a full briefing on the present state of your investigation. No flummery and no evasions, please.'

'Certainly, sir. Well, the first thing to note is that your friend Timothy Hayes has emerged as a thorough-going villain.' Percy nodded his satisfaction several times. 'The Brotherhood of Freemasonry seems to have a habit of producing undesirables in this area, wouldn't you say, sir?'

Tucker bristled visibly, a phenomenon which was always of interest to Percy. He glowered and warned, 'You must guard against this phobia of yours, Peach. Would you please now tell me the present state of your investigation?'

'Certainly, sir. And in turn you will no doubt give me your invaluable oversight. There is a wife – as admittedly there often is in these things. But a wife unlike any other in my now quite extensive experience. She makes no secret of her hatred of her husband, which seems to have amounted to an obsession. She's now admitted to us that she enjoyed dressing up in black from head to toe and playing the grieving widow. She's even told us that she had been considering how she might kill her husband in the weeks before his death. She maintains that someone else robbed her of that pleasure and that she hopes he or she escapes justice. She seems to be cocooned in a world of her own, where she doesn't seem at all affected by being a murder suspect.' Peach felt some of his own frustration coming out in this lengthy account of Tamsin Hayes.

'You should beware of the wife, Peach. Do not lightly dismiss her from your consideration for this crime.'

'A trenchant observation, sir. I shall bear it in mind. There is also a mistress.'

'Aaah!' Tucker tried to mitigate the banality of his eager monosyllable by nodding sagely several times. *Cherchez les femmes*, eh,

Peach?'

'I believe that Gallic viewpoint still has its followers, sir, even in these times of sexual equality. The interesting thing in this case is that Clare Thompson had been ruthlessly jettisoned by Hayes shortly before his death.'

'Hell hath no fury like a woman scorned, Peach!' Tucker delivered this triumphantly original view like a conjuror producing a white rabbit.

'Indeed, sir? I believe the correct quotation is "Nor hell a fury, like a woman scorned". I had occasion to check it out with my fiancée, sir. Which incidentally is another subject I need to—'

'Keep to the point, Peach, and don't try to obscure the matter and fob me off with quotations. Did this harpy kill Tim Hayes?'

'May have done, sir. She also has a husband. Jason Thompson. Rather odd-looking bod with unruly red hair and thick-lensed glasses, sir.'

'Crippen wore glasses, Peach.'

'Did he really, sir? Also had a black moustache and a short fuse, I believe.' He stroked his own very black moustache reflectively for a moment. 'Jason Thompson is very highly sexed, according to DS Blake, sir.'

'Has the man assaulted her, Peach? If there has been any interference with one of my officers, I shall—'

'Very gallant, I'm sure sir. I shall convey your chivalric sentiments to DS Blake, sir. Like you,

I find this difficult to believe, but it is apparently possible to be highly sexed without leaping astride DS Blake at the earliest opportunity.'

Tucker goggled at his DCI, another regular occurrence which never lost its fascination for Percy. 'This man sounds very odd to me, Peach. You should give him close attention.'

'Another of your insights, sir. Unfortunately oddness is not currently an arrestable offence, but I shall bear it in mind. DS Blake thinks that Mr Thompson's very active libido is entirely directed towards one particular woman, sir. He appears to be very uxorious, sir.'

Tucker assumed what Percy called his low-IQ goldfish look again and Peach took pity upon him. 'He is very devoted to his wife sir. Like yourself, in fact.'

Tucker passed rapidly from incomprehension to suspicion. 'Has it occurred to you that this man Thompson might have learned of his wife's infidelity, Peach?'

'Not only occurred but been followed up, sir. Jason Thompson has admitted returning to the Gisburn Hotel on Friday night after originally leaving for home at around eleven. He wanted to see whether Clare was up to any hanky-panky with Hayes, he says. But he denies killing him.'

'He would, you know, Peach! In the absence of any other suspects, I have to tell you that it is my opinion that—'

'No absence of other suspects, sir. Three more, I'm afraid. Not that we've closed our minds to others beyond them, of course. In accordance with your instructions.' He beamed with the irritating happiness which rectitude invariably brings to the righteous.

Tucker exhaled heavily. 'You have a habit of bringing unnecessary complexity into these investigations. I suppose I had better assist you to clarify your mind.'

'A consummation devoutly to be wished, sir. There's another woman, sir.'

A sigh which was this time positively theatrical. 'I thought there might be.'

'Did you indeed, sir? Your insights are quite disturbing, at times. This one is scarcely more than a girl, to experienced men like us. She's a croupier at the new Brunton Casino.'

'A hard-faced little bitch, no doubt, if she works in a place like that.'

Peach, despite a wealth of previous experience, was astonished anew by his chief's ability to prejudge an issue. 'Rather a nice girl, I would say, sir. Very intelligent and very pretty, but still with a touching naivety at nineteen. She's come up the hard way, with a single-parent background and not much money around.' He decided not to feed Tucker's prejudice by telling him about Jane Martin's brush with the law at sixteen.

'So how does this nauseating little saint become a murder suspect?'

'By being a date-rape victim, sir. Your Mr Hayes appears to have given her what we think was Rohypnol and had his evil way with her. Took her to his flat and dallied with her there, I'm afraid.'

'He's not *my* Mr Hayes, Peach! I never liked the man, from what little I saw of him.'

'Indeed, sir? Well, Miss Jane Martin felt quite murderous after this incident. She also has a boyfriend, sir. Boy by the name of Leroy Moore.'

'This is the black man from Moss Side you mentioned to me earlier in the week.' Tucker nodded happily at his mastery of key facts.

'This is indeed the man, sir. Moore has killed before, sir.'

'There you are, then. What on earth are you waiting for?'

'Evidence to warrant an arrest, sir. Even being black and having a previous record are not grounds for a murder charge, in these restrictive days.'

'Then go out and get that evidence.'

'Nothing tangible, as yet, sir. He has been doing some pretty dodgy work for Timothy Hayes, in the last year or two. Beating and intimidation, for a start. But as yet we've found nothing which would hang a murder charge round his neck.'

'You said Hayes raped his girlfriend. Would that not be enough to make a violent man take his revenge?'

'Motive, sir, not evidence. Moore had means, motive and opportunity.'

'Then get out there and find something to make it stick, Peach! Do I have to do everything for you?'

Percy bit back his first reply and said through thin lips, 'Your views are always of interest, sir. I shall relay your inclination to get out there and put yourself on the line to the lads and lasses downstairs. I'm sure they'll be chastened by the prospect.'

Tucker took a deep breath and said with immense dignity, 'I shall not interfere. It is not my policy to interfere, Peach, however incompetent my officers may demonstrate themselves to be. I think you have now wasted quite enough of my time.'

'You don't wish to hear about the person who has gained most of all by this death? Very well, sir. I am impressed as ever by your insouciance.'

Tucker gave the sigh of a grieving hippopotamus and said heavily, 'Who is this latest candidate, Peach?'

'Matthew James Ballack, sir. Divorcee of this parish and partner of the deceased. A man who had occasion to check out what happened to the firm in the event of the death of Hayes only two weeks before that event took place.'

Tucker leaned forward, steepled his fingers and pursed the chief-superintendental lips. 'Suspicious, that, you know.'

'I do sir, yes. You taught me a long time ago to look out for things like this.'

Tucker was as usual impervious to irony. 'I think you should give this man your full attention.' Then a thought struck him and he said apprehensively, 'You're not going to tell me he's a Mason, are you?'

'Afraid not, sir. That could have been a clincher, couldn't it? But he's still a prime suspect, in my view. On his own admission, he hated Hayes, though they'd started the firm together twenty-odd years ago. Ballack had a gambling problem and went downhill rapidly five or six years ago. Lost both his marriage and his standing and influence in the firm. He was in charge of brothels and on his way out at the time of Hayes's death – he reckoned this latest post was a deliberate humiliation and I'm sure he's right about that. He's now emerged from the shadows as the surviving partner and taken sole charge of what is still a private firm.'

'This looks like it, to me, Peach.' The well-groomed head nodded its satisfaction at its owner's acuity.

'Really, sir? Ballack says he left the Gisburn Hotel at about half past eleven but he has no witnesses to that. He says he now plans to clean up the firm and divest it of its more unsavoury activities. For what it's worth, I believe he is serious in that; it doesn't of course take him out of the frame for murder.'

'It doesn't indeed. I'm glad you realize that,

Peach.'

'One can't serve at the altar of detection with an archbishop without picking up a few things, sir.'

Tucker did not follow this at all – metaphors always confused him – but he gave his DCI a token hostile glare to be on the safe side. 'I don't think you should now be sitting here bandying words with me, Peach. You should be out there bringing in this man Ballack.' The archbishop of detection nodded his anointed head several times.

'You think the black man didn't do it after all, sir?'

'What? Oh, look here, you've just told me that this man Ballack has almost confessed to the crime, haven't you?'

'Well, at any rate, you think the wife and the mistress and the mistress's husband and the girl he raped are all in the clear.' Peach numbered them off on the four fingers of his left hand. 'You've certainly narrowed down the field for me with your overview, sir. This has been a most valuable—'

'Peach, just get out there and get this thing solved, will you? You're the man in touch with the case, the man I trust implicitly to see it through.'

'Implicitly, sir? This is really most touching. It fills me with confidence. I feel we shall have an arrest very soon now. Possibly today. To keep it within your mystic seven days, sir.'

* * *

Friday night, and the weekend stretching ahead of them. A month ago, when he had known nothing of Clare's affair with Tim Hayes, Jason Thompson had enjoyed this time, with no teaching on the morrow and two whole days with Clare stretching deliciously ahead of him.

Now he found himself searching for things to say, as he might have done with a stranger. 'The hour will go forward in three weeks. It will really feel like spring then.'

Clare looked at the clock on the mantelpiece above the wood-burning stove and spoke as if she had not heard him. 'This time last week you were driving to the Gisburn Hotel. This time last week none of it had happened.'

Jason wanted to say that yes it had, that the important thing, the thing which had burned his soul, had come long before that. He wanted to say that the death of Tim Hayes was an irrelevance, a fitting end for the man who had taken the dearest thing in his life away from him. He wanted to take Clare into his arms, to press his lips hard against hers to stop her talking about the instrument of his suffering. Of their suffering. Instead, he stared at the steady, tiny flame behind the window of the stove and said dully, 'We need to put this behind us, Clare.'

'Easier said than done, isn't it? But you're right, of course.' She made a huge effort, threw herself beside him on the sofa and took his hand. 'Of course you're right, love. You've always been my rock. You know that, don't you?'

'Not much of a rock.' Now, when he least wanted them, the images of her limbs entwining with those of Hayes came back to him more vividly than ever before and he could not put his arms around her, as he had so wanted to do an instant earlier.

She squeezed his hand and held it against her thigh. 'And I hope you'll still be my rock in the future.'

He wanted her, yearned for her, wanted to start all over again with the familiar, loved body. Yet he wondered if this was how it had started with Hayes, if she and not he had taken the sexual initiative. Jason found that he could produce nothing from himself, could only echo her sentiments. 'I want that as well.'

'Then everything will be all right.' She tried to infuse enough confidence for both of them into the words.

It was at that moment that the doorbell rang insistently, sounding like a knell in both their ears, fracturing the intimacy which had been in embryo between them.

'DCI Peach and DS Blake,' said Clare, attempting a smile as she led the CID into their sitting room. Somehow both of them had known who it would be at their door.

Peach didn't apologize for calling at this hour. He sat down on the very edge of the seat they offered to him, as did Lucy Blake. It was left to

Clare Thompson to say resentfully, 'I don't know why you should come here at the week-end. I said everything I had to say yesterday.'

'And I did likewise on Tuesday,' said Jason, taking his cue from his wife.

'Neither of you was completely honest with us. Hence our presence here tonight. This could all have been settled earlier if you had chosen to tell us the truth.'

The words had an ominous ring to Jason. He blinked a little behind the thick-lensed glasses. 'I told you everything I could.'

'No. You told us everything you wanted to, Mr Thompson. Perhaps, indeed, you told us a little more than you could.'

Jason shook the fiery red hair as if trying to clear his head. 'I told you that I'd held things back on Sunday. But I put that right on Tuesday. I told you then that although I'd originally left the hotel when I said, I'd taken out my own car from the garage here and gone back again. That I'd looked round for Clare and been unable to find her, and left about midnight.' He recited the facts as if checking them off on a list, assuring himself that he had left nothing out.

'That's where it begins to go wrong, isn't it?'

Clare tried to help a husband who was look-ing very apprehensive. 'Jason went back there to look for me.'

'And didn't find you.'

'That wasn't his fault.'

'No. Had you been where you told us you

were, he'd have found you immediately. You told us yesterday that, "I sat at a table at one end of the main bar whilst Tim Hayes talked to people who had been at the dinner. Waited until I was sure that my employer wouldn't need me again that evening." Had you been in that bar, your husband would certainly have found you there – he searched the hotel thoroughly enough.'

'I must have left before he searched there.'

'No. You insisted yesterday that you left the hotel only just before him. He began his search of the premises in that bar when he returned to the hotel.'

Jason Thompson's voice was full of panic now as he said, 'But we were both back here at the time of the murder. I told you on Tuesday: Clare drove into the garage just before me.'

'You did indeed tell us that. That is what I meant when I said that you told us a little more than you could. There was no meeting between you and your wife in the garage here as you claimed.'

A brief, terrified glance at his wife was more revealing than any words. He repeated slowly, as if trying to convince himself as well as his visitors, 'I saw the garage door still open and the lights of Clare's car still on as I turned into the drive.'

'No. Your wife did not return here until much later.' Peach was as calm as a man reading out a train timetable. 'She claimed on Wednesday that she was back here "before Hayes was killed", but that was a lie. Incidentally, no one except Hayes's killer knows exactly when he died.'

It was at this point that Clare Thompson's voice came in, as calm and resigned as her husband's had been uncertain. 'It's all right, Jason. You've done your best for me.' She turned for a moment to look directly into his face. 'You've always done your best for me. I know that.'

Peach gave the slightest of nods to Blake, who stood up and pronounced the formal words of arrest. He then said quietly, 'I think it's now time for you to tell us exactly what happened last Friday night. Don't you, Mrs Thompson?'

A long sigh of resignation, a pause whilst she organized her thoughts. Apart from this one wildness which had destroyed her life, Clare Thompson was, after all, a very organized woman. 'I watched Tim Hayes for a couple of minutes, deciding how long it was likely to be before he left. Then I went and locked myself away in the ladies' cloakroom. But that didn't work: I couldn't rest and I was frightened of missing Hayes as he left. So I wrapped myself up in coat and gloves and went straight out to Tim's car. Most people had left by then and the car was on its own. I still had a key to the BMW from the days when we had been together.' If she felt the sudden tremor in her husband beside her, she did not react to it. 'It was cold in there. Other people left in ones and twos, but it seemed a long time before he came out.'

'And by that time you'd found the weapon.'

She spoke directly now to Blake, as if it were important to her that her story was recorded accurately in the younger woman's notes. 'I knew about the pistol. I knew he'd taken to carrying it about with him in the car over the last few weeks. He said his wife had been behaving very oddly towards him.' She gave a sudden, startling smile, as if the irony of Hayes's fears about Tamsin had suddenly struck her for the first time. 'I've never handled a pistol before. I don't suppose I ever will again. But I had plenty of time to get used to the feel of it in my hands before he finally came out to the car.'

'Did you have a conversation with him?'

She looked at Peach as if he was very naive to ask such a question. 'I crouched down in the back of the car when I saw him coming. I'm not really a very big person, am I, Jason?' She gave her husband a glance and a smile, but the appalled man beside her could give her no answering reaction. 'He never saw me. I simply put the pistol against the side of his head and pressed the trigger. It was quite easy, really: much easier than I had imagined it would be.'

She walked like one in trance as they took her out to the police car in the drive. She sat very upright between Brendan Murphy and his female colleague in the back seat as it eased out and turned towards Brunton.

They had told Jason Thompson he could accompany his wife to the station if he wished. He sat staring straight ahead of him beside Peach as Blake drove behind the car containing his wife. His tousled red hair was unheeded now and those mobile hands were quiet in his lap. He blinked away the tears behind the thick lenses, an unlikely figure to be clothed in a terrible, tragic dignity.

$q$